Madhumita Bhattacharyya was a writer and editor with *The Telegraph* newspaper in Kolkata for a decade, interrupted by a stint in the non-profit sector. She is currently a freelance writer and editor, and lives in Bangalore with her husband, extremely bossy three-year-old and greedy dog. *Goa Undercover* is the third of the Reema Ray detective series.

ALSO BY MADHUMITA BHATTACHARYYA

The Masala Murder
Dead in a Mumbai Minute

GOA UNDERCOVER

Madhumita Bhattacharyya

PAN

First published 2016 by Pan
an imprint of Pan Macmillan India,
a division of Macmillan Publishers India Private Limited
Pan Macmillan India, 707, Kailash Building
26 KG Marg, New Delhi – 110 001
www.panmacmillan.co.in

Pan Macmillan, 20 New Wharf Road, London N1 9RR
Basingstoke and Oxford
Associated companies throughout the world
www.panmacmillan.com

ISBN 978-93-82616-38-2
Copyright © Madhumita Bhattacharyya 2016

Typeset by SÜRYA, New Delhi
Printed and bound in India by Replika Press Pvt. Ltd.

To my own particular Goa

PROLOGUE

It should have been nothing – a pair of sunglasses at the fringe of the water, tripping over each wave as it crashed on the beach, every breath of the vast ocean keeping them in limbo.

The owner of the glasses lay face down in the sand, in the posture of a sunbather praying to the rays to bronze her back. Except her arm was somehow askew, jutting out at an impossible angle. A closer look would reveal that it was not bent at the elbow, but an inch or so above it, the jagged edge of broken bone piercing through creamy skin.

To those present at the scene, the image would forever be accompanied by the smell of burning flesh; the taste of explosives on the tongue; the feel of soft, powdery sand kicked up by panicked feet desperate to be gone – an orchestra of terror teasing the brain till it woke screaming from its wide-eyed dream.

That there were only three deaths would be wondered at, given the density of the crowd at Sundown Bar just two weeks before Christmas. The name of Victoria Price would hang over the beach like a whisper: the nineteen-year-old Briton had the power to stop even the wildest of raves – if only for a minute of mute prayer.

Two other deaths were reported. Photographs were

published – a woman and a man who looked very much like Reema Ray and Terrence D'Costa. But these names would never be mentioned.

And that was as it should be.

ONE

A shot rang out. My heart was racing fast – too fast. If I didn't stop, I was sure it would stall, or my legs would give way, whichever came first. I had never pushed myself to the physical brink so thoroughly in all my life, and it had left every breath bitter, as if the acrid smell of gunpowder had settled deep within my lungs.

I saw shelter in front of me, in the form of the wide trunk of a tree. Ten seconds – that is all I would take. My mind screamed at me not to stop, but my body won the argument. No contest.

Once I reached the shade of the gulmohar, I squatted, trying to make my tall form as tiny as possible, while I swallowed air in greedy mouthfuls. I had never been leaner or fitter, and I willed my pulse to slow. If it obeyed, I thought I might still have a chance.

And then I felt it, even though I shouldn't have. A red laser beam, foreteller of imminent death, on the side of my head.

'Bang,' said my pursuer.

I threw my hands in the air. 'I give up. This is fixed! There's no way you could have reached me so fast.'

Shayak put down his weapon. 'I always hold something back in the field. I could have caught up with you with double the ground to cover. You must remember to always account for adrenaline.'

'Right. How come it never seems to work in my favour?'

'Oh, it does. Now imagine your plight without it. Stand up. Take ten. Then we'll start again.'

As I hobbled away, I knew ten minutes would not be enough for me to recover and save face for the next hour of torture Shayak had lined up for me. I considered the bloodbath: the two-hour training circuit had been the most gruelling of a two-month regimen I had started on, ahead of the first real undercover mission of my life. For the past month, we had been slogging it out at a Titanium camp outside Mumbai, set up for training security forces waiting to be deployed to the field in Titanium's operations as defence contractor. But the facility was currently empty, save for the training staff and Shayak. And of course my former ally Terrence, Titanium's latest recruit and my future (fake) husband.

Terrence and I were undergoing separate as well as joint training sessions conducted by a barrage of fitness and combat specialists among whom was Shayak, who was taking us through recon and combat practice. He said he was cramming one year of training into a fraction of the time.

It seemed crazy in retrospect, but it was I who had propelled us here, plunging us headlong into a dangerous and demanding course with all the enthusiasm of a novice who has no clue what pure physical exhaustion could be. What fear could make you feel. Just three months ago, I had solved two murders in my first month at Titanium. In doing so, I had discovered that the murderer had been trying to take down Titanium by putting Shayak, the nation's foremost security expert and former black ops soldier, at the centre of a scandal. And while the killer was now behind bars, there had been a hand at work behind it all that was yet to be revealed. A very powerful hand. Buoyed by success and fired up by a sense of urgency, it was my idea to go undercover to track the conspirator down.

How much of this was motivated by my desire to be Shayak's hero I did not dare to ask myself. I ignored the what ifs and maybes, the fleeting kisses and the shadow of longing hanging over stolen gazes. I focused squarely on the present, when every day our task was becoming more critical. In the three months since we had uncovered the plot to sabotage Titanium, the company had taken blow after blow. Though Shayak was exonerated and the real killer caught, many of the company's staff engaged overseas in highly sensitive projects had to be pulled out after Titanium lost its official endorsement. Some of that was the rub-off of Titanium finding itself in the spotlight, which is not a virtue for a private security firm. And some of it seemed to be the impact of forces that continued to act against Shayak and the company he had built.

Shayak had been away, first in Afghanistan and then Syria, overseeing the withdrawal of his men there. One by one, Titanium's teams in domestic government facilities were benched as well. The troops working with US contractors were still in place, which meant that either the government of that country was less vulnerable to influence or the reach of the people we were dealing with did not extend so far.

The whisper of scandal had also caused many corporate clients to fear the worst, and Shayak had had to devote much of his time in the past months trying to win back confidence.

Luckily it had worked, and thus far most of Titanium's private clients had been retained. But if we could not get to the bottom of the conspiracy, that might change, bringing the country's leading security company to the ground and leaving thousands of employees out of work – including me.

Thus, Shayak's insistence on working Terrence and me to the bone. If Titanium was to be restored even to a shadow of its former self, in an industry where trust was everything, it meant solving this case – and it would have to be soon. He was so desperate that he went along with my plan to go undercover in Goa. With so little evidence, and all of our leads pointing solidly in one direction, there didn't seem to be an alternative. We were going in armed with precious few answers. That was the sort of vulnerability that could put a target on our heads – out there where the bullets were real.

*

As had become routine, the morning after my hypothetical death by the tree, I could barely move. The session had continued well past nightfall, and the only part I had excelled at was hand-to-hand combat. My aim at the firing range was iffy at best, but it was my stamina that caused the most concern.

'Don't worry about speed so much, Reema,' Shayak told me over and over again. 'Worry about how long you can keep going.'

Shayak must have anticipated the jelly legs because he let me sleep till the shockingly permissive hour of 6 a.m. and had scheduled only a brief workout after which there was a breakfast meeting.

I walked into the conference room drenched in a cold sweat after my hot shower. Whoever said the only way to prevent post-workout stiffness was another workout had clearly never worked out a day in their lives.

'Sit,' said Shayak, pouring the coffee. A bowl of fruit sat in the centre of the table. Toast and eggs were brought in by the resident kitchen staff. There was nothing fancy. Food was there to keep our strength up and help us reach our training goals. Period.

Unable to bend at the knee, I collapsed into my chair, skimming over the soft board covered with pictures, documents and a scribbled web of names. A board we had become intimately familiar with.

With only days to go before we shipped out, we still knew next to nothing about George Santos or his ashram. The spiritual guru of British origin who had made Goa his home had more than a passing acquaintance with the man who had killed two people in an effort to sabotage Shayak. That's what we knew three months ago, and for all intents, that's what we knew now.

We needed leverage, and Shayak had promised some intel before we were thrown into the deep end. George had turned evasion into high art and the only reason Shayak hadn't severed ties and left him at the mercy of law enforcement was that there was so little on him that he would, no doubt, get off scot-free. So best to hedge our bets and go in with him on our side. Though which side he was really on was anybody's guess.

Shayak tossed two identical folders next to our plates. 'Everything we have on George Santos. Some of it you've seen before, news articles and the like, but the first few pages are new, and should be of some use to help you get into character. It might not seem like much now, but remember, in about a week, Terrence and Reema will be man and wife. You are going to have to make it look convincing, and the more at ease you are in your new environment, the easier it will be.'

I scalded my mouth on the coffee and looked through the literature. I did not like being reminded of our cover story at the ashram. George, as we knew, helped you 'find your way to the truth', took your money and sent you on your way. But on paper at least, there seemed to be more to it.

'Have you chosen your names yet?' asked Shayak.

Terrence nodded. 'Vishal Chowdhary.'

'Good,' said Shayak. 'Generic enough, with sufficient regional ambiguity.' Then he looked at me. The brief had been simple: choose two names that are comfortable, and that we wouldn't mind responding to. Nothing too memorable or exotic; just everyday names. 'Aparna Shenoy. Apu for short.'

He stared for a second longer than necessary, and something I couldn't quite define flashed in his eyes. And then he nodded, back to business once again. 'That should work,' he said.

'Where will we be staying?' Terrence asked.

'Soul Retreat Wellness Spa,' said Shayak.

Terrence let out a low whistle. 'Sweet.'

'Fancy, is it?' I asked.

'One of the fanciest.'

'As for your cover stories, I'll have a complete dossier tomorrow.'

We knew the broad strokes – we were a disenchanted

married couple who were moving back to India after a few years in Silicon Valley. We were not happy to return, and our marriage had hit choppy waters, causing us to seek George out before settling down in Mumbai.

'How much of this will we actually have to be a part of?' I asked.

'George usually insists on the participants attending his sessions, so you'll need to be there for at least some of it to avoid suspicion.'

'And what if the investigation goes on for more than two weeks?' asked Terrence.

Which was likely, given the scale of the conspiracy before us.

'He often has hangers-on, so I don't think that should be a problem. Or if you feel you've had enough time at the ashram to learn what you need to know, you'll be transferred to another base.'

I paused at George's picture. A head full of straggly dark brown hair streaked with grey. Skin lined by decades in the sun. Whenever I had met him in the course of the Maaya Island murder investigation, he had been wearing worn flip-flops on his feet, along with clean but frayed clothes. But it was the eyes you remembered most. Arresting. Blue. Disarmingly, deceitfully open.

I was skimming through passages extracted from George's tenets when something gave me pause. 'The body is one of the most honest routes to the soul, through the soul. In the Truth Temple, every path to knowledge is embraced. It is the only form of the divine we can be sure of.'

'This sounds awfully like it may degenerate into one big sex orgy,' I said.

Shayak gave a brief nod. 'I suspect most of these things do. You should be able to use the married couple cover to deflect some of that.'

'Really? Is the marriage institution likely to be seen as an obstacle to extracurricular sex, if it is the ultimate route to my soul's truth?'

'You can always say that your relationship isn't open,' Shayak suggested.

'Why would we do a thing like that?' asked Terrence.

Shayak ignored him, which was how he usually dealt with his newest employee's sense of humour.

'No one is asking you to do anything you aren't comfortable with,' Shayak said pointedly.

I trusted my ingenuity enough to know I would find a way around the problem. As for Terrence, I didn't anticipate very much trouble. I just hoped he wouldn't be spending all of his time chasing George's more impressionable students at the expense of the task at hand.

'Once more, from the top?' I said.

'Vishal,' Shayak asked, 'how long have you been married?'

'Almost five years,' said Terrence, without missing a beat.

'Age?'

'Apu is a smashing thirty, and I am thirty-two and showing every day of it.'

We had increased my age a few years, which I knew wouldn't be much of a problem. I had never looked young, even when I was.

'Maybe I could have allegedly cheated on you,' I interjected. 'Thus our strict no-extramarital-fraternization policy.' It might be the perfect story: not only would it make for a ready, convincing response to randy old men, if any, it would also ensure fewer distractions for Terrence, who engaged in flirting as others talk of the weather.

'Hey, how come I get cheated on and not the other way around?' he protested.

Shayak waved away the objection. 'Who would believe you would cheat on her?'

Terrence shrugged. 'Fair enough.'

'Go on,' prompted Shayak.

'George will give us access to his documents, and enough of his time to make sense of it,' continued Terrence. 'He and his assistant will be the only ones who know of the operation. Our primary objective is to insinuate ourselves as deep as possible in the ashram to track any suspicious behaviour.' And all under two weeks, preferably.

'And what do we know so far?' Shayak asked, turning to me.

'Precious little,' I said. 'George has been secretive, trying everything he can to slime out of cooperating in this investigation. But it was either that or be held as part of the conspiracy behind the Maaya Island murders.'

'What I still don't get is why he was so rattled by that,' remarked Terrence. 'He didn't do much at the end of the day, did he? He tried to leverage a contact to find out what he could about the investigation, supposedly at the behest of a friend. Hardly something for which he could see jail time.'

'Right,' I said. 'So what that says to me is that he would rather open himself up to an investigation he can control rather than rat out this friend prematurely, and draw attention to himself.'

'George is afraid,' said Terrence.

'You bet. It fits with all his evasions.'

'So why not just leave the country?'

'Who is to say this friend wouldn't hunt him down? He is powerful enough to think he can take down Titanium, and corrupt enough to need to. George might be slimy, but whoever instigated the double homicide is most likely much worse. Add to that the fact that George has too much to lose, and that he is arrogant enough to think he can hide it from us.'

'If his computer is anything to go by, he might be right,' said Terrence.

We had brought a copy of his hard drive and the search turned up nothing of note. I had been combing through the documents for the past few weeks after tech handed it over to me, but apart from a few cryptic files I couldn't quite make sense of, there was nothing. I had left the original with an expert in Mumbai – Neeraj, who had helped us in the past – to pull any available metadata.

'And yet we have no choice but to work with him,' continued Terrence.

'George is, unfortunately, our only good lead,' said Shayak. All of the information we had retrieved from the murderer – his apartment, hard drive, cloud – was useless. He was not cooperating; after his arrest, he had hired the best lawyer he could find and clammed right up.

'We also have motive,' I said. 'Take down Titanium – and you along with it – at any cost. Which brings us to the drug angle – and if we can find some sort of connection, that seems as good a place as any to start looking.'

'And here is what we know about that,' said Shayak. 'About two years ago, there was a huge drug haul confiscated from some trucks by the Mumbai Police. The stash was housed in a building where there was an explosion, leading to the deaths of DCP Daanish Alam, who had been called in to investigate, another policeman and three civilians. The drugs were removed before the bomb was set off. We were asked to investigate, but then were called off a few months later. Details about the forensics, etc. are here,' he said, passing around a sheet of paper.

'Then, just over three months ago, in a remarkably similar series of events, a consignment was intercepted in Mumbai, packed with synthetically produced drugs such as oxycodone and ketamine. Due to the echoes of the previous bust, our friend, the new DCP Ajay Shankaran called us in. There was a shoot-out, and though this time they couldn't make off with the drugs, three people died in the crossfire.'

Terrence and I already knew this much, but I could sense Shayak had made some headway.

'What we know now, after detailed chemical analyses, is that these drugs might be from the same source. There was just enough trace left from the first bust for us to see some similarities.'

'So they are both from Goa?' I asked.

'If my initial investigation was correct, then yes. The trucks had come from Goa, or at the very least, through Goa, because the drivers who had been apprehended had not been present when the cargo was loaded and could not give a definitive location. But the chemical analyses in conjunction with my original data that the explosives used in that first blast originated from an ordnance factory in Goa seem to confirm that Goa is the thread tying all this together. And it has become pressing – and personal – because the murders at Maaya Island were part of a concerted effort to ruin

Titanium after the conspiracy to infiltrate it and destroy evidence of this Goan drug trail failed.'

'Saving Titanium means solving this crime,' said Terrence.

'Exactly. And whoever masterminded the plot had made initial contact with the murderer when he was working for George in Goa. Even if George is only the "connector" he claims he is, he is closely associated with the people behind all of this,' I said. 'And that's why we need to go back into George's affairs for over two years. He can't have always been this careful. If we dig deep enough, we'll find his mistakes.'

Shayak pulled out a brown cardboard box from under the table.

'What's in there?' asked Terrence.

'Everything pertaining to Daanish Alam that was recovered from the first Worli explosion. If we are correct in assuming that the real objective of the blast was to kill Daanish, we need to learn what we can about his death, and his life too.'

'Isn't this box police property?' I asked.

'Yes, but since they didn't launch an investigation into his death per se, it was just lying around. Ajay has made it available to us.'

Ajay Shankaran, officer in charge of the Maaya Island case. We had worked together on it, and he had asked me out once, though with all the madness that subsequently ensued, I hadn't seen him since the case was closed.

'Once we are done with it,' Shayak continued, 'I've been asked to hand over the contents to his wife. She is coming here now.'

I opened it. A fragment of khaki uniform, bloodstained,

signs of charring. A belt buckle. A rusty key chain, at the very bottom of the box, holding one old-fashioned rusty key, and dangling from it, the remnant of a small lilac seashell.

'What does this key open?' I asked.

'The police didn't know – nothing at his office apparently,' said Shayak.

'We'll just have to ask his wife,' I said.

I returned to the forensics on the blast. Shayak's data connecting the explosives to the Goa factory was there, as well as the chemical composition of the drugs. The details of the five victims. Not much else could be salvaged from the site after the explosion and firefighting.

Shayak passed out another couple of sheets. 'The forensics from the shoot-out.'

My attention went first to the comparison between the two drug consignments. There were overlaps in the chemical fingerprint, but it hardly seemed damning.

'Just how little of the earlier drugs were found?' I asked.

'Honestly, there was only what we found on one of the two drivers, who had helped himself to some MDMA. So on that basis, we can definitely say that at least one of the drugs in the two shipments was almost identical.'

'Apart from that, every last pill was gone?'

He nodded. 'They weren't messing around.'

'So we are actually looking at a burglary and then an explosion?'

'Yes. The drugs were cleaned out of the building and then the bomb went off.'

'Why do you think Daanish was the target, then? Wasn't crores worth of drugs enough motive?' asked Terrence.

Shayak looked at me for an explanation. 'Sure – but why

bomb a building when you had already broken in and got what you wanted? It just isn't efficient,' I said.

'So you think the same people who sent the shipment and bombed the building later dispatched another shipment which got intercepted and sent in the firing squad to get it?'

'It is always possible that the drugs are being sold to a number of distributors, but the other methods employed – the way the trucks were loaded keeping the drivers in the dark, the origin of the trucks in Goa, even the way the consignments were shipped – point to the same people,' Shayak replied.

'Have any other shipments of the same kind been intercepted?' I asked.

'No.'

'It is very puzzling in its circularity,' I mused. 'Similar drugs, similar bust. What are the odds?'

Shayak nodded. 'This new evidence regarding the similarity of the drugs changes things. Hopefully we will learn more by going to the source of the drugs.'

'And also, maybe we need to relook at the second drug bust,' I suggested.

'The cops are all over that, aren't they?' said Terrence.

'Not as much as you'd think,' said Shayak.

'Do we know how the drugs were intercepted?'

'They claim it was a random discovery. The trucks were pulled over, and the drugs were discovered in furniture cartons.'

'Ajay called you in to investigate when he found irregularities.'

'And we were called off, and all hell broke loose soon after. Ajay is off the case too.'

'Why?'

'He has not been given a reason.'

'Can he be brought in?'

'I don't know. He is pretty ill at ease right now. The commissioner has made it clear that all collaborations with Titanium are off, even if we help close a case. I'll give it a shot, though.'

*

A guard entered the room to let us know that Faiza Alam had arrived. Shayak asked him to show her to the smaller conference room and organize a fresh round of coffee, grabbed the box and headed out.

Faiza was a pale woman, eyes shadowed by dark circles which cast a pall over her pretty features.

'Thank you for coming, Ms Alam,' said Shayak.

'Call me Faiza,' she replied.

'I know this is not easy to do. We wouldn't be doing it at all if it wasn't most necessary.'

'What I don't understand is the sudden urgency,' she said softly, her voice quivering just a little bit.

'New evidence has emerged that suggests what Daanish knew might be the key to understanding his death.'

She frowned. 'Didn't that terrorist group claim responsibility?'

'Yes. But there might be a link to more recent crimes – murders – which has caused us to relook at it.'

'I don't understand – why wasn't something done earlier in that case?'

'As you know, Faiza, there never was a formal investigation into Daanish's death, because it was deemed an accident. Now we feel he may have been the target of the explosion.'

'Not the drugs they stole?'

'In addition to that.'

'I don't understand.'

'Neither do we – not really. That's why we are starting from scratch. I want to know what Daanish was working on before the explosion. Anything that might point to a motive. We wanted to know if you remember something – anything at all – that might be of use.'

Faiza shrugged. 'Daanish never discussed his work with me.'

'Not even something big? What if he was in danger?'

'Especially then he'd keep it quiet.'

'Why?'

She paused. 'Daanish and I, we had problems.'

'Could I ask about what?' I had never seen Shayak being this gentle, as though Faiza might break with one loud noise.

'I don't see how it can possibly matter.'

'Maybe it doesn't. But knowing all the facts can only help us at this point.'

She sighed. 'A couple of years after we were married, Daanish went on a raid of some sort. He was shot. The stress of that caused me to miscarry. He blamed himself, and I went through a long period of depression afterwards. We never quite recovered from that; it caused a rift that we could never quite repair.'

'But you stayed together?'

'Only, I think, because Daanish felt too guilty to ask for a divorce.' There was no bitterness in her voice, only a sadness that she wore like a veil.

'Was there anyone else he may have confided in?'

'A lover, you mean? Believe me, I have asked myself that

question a million times, have gone through every inch of our house, but have found no evidence of it.'

'What about a friend?'

'Sometimes I think he didn't have any. He had become increasingly isolated, as though he had no interest in our life together, or his old life, old connections.'

'Was he travelling in the months before his death?'

Faiza squinted a little, trying to remember. 'Yes, I do believe he had been.'

'Do you know where?'

'Oh, I don't remember. Well, I think . . . no. He was never gone for more than three–four days at a time. There were two, maybe three trips?'

'Have you ever seen this?' I asked, holding up the key chain.

She took a long look at it. 'No,' she said, but there was a somewhat puzzled look on her face.

'You look like there is something you want to add,' I said.

'It's just that – the shell, it looks like something I had given to Daanish once.'

'The key chain, you mean?'

'No, just the shell. It looks like the one I found on the beach just after we were married.'

'Take a closer look,' I said, sliding it across the table.

'It really does look like the same one. It's so unusual, isn't it – that whorl of black against that spotless white.'

'Maybe it is the same one.'

'I don't see how it could be.'

Shayak took the key chain, inspecting it. 'It wouldn't have been hard to attach the chain.'

Faiza still looked sceptical. 'Daanish wasn't particularly given to sentiment. It is not like him to put so much effort into that stupid shell.'

'Maybe it feels like that now,' I said. 'But when you were first married, perhaps he was infected by a little romance?'

She smiled. 'Maybe.' I could see a flicker of light in her eyes, and I was filled with renewed regret at having to drag all of this up.

'What about the key?' asked Shayak.

'I don't know – it could belong to anything.'

'Are you missing any keys at home?'

'No.'

'It looks like it might belong to an old cupboard.'

'We had many.'

'Do you mind if we come over to take a look around?'

'Why?'

'It is the only thing that is unexplained amongst his belongings.'

Faiza shrugged. 'You are welcome to. I have moved back to my parents' home, but I brought all of our things with me. My only request is that you come when my father is out.'

Two

While we were still preparing for our true mission, my first trip to Goa was upon me, unexpectedly, thanks to a small company by the name of Santa Maria Travels. It was an establishment with a curious record. It was a small-time travel agency, and yet it had upwards of ₹9 crore revenue. It listed amongst its services adventure sports, scuba diving, snorkelling, fishing and charters, and yet the limited equipment for these never left a ramshackle warehouse. It paid tax, and no one had apparently audited it since its inception in 2005. Apart from a small office in Margao, there was no evidence of the company.

Shayak's forensic accountant had tracked down a few phantom mentions of this place in the records we pulled from George's computer and it had stirred his suspicion. That had led to a hunt for more information, very little of which was available, and that, coupled with the fact that we had come up dry on every other George-related lead, made a Goa trip at least worth a shot.

It was to be a quick affair. And though there was no time to soak up the scene, it only took me the duration of the drive from the airport in Dabolim to Panjim to fall in love. The smooth, winding roads rose and fell through verdant hills, crossing rivers over quaint bridges. I had expected a bustling, tourist-packed glitzy town, not villages and picture-postcard villas and romantic riverboats. And, perhaps the most special in a country where we are all packed in like sardines – for long stretches, there was no one in sight as far as the eye could see. Where was everybody? I drank it in, greedily.

Terrence and I stopped for a bite, in keeping with our tourist cover – or so we told ourselves – at Mum's Kitchen on Miramar Road. I realized then that I had never had Goan cuisine before, despite trips to several restaurants that claimed to serve it.

'The prawn curry,' I gushed.

'Yup.' Terrence smiled, digging in with his hands.

'I could drink the gravy like soup,' I said.

'Why don't you?' he asked.

And so I did.

We finally arrived at the Santa Maria office after 9 p.m., long past it had been locked up for the day.

We were not in disguise. Vinod, a young Titanium employee who was officially a driver and unofficially just about anything else, had been keeping watch for three days now. The office was on a quiet side street, and he had counted fewer than twenty people walk by it per hour after sundown. We parked the car and waited till there were no vehicles or pedestrians around. We had our knapsacks on, loose, printed cotton attire and our *Lonely Planet* in hand in case anyone was watching.

Vinod had made a set of duplicate keys for the shutter and the large deadbolt within. Making keys from scratch turned out to be one of the many talents Titanium had nurtured in its young, resourceful employee.

Of course, we didn't know what lay within. If this was a

cover organization for George's sinister activities, any amount of security might greet us, which was why inside our knapsacks was all manner of cracking-and-hacking gear.

But none of that, it turned out, was required. There was a reception, and a back room, configured for two employees. It was now empty. There was no safe. No suspicious locked cupboard. Just your usual ledgers and a dusty old PC that would have been sold for scrap by most serious businesses. We made copies of everything we could, took pictures, scanned documents, downloaded files, and by 5 a.m., we were out of there and on our way back to the airport.

So smug of George, I had thought, to leave it all unguarded. Till we started going through our loot at leisure, and I realized that cracking the information would be harder, much harder, than we had realized. The data would have to be analysed at length to help us understand it, to find patterns or anything else that might tell us what it was all about. When we got to Mumbai, we handed the loot over to Archana, Titanium's able administrator. George's giving us access to the ashram meant next to nothing for a man so adept at hiding.

*

It was strange to be back in the city that had been my home for only a few short, if eventful, months. At this point, I had been at the Titanium camp for almost as long as I had lived in Mumbai. Though nothing had really changed since I left, it felt as though everything had.

I was no longer merely a detective. As of the Goa trip, I was an undercover operative. Where was the old Reema who liked to bake when she was stressed and hang out with her friends and drink one cocktail too many? I couldn't remember when I had seen her last. And where was the girl who had met Shayak in a bar in Calcutta, over nachos and bad music, and felt the hum of excitement no man had ever caused?

And where indeed was that Shayak, so casually flirty, so utterly delicious? If *my* life felt different, what about *his* – how could he even keep his head straight? The roof of his world had caved in, and it was through sheer determination that he was still holding it up.

The new, inscrutable, slave driver Shayak we'd be seeing soon enough. He'd left the camp on official business of his own and would be meeting us directly at our first appointment.

Going under cover necessitated a makeover. I had been glimpsed in some of the TV news footage on our last case. But I knew it was more than that – not knowing who we were up against made this added layer of security just good sense. Only George and his assistant would know who we really were, leaving us free to investigate his staff and associates in the hope they would lead us to a man we believed spent some time in the vicinity of the ashram.

In the interest of discretion, I had called my friend Devika, my one-time boss when I was a food writer. A fashion editor, she knew style – and more importantly, she knew stylists. She was in Mumbai for a couple of weeks, staying at a swank service apartment in Colaba. When I had reached out to her for assistance, she had roped in Rahil Bhuiya, a new talent she had been betting on for the past couple of seasons.

She greeted me with a long hug. When we finally pulled apart, we were both teary. Devika was eight weeks' pregnant, so it didn't take much to get her going. And though I hated to admit it, I was more prone to waterworks than most people I knew when it involved the people I loved.

'I'm so proud of you,' she said, 'but I am also scared shitless of all this cloak-and-dagger stuff.'

'Forget that! I can't believe I am not there for the blow by blow on your pregnancy.'

'Trust me, you aren't missing much. A lot of head-in-toilet time.'

I looked at Shayak, who was standing in the corner, his expression unreadable.

'Why don't you two catch up first,' he suggested. 'I'll go in with Terrence for his session now.'

Devika nodded to Rahil, and he, Shayak and Terrence moved into the other room.

'When it comes to style, I trust you completely,' I said.

'Not about that, though, is it?' said Devika. 'What you want is more of a disguise – something a film stylist might do best.'

We needed advice on hair, accessories and clothes. They needed to be in keeping with our characters and make us look as different from our normal selves as possible. In Terrence's case, it was likely to involve facial hair, in preparation for which he had been growing a beard for ten days now.

'Rahil is the best of both worlds – he has worked in theatre before, and he is young enough to be open to this sort of thing. And given that he owes me his career, I expect him to keep his mouth shut about it!'

'How have you been, Devika?' I asked.

'The first trimester is brutal. My body is well past its sell-by date, Reema. If you want babies, do it soon!'

'Babies!'

'That's what I thought in my twenties too. And now look

at me. I can't sit, stand, or lie down without creaking like a
bag of old bones.'

'Nonsense.'

'Nope.'

'Still, I don't think I should be planning babies any time
soon.'

'No, no, you shouldn't be, not when you are about to go
off to play Wonder Woman.'

'I really would prefer Black Widow, I think.'

'Figures.' She shook her head, seeming more rattled than
I had expected. Devika had no idea what our mission was
about, and I was under strict orders to reveal nothing.

'I'm not alone, Devika. Don't worry about me.'

'Shayak will be with you?' The thought of that seemed to
give her comfort: she had met him in Calcutta, and had liked
him then.

'You know I can't share any of the specifics.'

'I'm not trying to set you up,' she said. 'I simply want to
make sure you have someone responsible looking after you.'

'I won't be alone,' I repeated softly.

'Poor Reema,' she said. 'You know how you feel about
him now?'

'No.'

'Have you talked about it?'

'Not since I moved to Mumbai. He had said then that the
ball was in my court.'

'I see how he looks at you –'

Just then Terrence and Shayak came out. I hushed Devika
before she could say any more.

Devika came in for my consultation. She had plenty to say
to Rahil. 'Reema here needs a new wardrobe for sure,' she

began. 'I've tried to help her, but I doubt she has more than five things in her closet that aren't black, and it simply won't do for Goa.'

He circled me, sizing me up. I wished Shayak wasn't in the room to witness my humiliation, the slob shaming I was certain would follow.

'It is your great advantage as a woman that you are unforgettable. Unfortunately, it is a serious disadvantage for an undercover detective who is trying to blend in.'

Not what I expected to hear. Rahil's history in theatre had left him inclined towards dramatics. 'Make me forgettable then.'

Rahil was almost talking to himself, mumbling away. 'You try to do this already by dressing in black. But not only will that not work in Goa, where you'll look like a fool in black, it doesn't work in the city either. It is impossible to make you inconspicuous. I can't make you into a fly on the wall. You'll be the centre of attention, never on the sidelines, wherever you go.'

I half expected him to click his heels and give me a bow.

While the compliment couldn't not make me smile, I knew it was hardly the truth. I could blend into the background if needed, as I had done many times in the past. I seldom sought out the limelight, and had become quite good at avoiding it. At skulking around in dark alleys, watching men and women do what they did when they thought no one was looking. I could be a man, with a hat, a baggy jacket and a slouch. Suspicious when you are in Calcutta and it is 20 degrees in the winter, but you hardly merit a glance when you are taken for a street dweller. I could be a sweeper in a sari with oil in my bunned hair and broom in hand. I knew the tricks to becoming the background score of any scene. In India, it was the poor who were faceless. I was lucky I was only playing a part.

And yet I looked into the mirror, trying to see myself through a stranger's eyes. The head full of corkscrew curls was the most distinctive feature, I thought. Then there was the height: I was well above the average height for an Indian woman, but there were ways to distract from that. Nothing else about my face demanded particular attention. Maybe the eyes. Large, Bengali eyes, I had been told. And high cheekbones.

Shayak, however, seemed to agree with what he had heard. 'I don't care if she looks good or not out there. We need to be sure she won't be recognized.'

The designer nodded. 'I think we will need a wig.'

'No,' said Shayak.

'I'll get you a great one. No one will be able to tell the difference. It won't be cheap, mind you.'

'It's not that. It isn't safe, it is too troublesome, and if someone catches wind of it, it is too suspicious.'

Rahil bit his lip. 'In that case, it pains me to say this but . . . that hair will have to go. And with curls like that, I'd say you have to go short – pixie short. Unless you fancy a 'fro.'

My hair? My hand flew to it, in an ineffectual effort at protection.

He shook his head again. 'But your height and body will always draw attention. It's like making a runway model disappear. Impossible!'

By this time, I was bewildered. I was more slender now than I had ever been, with the rigorous training and purely functional diet. But I had spent so much time in workout clothes in the past few weeks that I felt anything but attractive.

'What if we think beyond a makeover and think more

along the lines of a disguise. What if I am pregnant?' I suggested.

All eyes were on me. 'Are you now, love?' said Rahil.

'No, no. I was thinking of a fake bump.'

'That could work,' said Rahil.

'But it will slow you down. You need to be quick on your feet,' said Shayak.

'If you objected to a wig, how can you be comfortable with a fake baby?' asked Devika.

'It is so much less obvious,' I said. 'Plus, I need to be undercover only at the ashram. When I am in the field, I need to be myself, no?'

Shayak nodded. 'Yes, I suppose that's true.'

'So I'll need something light. And easily removable. Is it possible?'

'I can't see why not,' said Rahil. 'Only problem is that something light will need you to work much harder to convincingly mimic the gait of a pregnant woman.'

'It shouldn't be a colossal bump,' I said. 'A small one. Hopefully we will be done with this assignment before I am due.' The joke fell flat on my audience.

'You'll need a good quality bodysuit,' said Shayak.

Rahil waved his hand. 'I can get you the best. But there are issues. You won't fool anyone if you are naked. And given that you'll be in Goa, it'll be best if you stick to a one-piece swimsuit.'

From his face, it appeared he thought this was an issue. I didn't think I'd be hitting the beach much – or getting naked with an audience. 'Let's do it,' I said. I looked to Shayak and he gave a nod.

Rahil jotted down quick notes and handed them over to

me. Directions for the hairstylist. Points for Devika, who would be acting as our personal shopper. A little sketch of the spectacle frames he thought we should buy.

'You and Terrence are returning hipsters from the Bay Area. You'll work the look, I can tell,' he said to me. 'But he'll need some practice to get the Goa boy out of him.'

With that, he left. Devika trailed after him to discuss some additional points, leaving me alone with Shayak.

'Well, all this hard work has finally got me into shape,' I said.

Shayak looked crestfallen. 'You were perfect the way you were.'

'You don't like me thin?'

'You are gorgeous as a waif, and you'd be gorgeous the size of a house. This just reminds me of what I've put you through and I don't like it.'

'What, carrying Terrence's baby? It's nothing short of a dream come true.'

He scowled.

'Look, Shayak, last I checked, you were not the one killing people, selling drugs and setting off bombs. So stop taking credit for everything and let's get out of here. We have loads of shopping to do.'

Devika, Terrence and I headed to the mall, while Shayak had other matters to attend to – or perhaps he could think of nothing worse than spending the day shopping with us. To accentuate the bump, we were sticking with maternity wear for me. While Terrence needed many pairs of shorts and printed T-shirts. We then got our glasses and swimwear, after which I left for my next appointment.

★

I reached Faiza's parents' two-storey home in Bandra, which was painted a sparkling white. Inside, Faiza and Shayak were waiting.

'I have managed to send the servant away as well, so we have the house to ourselves,' she said. I wondered how much of this was for our benefit and how much to ensure tales were not carried back to her father. Faiza was a woman who was afraid of everything – I had met her before in so many other women, constantly waiting for something to go wrong, or someone to bark at them or the sky to fall. I thought I was an empathetic person, but sometimes women like Faiza just made me want to shake them.

We walked up a flight of stairs and Faiza led us on to a landing. 'These two cupboards belonged to Daanish and me.'

I wasn't sure what we were trying to find, but one thing was clear: there was no point looking for any trace evidence, after years of – judging by the gleam of the wood – polishing and daily cleanings.

Shayak tried the seashell key; it didn't work. Faiza opened the cupboard, which was stacked with linens and toiletries.

I looked at Shayak.

'What about that cabinet?' Shayak asked.

We walked over to it and once again, the key from our box was a mismatch. Inside there were piles of clothes with laundry tags. This house was clearly run with the zeal of a hospital.

'Where are Daanish's old things?' I asked.

'We gave away his clothes to charity. I only have one of his old uniforms and a few other items.'

'Any papers, a computer or books?'

'We gave away all his old books to the local library. Papers and all – well, he didn't bring any home from work. The computer was also office property, so that is gone. Some of his other items – certificates and so on – I have kept.'

'Can we see them?'

She led us into a bedroom. It had a large four-poster bed, an antique almirah with a mirror that filled an entire wall. At the foot of the bed was a wooden dowry chest. The intricate carvings were Kashmiri, and the walnut wood had withstood time with elegance. This piece alone had not been varnished or polished recently.

'This too was with me in our house. Whatever I have of my old life is in here.'

Once again, our key didn't budge. Faiza unlocked the chest and opened the heavy wooden lid. There was a shallow layer on top that held small objects, including the certificates and a stack of photographs.

'Do you mind?' I asked.

She shook her head. 'I don't like having them out, but you are free to take a look.'

I held on to them as Shayak lifted the wooden tray to reveal a single chamber underneath.

Right away, I saw the uniform. An intact version of the bloody fragment I held in my hands yesterday. Highly decorated. Trim. Spotless. I felt a moment of grief for this man I had not known.

Underneath that, wrapped in plastic from the dry cleaners, was an ornate pale yellow garment covered with zardozi. Below it was an identical packet with a black item inside. The wedding sharara and sherwani.

We were raiding this woman's memories. I didn't want

to rifle through these things. I tried to touch as little as I could.

The wedding clothes were bulky and the chest was not large. There were a few other ornate items of clothing, without the plastic covering, which looked like they had been worn more often. And there were some smaller objects tucked neatly into the sides: a man's watch, a half-empty bottle of aftershave, a pair of worn slippers, a mixed tape of Kishore Kumar songs. Items without value to anyone but their previous owner and his wife, for whom they had become ghosts impossible to exorcise. So she hid them where she knew they were safe from the world, and out of her view.

Finally I turned my attention to the photos. They were dog-eared and fraying at the edges; these had been taped on to mirrors and put into photo frames. Too intimate to contemplate on a daily basis, they had been removed and stowed away, while other, more formal photos – posed at their wedding, taken at a commendation ceremony by an official police photographer – remained on display. I flipped through them quickly, trying to get a sense of the man who had coloured every aspect of this investigation – a man I would never know.

A handsome face, quite pale, half-turned away from the camera, a light brown eye laughing as a large, fine-fingered hand made to cover the lens, pleading with the photographer to stop.

A young woman, so much more carefree than the sedate form standing beside me now, in ankle-deep water, hitching a long skirt out of the path of the wave, a smile breathing life into shy eyes.

A close-up of two grinning faces, squinting into the

camera, his arm outstretched, not wanting to interrupt a moment cocooned in togetherness by asking a passer-by to take a picture.

They made a handsome couple, in the first throes of love. He was a good-looking man, and Faiza, emboldened and confident, seemed like a different woman. All the pictures here would be at least five years old, by Faiza's timeline, before resentment had frayed them apart.

I handed the photos back to Faiza, and found her looking at me quite intently. She took the prints and placed them back on the tray. She was about to close the chest again, when something struck me. 'Wait a minute,' I said, taking a step back.

I inspected the chest from a distance and then squatted on the floor. Then I reached into the chest, feeling along the bottom.

'This main cavity looks quite shallow compared to the depth of the chest. Are there any other compartments?'

'No,' said Faiza, giving me a confused look.

I leaned over to inspect the bottom, and Shayak joined me. 'What are you thinking?'

'It could be nothing, but these old dowry chests often had secret compartments.'

Shayak had encountered my Cold War fixation before. What he didn't know was that it extended to all arcane objects of spy craft. Secret compartments and locks were a gorgeous part of the past that had crept away from us, in the rush for digitized safes and Swiss bank accounts.

'How long has this been in your family, Faiza?'

'Well, this belonged to Daanish's mother. She didn't have a daughter – Daanish was an only child – so it was part of my trousseau.'

We emptied the chest as quickly as we could. The bottom felt almost impenetrably solid. I felt around for any secret levers or panels, but could find nothing.

I kneeled on the floor again to take a closer look. The intricately carved exterior was a beautiful hardwood, and it was also the perfect place to hide a secret.

'Look at the joint here,' I said, pointing to a corner of the base as my excitement mounted. There was an almost imperceptible gap. I was sure the front of this was a false cover that opened to reveal something. Maybe a drawer?

After a few more moments of feeling around, I finally found it. A small lever that slid up, worked into the whorls of the design. And then I found its counterpart on the other side. I pulled, gently, tenuously.

With a thud, the front of the base fell to the floor. Inside was another wooden panel, about eight inches tall, and in its centre was a keyhole.

Wordlessly, Shayak passed me the key and I slipped it in. There was a click.

Faiza quickly kneeled beside me.

'Don't touch anything,' said Shayak.

This was a little time capsule: this secret compartment had been, in all probability, opened, touched, handled last by Daanish Alam. Here was a chance to find a clue as to what had gone on two years ago.

Shayak handed me a pair of latex gloves and pulled on his own. 'You do the honours,' he said.

I directed the beam of the flashlight inside. I could see only one item. I pulled it out. It was an old-fashioned leather-bound diary. I flipped it open, curbing my greedy fingers, forcing them to treat the pages gingerly – as though they might fall apart like some ancient manuscript, even though the journal was a sturdy, modern one. I wanted to shield it from Faiza's view, in case it held contents that might be painful to her.

But instead, I found a scratchy hand of cryptic, indecipherable letters and numbers.

'A code?' I said, almost under my breath, to Shayak.

He nodded. 'Faiza, have you ever seen this?'

'No,' she said, clearly shaken.

'And this script?'

She shook her head, bewildered. 'What is that?'

'I don't know,' said Shayak. 'Can we take this with us?'

She nodded and stepped back. We bagged the diary and did our best to dust the secret compartment for prints.

Peeling off our gloves we stood up and headed towards the stairs. Shayak had moved ahead, and I looked at Faiza, her face even paler than usual.

'What's the matter?' I asked.

'The seashell. It meant something to him. He used it to guard his secret.'

We had pulled a Band-Aid off a still raw wound. But maybe Faiza could be left with something to hold on to. 'Of course it did,' I said softly.

'I just remember him being so angry all the time. And me too.'

'Faiza, our memory has a nasty habit of hijacking all of the happiness we once had, leaving the guilt and the bitterness behind. It is what regret is made of. You can't let it win.'

She turned away with a little shake of the head, and I could almost hear the tear slide down her face.

★

My last appointment of the day was at the hairstylist, a swank affair that Devika had booked.

A gorgeous man, with the most beautiful poker straight hair, wielded the scissors. I had never been one to make conversation with my stylist, but for some reason, that day I did. Maybe it was the fact that he was from Darjeeling where I had spent so many lovely summer days, and I suddenly felt a long way from home. Maybe it was because it was my last evening being me for a while. Maybe I needed something to distract me as I watched the curls fall away from my face.

I had never had short hair before. Even as a child, I remember it like a crazy cloud around my head, and hanging down my back. I didn't think I was a person given to vanity, but I didn't know if I could feel like Reema Ray without my hair.

And then he was done. It was all according to Rahil's plan – very, very short. It was still curly – my hair would take a boatload of chemicals to flatten – but with a little bit of product, it looked so completely cool. I left, wondering why I had never done it before. I might still look like the old Reema – but only just.

I went home, showered and packed my new clothes away to join the rest. Finally, I had time on my hands, and for the first time in weeks, energy to spare. I called my mother, who had no real idea what I was about to embark on. The next morning, Terrence and I would be flying to Dabolim airport, Goa, where a self-drive car would be waiting for us. From there, we would head to the resort where we would be in George's care. And I couldn't tell her about it.

After I hung up, I thought I might call a few more people who would not hear from me in what might be months.

News of our safety would be given to our immediate families periodically, in case we were unable to communicate ourselves, but it was unlikely that we would be talking to them for any length, any time soon.

But I couldn't bring myself to call friends whose questions would go awkwardly unanswered or who would have to be told outright lies. So I thought I'd have a quiet night in, but then found I couldn't keep still. I blamed it on the relatively sedentary day I'd had after weeks of my Olympic-grade training regimen. I had to head out.

Without thinking about it any further, I took the elevator down and walked over to Shayak's building in the same complex.

But going up thirty floors to the penthouse took long enough to spark off the doubts in my recently-shorn head, and I told myself that this impromptu visit was just about seeing him once before we left. One last meeting not as Apu Shenoy, about to enter a dangerous world she had no clue about, but as myself, no disguises.

Getting out of the lift, I saw the angry holes in the walls, where the surveillance cameras had been torn out. He had taken all of them down after the meltdown and security breach at Titanium. It was an ugly reminder of how hard it would be to find people to trust in the days ahead. And how much was at stake.

Before I could change my mind, I rang the bell. Shayak came to the door, looking gaunt and worn. He stared long at my hair, and there wasn't even the flicker of a smile. I was beginning to think that he would turn me away when he took a step back and let me in.

I followed him into the living room, where my eyes went

to the bottle of whisky on the coffee table. It was half empty. This was a Shayak I had never seen. With his heart broken, spirit bleeding, body bruised. His life's work was being attacked from all quarters, and there was no telling how far it would go.

'This came for you earlier,' he said, pointing to a black suit cover.

'What is it?'

'See for yourself.'

I unzipped it − it was, bizarrely enough, the baby bump. It was a flesh-toned silicone belly attached to a full bodysuit. It looked like a part of a hacked-up mannequin.

'Wow, it looks so real!' I felt around, a little disturbed by the exceptionally lifelike belly button. 'It is going to be hot in this thing.'

Shayak was watching, grim.

'What's wrong? And please don't give me any more crap about feeling responsible for me.'

'It might seem like crap to you, but you show up here without your hair, ready to put on a plastic baby and expect me to feel fine about it?'

I was filled with the most irrepressible desire to laugh.

That seemed to rile Shayak even more.

'So you don't like the hair, then?' I said.

Finally, the glimmer of a smile. 'Like I said earlier, you'd look gorgeous bald, Reema.'

I felt myself flush, and flopped down on the sofa with more cheer than I'd felt in a while. Shayak could be a sourpuss if he wanted, but I was heady. 'Did the diary tell you anything?' I asked.

'Most of it is written in code I haven't been able to break

yet. But there is one section with a few numbers that leaped out at me.'

He sat down next to me and opened the book, and I leaned over to see. 'This is a rare instance where Daanish seems to have got sloppy.'

Shayak pointed to where a page had been torn out of the journal. He had rubbed a pencil over the following page, revealing the impression of what had been written on the missing page.

'There is a series of numbers here,' he said.

I peered at it. 'Looks like a licence plate number,' I said.

'Yes.' Shayak nodded. 'The truck that was intercepted by Daanish. But this next number, 41438211, I haven't figured out yet.'

Not surprising for the truck licence plate number to be in his notes. He was investigating the drug haul when the bomb took his life. The other set of numbers too appeared to have been written in haste across the page, unlike everything else that was methodically and neatly written in a close hand. A code like the one Daanish seemed to have been using would take patience, and even its inventor would need to follow a key while writing in it, which did not lend itself to hasty scribbling.

I pictured him, phone in one hand, pen in the other, taking quick notes and tearing the sheet away.

'Perhaps it's a serial number of some kind.' Shayak shrugged. 'It's not a phone number, I already checked. Now, what might really help us is if we could figure out what the number means, and also decode the contents of the diary *after* the torn page. They would have been the product of the forty-eight hours between the confiscation and the explosion.'

I nodded. 'Do you mind if I take a crack at the diary?'

'You think you can decipher it?'

'I think it might need a keyword.'

'Like a Vigenere cipher?'

'Or a variation of that.' Unlike simple substitution ciphers, which are easy to crack, a Vigenere cipher is a polyalphabetic cipher that requires a keyword for the reader to be able to break the code.

'Be my guest. I'll keep a copy and give you the original tomorrow.'

He sat back down and ran a hand over his brow. He looked as though if he closed his eyes now, he would not wake up for days.

'We'll stop it, Shayak. We'll find out who is behind this, and what all of this destruction has been for.'

He nodded, but there was no fire in it. He poured us both a measure of Scotch. 'I know we will. We have to. The question is: will Titanium still be left standing at the end of it? And will it all have been worth it?'

'It will be. It has to be. I am not ready for unemployment just yet.'

For the longest time, he stared out of the window into the darkness of the sea, and the lights twinkling in the high-rises that lined it. 'I couldn't help hear what you said to Faiza,' he said.

My words about regret. All of a sudden, I felt like such a fraud. I, who had turned away Shayak claiming that I could not be involved with him, my boss. I, who had been going to bed every night wondering what it would be like to have Shayak there beside me.

The whisky warming my throat, I ran my hand down his

arm. I would like to tell myself that it was without thinking, but that would be a lie. On the cusp of going under cover, it was as though I were someone else.

Maybe regret was not Apu Shenoy's thing.

He grabbed my fingers and looked at me. When I didn't pull away, I saw a shadow of his old, playful smile. 'Strange soul. You don't want me when I am at the top of my game, but you want me now that I am lying in the gutter.'

'I think you know that I've wanted you always. Want was never the problem.'

I reached for him again. For the first time, I was not afraid. The worst had happened, and we were here, still standing, about to encounter more danger than I had ever dreamed of. And I'd be a fool to continue to ignore what I felt.

So I kissed him. With all the longing of the months gone by. A kiss to make up for all those I'd held back. A kiss to make us forget.

He tore his mouth away from mine. 'Reema,' he said with a ragged sigh, leaning his forehead against mine.

I felt intoxicated, though not by the liquor. Why did he stop?

'I hate sending you out there with Terrence.'

I heard a nervy little laugh emerge from my throat, but it wasn't amusement I was feeling. 'I can handle him, he's harmless.'

'About that I have no doubt. It's just that Terrence is not who I would like by your side during this mission. I should be the one with you.'

'You have too much going on. You can't be stuck in Goa indefinitely.'

'I know, I know. And yet it is where I want to be. Which is why, Reema, I will finally admit that you were right to stop us from happening,' he said, getting as far away from me as he could on that sofa. 'What we are going to do is hard enough without compromising our judgement with this.'

'Maybe by ignoring it we are making it worse?'

'Reema, I wish what I wanted was so simple that sleeping with you would help get it out of my system. But that is not the half of it. I want all of you, and so badly that I am afraid if you touch me again, I won't stop myself. But I won't sabotage us.'

I wanted to ask him what he meant. If, when it was over, it would finally be our time. But what if this never got over? There was so much we didn't know that the question seemed too dangerous to ask. And maybe I just didn't want to hear the answer.

Had I not erected the walls earlier, things might have been different now. But what if our brief flare of connection had burned itself out when life became too tangled?

'How bad was it over there?' I asked.

'When you are in battle, you measure defeat by the number of bodies you send home. I got everyone out, so I am feeling positive on the whole.'

'You know you can tell me to do anything.'

'And I have. I am already putting you in far more danger than I should.'

'I knew the risks when I volunteered.'

'No, you didn't. And in many ways you still don't. How could you, when you have no idea what you are up against?'

Suddenly, my high was gone. 'Do you always have to be so condescending?'

'What am I saying that is not true? You are no more than a girl with a dream of being a hero.'

'The best thing I can say about that statement is that it is not chauvinistic,' I snapped, getting off the couch as quickly as I could. 'But that in no way stops you from being a pig.'

Shayak stared coldly. 'What do you know of terror? What do you know of blood on your hands? The thrill of danger has already gone to your head. Do you think I haven't been there? Do you think I didn't enjoy it too? But then, after a few missions, all you remember is the waste, and all notions of heroism are shot to the ground.'

Later, when I played this conversation in my head over and over and over again, it would strike me that these words were totally unlike the Shayak I had known so far. Even in the face of evil, he had never been given to melodrama. This was coming from pain. But at that moment, I was not in a listening mood.

'If you think so little of me, why did you give me this assignment in the first place?'

'Because I am a selfish prick. I need answers, and I think you are my best chance of getting them. Believe me, if I could afford to go undercover at this point, we wouldn't be having this conversation.'

'So you don't want to take Terrence's place beside me. You simply want to cut me out.'

'And I'd be doing you a favour.'

'Need I remind you that I got you out of jail a few months ago?'

'You are a good investigator, Reema. You might even be a great one. But this is war. What we need are soldiers.'

'Nothing like a vote of confidence before sending me into battle, boss.'

And with that, I stormed out. It was hard, though, to summon an ounce of dignity lugging that ridiculous baby bump out with me – especially when all I really wanted to do was hurl it at Shayak's thick head.

THREE

'Sweets, will you pour me some tea?'

Terrence looked over the top of his newspaper and shot me a saccharine smile. I choked back the bile, but only because of the people sitting at the next table.

I picked up the teapot. Terrence, it seemed, was going to milk this for all it was worth. Being married – even if it was only fake – to Terrence was probably my least favourite part of this assignment. But for the sake of appearances, I satisfied myself by adding one . . . two . . . three . . . four – that should do it – spoons of sugar to his cup before giving it a good stir and passing it back to him.

'What time is the first meditation camp?' I asked.

'Truth Temple, you mean.'

What George Santos called the core sessions of his programme, I thought with distaste. Maybe being Mrs Terrence wasn't so bad by comparison.

'It's in thirty minutes,' he said, taking a sip of the tea and spitting it back out.

'What's the matter?' I asked.

'Nothing,' he said, setting the cup down. 'I just remembered I wanted to cut down on caffeine as part of my cleanse.'

I had been Mrs Vishal Chowdhary for only twenty-four

hours and I could already take a masterclass in passive aggression. 'And yet you wouldn't think of giving up on a few of your daily beers,' I said, taking a sip of my beautifully brewed black coffee. I had feared this retreat would call for sacrifice of all sorts of pleasures, and have us chugging wheatgrass shots early in the morning, but I had underestimated George's business sense. Why impose deprivation when you can hand people total spiritual enlightenment and a wallet-lightening minibar bill at the same time?

'I'm Goan, remember? Cut me some slack.'

'Shhh!' I hissed. Terrence D'Costa was Goan, Vishal Chowdhary was quite deliberately not. He realized his error and looked suitably contrite. Thankfully, no one seemed to have heard us.

I rested a hand on my fake bump. I would have to watch what I said, did and even consumed in public to stay in character. How I wished to just enjoy Goa the way countless others did. A drink at a beach shack, a plate of calamari, a night of dancing.

Though the upside of sharing a room with Terrence was that he could order what I wanted and I could happily eat and drink without arousing suspicion. Such were the silver linings I was searching for. If I hadn't been cohabiting with Terrence, perhaps the need for alcohol wouldn't be so pressing. Perhaps if I could shake off Shayak's rejection, my moods wouldn't be as barometric as those of the pregnant lady I was playing.

A spot of meditation might also dull the edge, I thought, as we headed for the opening session of the two weeks of hell we had embarked upon. The map of the property led us to a large pagoda on the beach. It was open, close enough to the sea that I all but felt it on my skin. Immediately I felt myself relax. Settling down on one of the floor mats, I looked around me. The sound of the gentle waves would be the background score. It was hot, but the breezes blew away any discomfort.

People were still filtering in, but I wasn't surprised to see that the majority of our fellow participants were foreigners. Largely white. Some affluent seniors. Some younger men and women in their thirties and forties, wearing the loose, flimsy cotton clothes all foreigners seemed to favour. The Indians present were dressed in designer loungewear. I thought one man looked vaguely familiar — if I wasn't mistaken he was the spawn of a wealthy mill owner. George's reputation amongst Mumbai's elite seemed intact.

'First lesson of the Truth Temple. This is not an episode of Charles Manson and the Freak Show,' barked George, walking around the room with frenetic energy. He was wearing a spotless white linen shirt and matching trousers, his feet bare. 'People come to Goa for all sorts of things. I am not one to judge. But that is not why we are here. I am not going to have you drop acid, smoke weed, take E or whatever it is young people do nowadays to forget their troubles. That is the easy path to gurudom — get 'em high enough and even the shallowest bunch of morons will be convinced they are having an epiphany. Not here. Here we want to remember — because without knowing where we've been, we can't even begin to conceive of where we want to be.'

He looked around. His expression was more amiable than his words sounded, but most of the younger crowd looked intimidated.

'Cold beer, however, is never a bad thing.'

Laughter all around.

'Statutory warning: This experience *will* change your life. I shit you not. If you aren't prepared for that possibility, if you are one of those people who are in love with themselves, just the way they are, then walk out right now. You can enjoy your time in Goa and then you can go home, a little fatter, a little poorer, but otherwise none the worse for wear.' George looked around and one fellow raised his hand.

'I'm not your headmaster, Kapil, you don't need permission to speak.'

'If we leave now, do we get a refund?' The young man's smile was cocky.

'You think that's funny?' said George, suddenly icy.

Kapil was silent, assuming the question was rhetorical.

'Do you?' he repeated.

'Uh, no?'

'Good. Because the truth is not a blender with a thirty-day money-back guarantee in case you aren't satisfied with your product, or if you suddenly decide in your fickle little head that you don't want it.'

Kapil looked embarrassed, staring down at his bare feet. No one moved, in fact, and despite what George had said, I did feel a little like he was our headmaster, or the coolest teacher in school whom all the girls had secret crushes on, and that one of our own had received a dressing-down, marking him out as seriously uncool.

'You won't often find me taking myself seriously,' said George, 'except when it comes to money.'

A twitter of laughter, the loudest from Kapil.

George was definitely not your average spiritual guru, but this he did have in common with the best of them: magnetism.

He wanted to get you to like him so much that you wanted to be like him, or be with him. I could already see the beginnings of silly smiles on some faces, the younger faces. The older ones would take a while longer to crack. But they would get there, and I could well imagine that this was a state of mind conducive to emptying your wallets with speed.

And speed was important. Unlike many cult leaders, George did not demand long-term devotion. His product was a short-term one, though repeat custom was welcome.

He continued, his tone upbeat, which I found hard to reconcile with the hardened vein of cynicism I had witnessed in Mumbai, and seen glimpses of now. 'That doesn't mean we can't have some fun. Today, we'll ease you into it. As promised, we have a Goa tour lined up for you tomorrow. We'll get that out of the way so the rest of the time is without distractions. Later today, after we get things going here, we'll take a break and there will be a party where we will, like civilized adults, have a drink, maybe even a few. Try not to get too shit-faced. Use the time to unwind. Get to know those around you. The people you are sharing this lovely patch of earth with now are going to be your companions, your witnesses, your confessors, as you venture into the darkest part of yourselves. And it is thanks to them that you'll come out the other side alive.'

George then shifted gear. It was down to work. He and one of his assistants walked us through a crash course in meditation 101, George style. Which meant no style at all. We could do whatever we wanted at the sessions to connect with ourselves. There were some rules to follow, but nothing that would make you bust a gut. No talking. No phones. No loud chanting. Stay inside your head, and see what you find there.

After a few minutes of observing the sincere chanting, humming, yoga-practising lot, I made the most of the licence to go freestyle and got away from the room. I went for a walk on the beach and then, about fifteen minutes later, returned to the tent to sort through my thoughts, trying to bring my newfound sense of calm to bear on the case. It was hard to stay in the moment and feel a sense of urgency in this beautiful setting. Crime, in the face of beautiful breezes and sounds of the sea, seemed a world away.

But perhaps I could use it to my advantage. Sometimes what you needed as an investigator was simply time to be still. Caught in the hustle of daily life, it could be a challenge to tune into others.

★

At lunch, finally, we were meeting George for some one-on-one time. We had arrived the previous day, but he had so far managed to avoid us altogether. The manager of the event, Shyama – the only other person who knew why we were really here – had been handling us with seasoned hospitality while betraying nothing.

When we got to George's luxurious villa, he ushered us to a terrace secluded from view by palm trees. George lit up. He waited for us to start, flicking away the ash in a coffee mug.

'Why did you get rid of your beard, George?' I asked.

'Oh, that is my off-season look.'

'You like to charm your students with your bone structure?'

'Cheekbones speak volumes.'

'I look forward to watching you work. But about our investigation? I think we've given you enough time to consider your options,' I said.

He looked at me as he took a drag. He knew my baby was a silicone sham, and he made no effort to blow his noxious fumes away from me. 'I'm not kicking you out, am I?'

'We also expect some real cooperation.'

'What more do you want? I've told you what I know. I even have a whole stack of files over there,' he said, pointing to a bag in the corner, 'for you to go bug-eyed over. Hell, I've even handed over my computer to you!'

'The hard drive is suspiciously clean.'

'Didn't I tell you I was above board?'

'I'm willing to pick my battles, George, but don't waste my time.' Every single crumb George had thrown our way since agreeing to cooperate with our investigation had led to nothing. It was getting old, fast.

He didn't react, but I saw the flash in his blue eyes. If George was a con artist, as I believed every guru essentially was, his eyes did half the work for him. Expressive, twinkling, watchful, making you feel you were at the centre of a beautiful, bountiful universe. The glimmer was brief. It was not hostile; rather, it was curious.

'If I have understood correctly, there are two aspects in which I am related to your case. One, I knew the killer before he got the job at Titanium.'

'Yes, Rishi claims you told him about the job opening,' I said.

'Yes.'

'And you don't remember who mentioned it to you?'

'No. I don't, as I have told you several times before. Two, I had called Afreen, one of his victims, to find out what I could about your investigation into the murder of Ashutosh Dhingre. Correct?'

'Correct.'

A quick nod. 'Tell me what you need to know. Be specific and so will I.'

'You can't remember who told you about the Titanium job, neither do any of your staff – and you have asked. Strange man appeared, bought drinks at your bar, happened to mention the perfect job for Rishi to you, and you passed on the message.'

'Something like that.'

'For the moment we assume that is true. But we do know that Rishi was tied to you in some way, because he built your computer network.'

'Correct. But I still did not know him personally.'

'Then who was it that asked you to make that call to Afreen? Who needed information on the Maaya Island murder investigation?'

He shook his head, irritated. 'We've been through this before. I can't tell you.'

'Why?'

'My one rule is to never burn someone who wouldn't hesitate to hang you out to dry.'

'You really don't understand this, do you?'

'I think I understand better than you think.'

'George, your cooperation here is non-negotiable.'

He laughed. A short, dry laugh with just a slight edge of cruelty, reminding me that here was a man I knew nothing about. I stared him down, both of us unflinching. Time to try a different approach. 'If you give us a name, we won't reveal who gave us the lead. The most likely source for us would be Rishi, anyway, seeing as he is in custody.'

'You are assuming the person knows Rishi.'

'Yes. If they planted him in the Titanium job to begin with, they must.'

'Ah. So now we come to it. You think the person who asked me to make the call is the man out to get Titanium. The conspirator-in-chief, as it were.'

'Don't act as though this is news to you, George.'

'Then tell me why he wouldn't have just called Rishi up to ask him directly what was going on? Why would he have needed me? Why expose himself like that?'

He had a point of course, though not one we hadn't been over a thousand times during the months of training. 'Rishi was not exactly operating on script, was he? He went from saboteur to murderer overnight, and that doesn't seem to have been part of the larger plan.'

'So he was a rogue operative who needed to be reined in. Fair enough. But as far as I can tell, the person who called me had no connection at all with the murders.'

'How do you know that for sure?'

He shrugged. 'Call it an educated guess.'

We were getting nowhere. Time to pull out the ammunition we had. 'Would your answer be the same, George, if I told you we had a file containing certain dates of financial transactions made by Santa Maria Travels?'

'What?'

It blazed for only a second, but there was no mistaking the alarm in George's eyes. We had, at last, found an exposed nerve.

'It can be traced back to you, and it leads to an account in Mauritius.'

'How did you find out about that?'

No response.

Finally, he shook his head. 'You have this whole thing backwards.'

'Then straighten it out for us.'

'It's not that simple.'

'It never is. But you can take solace from the fact that you aren't of interest to us at the moment. And if you help, we'll make sure that, for the time being, you are of no interest to the police either.'

'This is blackmail!'

'If the situation calls for it.'

He downed his drink. He knew when the game was over. 'Don't put this in a report. Treat it as a lead. Keep my name out of it.'

'We'll do our best.'

'Satish Savarkar.'

'*Minister* Satish Savarkar?' said Terrence. 'What does he have to do with anything?'

'Former minister, if you are getting technical about it. He called me, said he had heard one of my followers was on the island and that he was very interested in finding out some information.'

'Where is he?'

'At Aguada. Not the hotel, the Central Jail. I didn't ask why he wanted to know. But the urgency was clear, and he is the sort of person I make it my business not to cross, as I was saying.'

'So you tried to get in touch with Afreen.'

'But she resisted. Who knew she had so much spunk?'

'Was there any blowback?'

'If Afreen hadn't died, maybe there would have been. But I didn't have to own up to my failure to control my former pupil in the end.'

'And you are sure Savarkar wasn't involved in the Maaya Island murders in any other way?'

'Quite sure.'

'Why?'

'The person you are looking for has a great deal of finesse. A fine conductor who has long-term vision, willing to plan for every eventuality. Satish Savarkar is a blunt weapon grabbed in haste.'

'You know him?'

'In passing.'

'Elaborate, please.'

Another cigarette was lit. 'This ashram is known for its parties. For Afreen's batch's graduation, as it were, her boyfriend Gagan – who owns the property we are in right now – brought his posse. Satish was amongst them.'

'So then why didn't Satish just call Gagan for help in contacting Afreen?'

'As far as I know, things went sour between Afreen and her lover soon after she left here. It wouldn't be the first time a couple split up after attending a workshop,' said George, with the merest hint of pride. 'She wanted to change her life – he made it happen when he asked me to get her a part in my friend Adil's film. I arranged for that. She attended our ashram and then Gagan's little pet decided she deserved more than to be a rich man's toy.'

'We need to meet Satish, as well as this ex-boyfriend of Afreen's.'

'I don't know about that. Gagan has been overseas a lot, but I'll find out. Though, honestly, he isn't likely to give you much. And about Satish, sorry, I can't help you there. Aguada Jail is a little beyond even my reach.'

★

'What bollocks!' said Terrence as we walked away.

'I am not so sure about that,' I said.

'What! You actually believe him?'

'Which part do you specifically disbelieve?'

'The whole thing! He is still jerking us around. Satish Savarkar, my left —'

'I have to disagree.'

'So now you trust that two-faced fraud? Savarkar called, but had nothing to do with it. He knows Rishi, but has nothing to do with him any more either? How convenient.'

'So many of our assumptions are far-fetched. What we have is one crime, and too many people who seem to have a hand in it.'

Terrence didn't seem to be paying attention. 'George is all about denial. From the get-go.'

'Even so. I think we have a few facts which seem connected because they happen to have something to do with George, but are actually quite disparate.'

'What do you mean?'

'That it is not all as neatly packaged as we think. Just because he knows some people connected with this case doesn't mean he is complicit. If you see George as the connector that he is, it makes more sense. Goa is a small place, am I right?'

'Right.'

'So he happened to know Rishi for legitimate business purposes. They were working together. That is where our conspirator found him. Nothing sinister there: plenty of people spend time in Goa and the ashram is very popular. Then he happened to know Afreen's boyfriend, which is what connects George to Afreen, which is why Satish sought him out. How many times have you walked into a party of a friend and found another one of your friends there, and you had no idea till just then that your two friends knew each other?'

'It's happened.'

'Come on, it happens so often that you'd think we lived in a village, not the second most populous nation on earth. We make a big deal of it because we always see ourselves at the centre of every story, and we love stitching everything else around that.'

'You've lost me, Ray.'

'We're focusing on George by virtue of the fact that we are aware of the role he played in this. And it is true he is our only lead. But he may be innocent, despite how it looks, because we aren't looking at the whole picture. We are merely looking at one slice of reality, from one angle, and we may well be reading things into it that are not there.'

'Meaning what?'

'Meaning I am willing to take George at face value – for now.'

'And what about Santa Maria Travels?'

'What about it?' I asked.

'Just see how he reacted when you brought that up! There's some weird shit going on there.'

'Yes, but what about? There is absolutely nothing that isn't purely coincidental to link George's activities – illegal though they may be – to the Titanium conspiracy. Let's figure that out first before we jump to any conclusions.'

'So you are saying we are wasting our time here?'

'Not at all. We still need to maintain a watch at the ashram and its extended universe, including the Sundown

Bar, where Rishi's recruiter had found him.' Somewhere in
the ecosystem surrounding George Santos, there were people
lurking about with deep roots in this business, and we had to
maintain cover if we hoped to find them.

Terrence looked far from convinced, and I couldn't blame
him. So far, our hunt had only resulted in more questions.
What we hadn't told George was how little we had managed
to decipher of the Santa Maria files. Our gracious guru, it
turned out, was far more technically savvy than he let on,
with his worn rubber chappals and seeming Internet aversion.
His bookkeeping was complex and almost impossible to
follow. But at least now I had his reaction that told me in no
uncertain terms that with Santa Maria at least, we were very
much barking up the right tree.

It was something, in a world of nothings where we were
grasping at ever more flimsy straws.

FOUR

A few hours later, I found myself taking far more time than usual to get ready for the party. I was out of my element in a beach full of strangers, with an adopted name I was convinced I wouldn't respond to and uncomfortable in my own clothes. It was still very much a disguise I did not feel. I looked in the mirror in another attempt to commit to memory how I looked, to see how others might see me.

Hair short, short, short. I would have to stop reaching up and revealing my shock. I had never noticed it before, but apparently I was given to absent-mindedly running my fingers across my scalp, feeling my way along the length of one thick curl. When I had it coiled away in a bun, I'd feel the tendrils as they escaped.

But this was a minor problem when I had the show stealer, my baby bump. I rested my hand on the gentle curve. It wasn't much, but the trick was to draw the eye to it, make it my defining feature. I had been wearing it even when alone, only taking it off before getting to bed. I needed to get used to it, though the hardest part about it was the sweatiness underneath it all.

I tried to touch it absent-mindedly, as I had seen so many women do. The gait was much harder to mimic. I had read that the hips spread within weeks of conception, in preparation for the changes to come. A little bit of a waddle was hard enough, and it was even harder to remember to do.

I finally focused on my face. The same old face. But somehow, it seemed completely alien. The new hair brought out my features in a way I had never noticed before. Or maybe it was me – my gaze altered by the isolation of living incognito.

My cheekbones had suddenly grown angles I never knew they had. My dark, dark eyes looked even larger behind hipster eyewear. The shade of orange-red lipstick was one Reema would never wear.

My navy singlet was just short enough to bare the few inches of skin between my hip bone and navel. The prosthetic was good enough that no one would know it was a fake with just a little on show, especially by the light of the moon and the flickering lanterns I had seen being put up.

The wide olive linen shorts fell just above the knees, and below that were colourful chappals and toe rings – genius touches, thanks to Devika, which made me look like the perfect NRI tourist who had taken in a spot of jewellery shopping.

I was as ready as I'd ever be.

I found Terrence on the phone on the balcony, where he had been sent off to give me privacy as I got dressed. I saw the look on his face before he hung up, and I was left in no doubt of what I saw. Terrence was a man in love.

Actually, if I was to be perfectly honest, my *true* superpower was this: I could take one glance at someone looking at the object of their affection, talking to them on the phone, like Terrence, even so much as thinking about them, and know it. Even if they didn't know it themselves. I had a strike rate somewhere in the high 80s. My friends, through school, college and beyond, made good use of this skill of mine when they had an unrevealed crush and were desperate to know their chances.

So much for his bravado. My chill towards him thawed several degrees. Terrence's desperate attempts at flirting covered up a longing for someone who was, for reasons unknown to me, just out of his reach. He was far from a threat, his cheesiness merely a cover-up. I almost felt sorry for him, so I didn't even mind when he slung an easy arm over my shoulder. I gave him a smile, which he should have recognized as a relatively rare occurrence. But Terrence was still so lost in that phone call that he didn't notice.

'I hate this part,' I mumbled, as we reached the beach. The party was under way, one long table laid, studded with flickering candles. Waiters were walking around with trays of drinks and canapés. 'It's hard enough for me to hit it off with strangers without all this. . .' The word left unsaid? Deception.

'Just remember: if you act like you are in the middle of a conversation, you will always have something to say.'

'That is the most bizarre advice I've ever heard.'

'Try it.'

In keeping with this pearl of wisdom, we didn't bother with names and introductions. We walked up to one of the groups where a blonde in her forties was mid-anecdote.

'And I was like, I don't have a job, a husband or family, and I'm just not sure if I should head back home and try to work things out, when I started wondering why home was where home was in the first place if there was nothing tying me to it, and it was this whole downward spiral.' Her arms, with their beaded bangles and multiple rings, twisted through the air, mimicking her words. 'This other guru, all she had to say was that I should try om chanting. And I was like, I am chanting till I am frickin' blue in the face' – she really was the most spectacular shade of aubergine, though probably due to too much sun – 'and I don't really think it's helping. And at the end of the day, if a few prayers do the trick, why didn't I stay home and go to confession! They dish out Hail Marys by the armload!'

Laughter all around. A man, potbellied, nodded. 'I know what you mean. I tried the whole Buddhist thing a while ago. Went to all of Richard Gere's favourite places, and the silence just killed me. So I left, came to Goa and someone pointed me in the direction of George. Too early to tell, but at least the drinks are good, right?'

'At least there *are* drinks!' I laughed. And so did everybody else. Till I remembered I couldn't have one. I glared at Terrence and his beer as I picked up a glass of pineapple juice from a passing tray.

'Arre! No pineapple juice. Please!' screamed a woman as she snatched the glass from my hand.

'Uh, why?'

'Bad for the baby, na?' she said, with big round eyes, dropping her voice as if this was the part she was embarrassed about.

I put it back and had a fresh lime instead, afraid to argue too much because I was sure this was information every pregnant woman should compulsorily have.

'Sorry, I'm Malvika,' she said with a smile.

'Apu.' I nodded. She was an older woman – early fifties perhaps. Slender, fair, fine of feature and warm of face. Diamonds. Loungewear. LV. Delhi would be my guess.

'Thanks for the warning,' I said. 'I'm pretty new to this.'

'Three babies down,' she said with a laugh. 'Second grandchild on the way. I am an encyclopaedia of all things baby. So ask away.'

'Is this your first time here?' The last thing I wanted was to swap old wives' tales with a grandmother.

'No, I am an old hand here. This is an annual pilgrimage. When the rest of my friends go to London for plastic surgery, I come here and go back with a glow,' she said with a wink, which made me sure she wasn't just endorsing the rejuvenating powers of meditation. Hadn't I seen her sidling up to one of George's yoga teachers earlier?

'Really?' I said, as wide-eyed as I could manage.

'If you let him, George will expand your mind in ways you wouldn't believe.'

'What do you mean?' I asked, almost afraid of what juicy nuggets she would dish out next.

'It will depend on what you need. I, for instance, was deathly sick of all the boxes I had lived in all my life. Daughter, mother, wife. I know everyone says this, but once you get to my age and suddenly find yourself alone, you really *feel* it. My children are grown, thank God. My husband is gone, thank God. My parents have passed on. Where does that leave me? I had no idea till I started coming here four years ago.'

'And what have you learned?'

'That boxes are useless. I have no use for them any more, and I should have chucked them into the bin years ago. Nowadays, I do what I want, when I want, why I want. But it is harder to do than you'd think. Even with money, which I have, thank God, you get sidetracked so easily. So I come here for a sort of refresher course in not giving a fuck.'

'And have you found out who you are when you are not in a box?'

'It's a process. Not easy giving up fifty years of conditioning. I find that I like sex. I like wine. I don't like travel. I love my children and being a part of their lives. But I also like my job. I am a businesswoman and I am damn good at it, and I have no intention of giving that up, not for any grandmotherly duties I might be expected to assume. Though I enjoy those too. And that brings me to the hardest part of giving up the boxes: saying no.'

As we chatted, the surprises just kept on coming. If George could awaken all this in a woman of obvious intelligence and power, I might have to admit that I had seriously underestimated him. If this case was a complex riddle, George was one of the most puzzling parts of it and I knew that solving it would mean cracking him at some point.

The rest of the evening was a blur of new people and fantastic food. As I had suspected, the single men there were on the prowl, but a few complaints about my rocky marriage were enough to trigger sympathetic nods and a hasty departure. When I returned to the room in the early hours, I was exhausted and cursing my latex fanny pack, but even I had to admit to having had an unexpected amount of fun.

FIVE

The next morning, Terrence and I split up. He would keep an eye on the group while they were on the day tour, though I really didn't feel there was much to find there. But we were still in the due diligence part of our investigation, open to any possibilities. George would be there, and keeping an eye on him seemed smart.

I stayed behind to attempt to penetrate the shiny surface of the ashram operation. With fewer people around, and George gone, I hoped to catch his minions off guard.

There was one young man in particular I thought I could corner. He was a waiter at the restaurant by the name of Dhrubo. I had spoken to him over the breakfast buffet and learned that he had been working there for three seasons now. Something about the way he said 'scrambled eggs' convinced me he was Bengali.

I found him in the coffee shop, empty after the bustle of the morning. He was at the billing station when I wandered over to a table near him. He looked at me and smiled. I smiled back and he quickly came over.

'Can I help you, ma'am?'

I was counting on the Calcutta connection to break the ice. We Bengalis were a provincial lot. Nothing excited me more than meeting kinsmen in unexpected places. And while

Apu Shenoy was definitely not a Bengali, nothing could stop me from inventing a childhood in Calcutta.

'I know I just finished breakfast an hour ago, but this baby is insatiable,' I said with a smile.

He looked down awkwardly, obviously uncomfortable around pregnant women. He handed me the menu and I scanned it. In the dessert section I saw something that might serve as a sweeter icebreaker.

'Mishti doi!' I yelped.

'Mishti doi mousse,' he clarified.

Because this was an establishment too fancy to serve up the real deal, straight up.

'It'll do. I've had the most crazy cravings of all things that remind me of home lately.'

'You are Bengali?' he asked.

'No, but I spent many years in Calcutta when I was growing up.'

His smile grew bigger. 'Are you from Calcutta?' I asked.

'Yes. Dhrubo Chatterjee, ma'am.'

With that, he left to get the dessert. And a coffee too. Once he was back, he seemed more inclined to chatter.

'How long have you been in Goa?' I asked.

'Three years here, two years before that doing my hotel management.'

'Like it?'

'The work is good.'

'Must be a lot of fun.'

He smiled a thoughtful smile.

'No? Not fun?'

'After a while, it is just like any other place, ma'am.'

'You want to go back to Calcutta?'

'That would be nice. Or maybe another big city.'

Go figure. If you lived in the city, you wanted to live by the beach. If you lived by the beach, you wanted to live by the mall. Anyhow, I wasn't there to judge; I was there to pry.

'Calcutta is really something special,' I said, with what I hoped was a wistful look.

'Yes, ma'am,' said Dhrubo, nodding enthusiastically.

'Park Street, College Street, Gariahat! Such a buzz! And the food!'

I looked at Dhrubo's face and he seemed to be one more exhortation away from tears. Time to get down to business. 'This ashram must be pretty interesting.'

'Yes, surely.'

'Is George here through the year?' I knew he held sessions through the season in Goa, when foreigners flocked to the place. We were one of the first batches of the year. But what did he do for the six months when Goa was all but abandoned, especially by the foreign tourists who formed the bulk of his bread and butter?

'He comes and goes.'

'And his followers?'

'They come and go as well.'

'It's all so strange. I don't know what I am doing here,' I mumbled, taking a spoon of the mousse. It was vile. Overly sweet, heavily scented with cardamom. I chased it with coffee.

'Why, if I may ask, ma'am?'

'This whole thing seems so . . . fake to me.'

'Just wait, ma'am. George sir has helped many people.'

'You think so?'

'Why else would they come back, some of them every year?'

Because they were sheep looking for a shepherd? 'I don't know. I just don't think it will help me. Also, some of the other people here seem very strange to me.'

He maintained the dignified demeanour of a seasoned hotel staff. He couldn't ask questions, step out of line. But he was waiting for me to say more.

'They don't seem to care who's married, who's not. . .' I let all that tantalizing moral outrage hang in the air.

He looked down again.

'I don't even know if it's safe!' I whispered. More of a stage whisper.

Finally he broke. 'About that, you should be careful, ma'am.'

'What do you mean?' I asked, eyes wide.

'Nothing, nothing,' he said, embarrassed, pouring more water into my glass though it was already almost full.

'You know, if it weren't for my condition. . .'

He starting talking almost instantly – anything to stop me. 'A few years ago,' he said in hushed tones, 'there was an incident with one of the female staff.'

'What kind of incident?'

'You know . . . some improper behaviour.' He blushed.

'How do you know?'

'The whole hotel was talking about it, because of who the man was.'

My eyes were saucers in my head.

'Who?'

'The owner's friend from Mumbai,' he said, looking around, dropping his voice further, 'Johnny Brar.'

'Really? The arms dealer?'

He nodded.

'Who was the woman?'

'Arti. She was very smart, very smart. Part of the management team.'

'What happened?'

'No one knows, but George sir had to intervene himself.'

'And then?'

'He made her the manager of Sundown Bar. To get her out of here, I was told, without official complaint.'

'That is his bar, isn't it?'

'No one really knows. But he has something to do with it for sure.'

'Anything else I should know?'

He pursed his lips. Just then, another guest came in and he hurried away from me. He seemed relieved not to have to continue the discussion. He had already said too much.

*

Terrence returned from his tourist jaunt. Predictably, he hadn't noticed anything unusual amongst the new groupies. The ones who were returnees didn't go anyway. He filled me in on the way to Aguada Jail, which was about two hours to the north.

'Watching George work a room, or a bus as it was in this case, is really something. He has a gift,' said Terrence grudgingly.

'And what is that?'

'Charm. He talked to everyone individually and reached out in some way. Even with me. When it was too noisy for anyone else to hear, he asked me a bunch of questions about my family.'

'My husband's family or Terrence's?'

'Terrence's. Don't worry, I didn't tell him anything. Not that it would make a difference. I have a feeling he could find out just about anything he wanted to, about either of us. And probably already has found out what matters to him.'

'I have absolutely no doubt you are right. But there is no reason to make it easier than we have to.'

I told Terrence what I had learned.

'This Arti chick works at Sundown Bar?'

'Yes. I think it's time to check out that place for sure. George said his staff didn't know anything, but who knows if he's even asked them.'

The rest of the way, the silence was broken only by Terrence occasionally recounting a nugget from his guided tour experience. The drive from south to north was beautiful – serene, sun-dappled, charming. But any sightseeing stops were out of the question.

And then we were in view of Aguada Central Jail. Most tourists visit the seventeenth-century fort without even knowing that there is a functional jail right beneath them, just below where the tourists cavort, with their cameras and cigarettes and beer bottles. Just up the road beyond the fort are luxurious resorts with brash, rich tourists and cute cafes with European names.

I remembered what Rishi had told me when I first got to Mumbai, and he had made a passing effort at friendship. There are many Goas, he had said. You would have to find the one you liked the best. But even then, the contrasts between one side of Aguada hill and the other were so stark that they would make the most innured Indian's head spin.

We parked outside the metal gates to the jail, and were stopped at the gate. The guard took our ID cards and went inside. Once we were cleared, we were allowed in.

The jail had everything your average VIP prisoner might want. A cooperative warden, a view of the sea, five-star hotels and restaurants smiling over it from where meals could be obtained at short notice. But after nine long months of being locked up in a cell, it was home-cooked food, we had been told, that Satish Savarkar usually craved. Having failed to secure a free permit for tiffin brought in from home on a daily basis, he had induced the superintendent to find amongst the prison population an accomplished cook, who was given kitchen duty and ensured the former minister's dal-chawal-subzi, and occasionally even fish or chicken curry, were prepared with provisions obtained specially – and only – for him.

So it was no surprise when, after waiting a while for the jail superintendent to finally emerge and let us into the interview room, we found Satish Savarkar looking none the worse for wear, dressed in a greying but clean kurta-pyjama, not so very different from the scores of politicians on the election trail. He was fiddling with a cellphone, freshly showered and smelling of the talcum powder he had liberally sprinkled on his body, thickly layered on his neck.

'Good morning,' said Terrence. 'Thank you for meeting us.'

'The request came from someone I can't refuse, but I still don't know what any of this is about,' he said and smiled grimly, revealing teeth deeply stained with pan masala.

Shayak had dug deep into his ministry of defence contacts to set up this meeting. Thankfully, having worked in a top-secret division of the armed forces for many years, he had some friends whose loyalty remained unshaken by a little public smearing. For those who had worked with him personally, trust was not so easily broken by the politics and pressure that had lost him his government contracts.

'We are here because of your interest in the Maaya Island murder investigation.'

'Kya matlab?'

'When Ashutosh Dhingre died, you wanted information about it.'

'So? Is that a crime? I thought you had caught the killer anyway.'

'Yes, we have. But because Afreen turned up dead soon after your intervention, we have to ask why you were interested in the first place, and why you reached out to her in particular.'

'Arre, what a strange question! If I had known Kimaaya Kapoor, I would have called her. I called Afreen because I had access. But why does any of this really matter? In case you hadn't noticed, I am in jail for alleged crimes far worse than making a phone call.'

The man at least spoke the truth on that front. He had been the first one imprisoned during the crackdown on illegal mining in Goa. He was the minister-in-charge of the portfolio, and no amount of politicking could save him from accusations of spearheading the loot and pillage of the state's natural resources.

'We are not here to put you on the spot. We simply need to know why you wanted to find out about the investigation.'

'So you tell me, why should I help you?'

'Since you are blameless, why not tell us what you know?'

He shrugged.

'Why did you agree to see us?' I asked.

'As I said, a call came in from a person I couldn't refuse. But if you want to know more from me, you also need to be honest.'

Satish Savarkar wanted to know what we knew. I would have to give him something to get something. 'We have, as you have pointed out, already put the murderer behind bars. But now we are looking for someone who might have something to gain from certain other possible outcomes of the investigation.'

'Such as?'

'Seeing Titanium compromised.'

I could tell from his face that we had hit close to home. There was something, after all, to this theory.

'You called Gagan, Afreen's ex-boyfriend,' Terrance prompted.

'I did. But he couldn't help because he had not spoken to that whore for months. Said he knew nothing about her life any more. So I called George. He has a reputation for being a shrewd bastard. Knows how to make friends and keep them. He said Afreen had been a good sort, he thought she would help. But then she was killed, so it all came to nothing.'

'Why did you want to learn about the murder investigation?'

'I had a vested interest.'

'In what?'

'That I can't tell you.'

'Why was Titanium a threat to you?'

'Sometimes the best defence is offence.'

'Your riddles are not of any use to me,' I said.

'But it is all you are going to get. Jail has taught me many things, but mainly that nothing else really matters as long as you are alive. That is why I will not give you what you need, because I know that when the man you look for is pushed against the wall, there is almost nothing he won't do. Ask yourself, what does a dead man have to be most afraid of?'

'What is that supposed to mean?' I asked.

'Aren't you the detective? Figure it out.'

'If he is so dangerous, don't you want to see him behind bars?'

'If I thought it would diffuse the threat.' He paused, and then continued. 'Find out why this man is so afraid. Why go through all this trouble to discredit someone when he could simply kill him? Because he knows getting rid of Shayak will solve nothing. That is the only reason your boss is still alive. And that tells me you already have everything you need to find your man.'

And that was the end of the interview. Satish called the guard and had us escorted out.

Six

We left with Savarkar's words echoing in our brains. He was infuriating in his secrecy and wordplay, and I hadn't expected it. But I also hadn't expected the meeting to leave me so shaken. He was right: the only reason Shayak was still alive was because there was no point in killing him.

Shayak had conducted an independent investigation into the bomb blast that had ended with several dead and a huge cache of drugs stolen. That investigation was what led us to Goa. But having been called off by powerful forces, his work had not even been well begun.

Did Savarkar have enough clout to have pulled strings to stop Shayak's work?

'Terrence,' I said, 'do you know how Satish ended up in jail?'

'After the report on corruption in mining came out, it was pretty much unavoidable. He had approved massive amounts of illegal excavation and was found in possession of cash over ₹25 crore – it was spread out on his dining room table like a buffet.'

'Jesus. Probably just the tip of the iceberg.'

'Yup. The rest is sure to have been spirited away in offshore accounts.'

'How many years of jail time did he get?'

'About four years. That's including all his little excursions on bail and to the hospital. He knows that if he hangs tight he'll be out real soon. Fort Aguada Jail is a pretty peaceful place. Quite porous.'

'What do you mean by that?'

'People escape from there all the time. How rough can it be inside?'

'Rough enough for a man like Savarkar, accustomed to such wealth.'

'Yeah, but if people can get out, can you imagine all the things that are getting *in*?'

Point. 'We need to find out what Savarkar is getting, aside from home-cooked food. Maybe if we can cut him off, he'll talk.'

'It's a long shot.'

'No doubt. But what else do we have?' Suddenly I was struck by a thought. 'Do you know how Savarkar got *arrested*? How did the police get lucky enough to raid his house when he had so much cash literally just lying about? There must have been a tip-off, together with some very eager enemies looking to get even.'

'You could be right, but these things never make it into the open, do they?'

'We need to take a look at the evidence against him. Maybe we can find the leverage we need to get him to talk.' I could only hope that if we came back with more, Savarkar would give us more in return.

'Let's put it in the docket to Archana. I'm sure she'll be able to rustle up something.'

*

We were back at the ashram in time for the pre-dinner session. After being gone for most of the day, we had to show our faces, no matter how painful it was.

We were early, and settled down on our mats. I started doing some stretches, feeling desperately out of shape after the abrupt cessation of our strenuous workout routine of the last few months. I was continuing morning runs on the beach, and though lovely, it was nothing compared to what we had been doing.

People filtered in, getting settled, and I was struck by the sense of peace on the participants' faces. Was George working his magic, or was it the place itself that was so serene, so soulful, so soothing?

George was the last to enter, and he seemed to have shed the frenetic energy. Waiters brought around drinks of pineapple and tender coconut – tart, crunchy, oddly energizing. I drank up before anyone could tell me not to.

George started. 'Hopefully, by now you are getting the hang of spending all of this time with yourself. Today, I want to leave you with a thought that I hope will stay with you for tonight, and through the rest of your time here. Remember this when you try to peel the layers back: our truth is made up of the stories we tell ourselves.'

He paused to let this sink in.

'Think about it. All those little narratives that build our characters in our own heads. The one that got away. The hero within us. The dream we always wanted to pursue. Is that really who you are? What is your real truth? What do you really want – today, not yesterday, not what you will want tomorrow, not what your parents told you to want, not what you thought the neighbours would admire from afar. These questions are far harder to answer than you think, because we have all bought into our own bullshit. It took years to create this pack of illusions and lies, and I am asking you to undo it in days. Is it fair? No. Is it necessary? You can bet the rest of your life on it.'

He sat down now on the short wall of the gazebo, his hair turned into a halo by the setting sun. 'We are getting into choppy waters now. There are many ways in which this could work. I will leave you, as the best judge of you, to think about how you want to accomplish this task, with the tools we have given you so far. But I can promise that it'll be worth it, for by the end of it all you will learn what really matters to you. And then you can start rebuilding from scratch.'

'I am lost,' said Sabrina, one of the younger participants, from England.

'Then let me give you an example. A lie that I see people telling themselves most often is that they want to live lives without baggage. That they are looking for some sort of closure so they can have more meaningful lives. Really? Just think about this. What would such a life look like? Is a person without baggage someone who leaves little suitcases behind everywhere the moment she is done with them? Recognizing exactly when she has no need for the knowledge of the past? That would be incredibly clever – and incredibly foolish. For there is a great deal of useful stuff in there with all the crap.

'I say this whole trope is a lie. What you really want is to forget your mistakes, your embarrassment, your pain, because it is dragging you down. It is the source of shame. Stop trying to leave it behind. Yes, you failed, you were rejected, you were fired. Instead of running away from it, embrace it. Ask yourself what you might do with your baggage to make it work for you.'

'How is that a lie?' asked Kapil.

'It is self-deception. The only thing worse than that is self-denial.'

'How?'

'The great middle-class burden is to be responsible. In India, that involves taking a job to earn the most money, to make our parents happy. I see people in every batch who are approaching the middle of their careers and are finally questioning that path.'

I looked over at Malvika; she was watching on with serenity. She didn't look blinded by the man – she seemed to really be weighing his words. These were the messages that had brought clarity to her life once. And she kept coming back for more.

'These are just examples. For some of you,' he said, 'it is relationship trouble.' George continued his spiel but by then I was distracted, not for the first time, by Olivia Stein.

I had observed there were certain types of people who were drawn to George's ashram. Perhaps ashrams in general. There was the drifter, the kind Goa seemed to be full of. There was the sincere seeker, who needs a new guru every season. George had built enough of a reputation to attract people on the lookout for penny wisdom – self-helpers with the urge to follow. And there were people like Malvika, who seemed to draw something from the experience, enough to return year after year.

Olivia didn't strike me as fitting into any of these categories. She was pleasant enough, attended all the sessions as far as I had seen, and was participative when called upon to be so, but the rest of the time, she kept to herself. And yet, twice I saw her engaged in rather intense conversation with George. When she saw me watching on one occasion she looked away quickly – too quickly. And now George seemed to be engaging with everyone in the room, including me, his undoubtedly fake student. But he seemed to be skirting around her.

I would have to find out more about Olivia Stein. One more for the docket.

SEVEN

I felt my phone vibrate, and I heard Terrence's do the same. George must have heard it too because he turned around to glare. No phones were allowed in the Truth Temple.

The numbers we had were untraceable and unknown to all except Shayak. We excused ourselves and found identical messages. He was in Goa, and he was summoning us to a place called Mathew's, ASAP. Terrence knew where it was, and we lost no time getting into the car. We travelled for over forty-five minutes to Quepem, leaving the sea behind us, heading towards rolling green hills, and though it was dark for the most part, it was clear that this Goa was as lovely as the beach version. I breathed in deeply, the smell of the earth and the trees warming me despite the exhaustion of the day.

'Goa is so lovely, how can you stand not to live here?' I asked Terrence, mainly because I couldn't stand the suspense any more. Would it have killed Shayak to have told us what the emergency was about?

'I've grown up in Calcutta for the most part. After the city, Goa can seem a little small.'

'I think I'd put up with anything if this were my home.'

'I don't think the beach bum lifestyle is for you, Ray.'

'Who said anything about being a bum?'

'You intend to start up a private detective agency here?'

'Maybe a small cafe.'

'A woman of many hats! I didn't know you cooked.'

'Yeah? Well, I do. And I'm pretty good at it too. And maybe I am ready for a life I can't imagine just yet.'

'Sounds like George is getting to you, Ray. I'd be scared, very scared.'

We reached the town and followed Shayak's directions to the restaurant. It was a small, plastic-sheet-roofed shack set back from the road, the red plastic glowing like embers. We got out of the car. Five plastic tables and mismatched chairs were the only furniture here. No tablecloths, not even dirty ones.

But it didn't matter. For when I walked in, there was only Shayak and I. It felt like a lifetime ago that we had argued in his apartment. As long as Shayak kept looking at me like that, I found it hard to remember why I had been so angry.

But then it came back with a sting: he had turned me down. And yet, now, in those eyes burned an intensity that seared me to that little spot of earth. Regret, sadness, fear.

And that's when I knew the news was bad. I forced myself to sit down.

'Savarkar has been killed,' he said in a soft voice.

I let out an involuntary gasp. 'What? How? By whom?' asked Terrence.

'Looks like a fight among inmates. He was stabbed by one of the prisoners.'

'Just hours after our visit?'

'Within an hour, in fact. Either it was planned before you went in, which would make it a very neat coincidence, or they found out you were coming, surmised the reason and ordered a hit. No doubt that it was a contract killing. I don't need to tell you that this changes everything.'

'What do we know so far?'

'They will be releasing the news tonight to the media. This is Goa, so they have managed to keep it under wraps till now.'

'Why?'

'Savarkar is a powerful man with much political clout. He comes from a dynasty here with deep roots. I think they wanted time to manage the fallout.'

'Goans are not likely to riot at all, even less so if it's cocktail hour,' said Terrence.

'I am giving you the unofficial line. I came as soon as I heard.'

'How did you get here so fast?' asked Terrence.

'Chartered flight. Sorry to drag you out all the way, but I need to follow up on a lead.'

'What lead?' asked Terrence.

'I'll tell you if it pans out. But what we have learned so far is that Savarkar had a cook, a fellow inmate, who obviously had access to a kitchen knife. He turned on Savarkar after serving him tea. Stabbed six times. Bled out before he reached the infirmary.'

'Is the security so bad?'

'These VIP guests have the whole jail at their disposal to do their bidding. This requires a certain amount of laxity. This cook was apparently hand-picked as being mild mannered and calm; but he must have some deep gang connections to make something like this happen.'

We were with Savarkar for about thirty minutes. Before that, we were in the office waiting for the superintendent for about forty minutes. Shayak had made the call to his contacts to arrange the meeting the day before. My money was on the machinery for the execution being put in place as soon as Shayak's request went through, as the news of our impending meeting filtered through the jail grapevine. It was the only scenario that made sense.

'What about the autopsy?' In my first murder case for Titanium, we had worked closely with state forensics. But things had changed.

'It is happening, and I don't expect to see anything more than the official report. Which might be okay in this case, because the death itself seemed pretty straightforward. Plenty of witnesses, too.'

'And the murderer?'

'No trouble there. He was in jail to begin with, and there he shall stay. Not saying who put him up to it. Claiming that he hated Savarkar and his insatiable appetite for bhindi.'

Terrence managed a sad laugh. 'Poor sod. Hope he doesn't end up dead next.'

'I am grasping desperately at silver linings here, but at least this gives us our next lead,' I said.

Shayak nodded. 'We start looking into the life and times of Satish Savarkar. But we still don't have a lot to go on.'

'And yet, just the fact that we reached out to him scared someone enough to get him killed,' said Terrence.

Our investigation would have to move far quicker than we had planned. The strategy had been to peel away at George's ashram to uncover leads. Now we had another dead body. And while the perpetrator was behind bars, we knew there was a brain behind it all – and that is whom we needed to find. No one else would be looking for him. Or her.

'The conditions at the ashram – with sessions to attend, housekeeping constantly in and out of our rooms, no real

Internet or other resources – is hardly ideal if we are to conduct an investigation of such a scale,' I pointed out.

Shayak nodded. 'We are going to have to shift gear. We'll set up an operation room somewhere close to you. Archana and Vinod are already on their way by road from Mumbai with almost everything you need. Give them a couple of days.'

'Great,' I said, partly because that meant less time at that bloody ashram.

Shayak turned to me. He was all business now. 'Anything else to report?'

'I think I am making some headway on the diary. With that number we found, 41438211.'

'You've figured out what it is?'

'As a matter of fact, yes. Archana had the team look into licence plate numbers, addresses, even prison IDs. When we turned up nothing promising, I broke it down. I tried searching for various combinations of the numbers till I finally struck upon one that clicked, with some well-placed dashes and what not. What if the second half was a date? 3/8/2011? And what if the whole thing was a serial number that included the date as a part of it? I've seen enough court files for this to have rung a bell. Then I started that search – and it turned up something quite interesting on a legal database: the numbers coincided with a case number in, of all places, Goa.'

'What case?'

'Daaku Singh vs State of Goa. The number of the bail warrant. A case of extortion and corruption.'

'What do you know so far?'

'Very little. He was accused of extortion by putting the fear of death in someone – or something like that.'

'Brilliant work, Reema. Drop everything else,' said Shayak. 'That is where you start.'

Terrence cracked a real smile this time. 'I think I know how to move this forward,' he said. 'You'll have to come home with me after all, Reema. My cousin, the bright spark in the family, is one of the best lawyers in town, and is a conspiracy theory nut to boot. He's up to his ears in PILs. He'll know all about this and its dirty innards.'

Shayak gave him the go-ahead and Terrence went out to make the calls to set it up.

Shayak stared after Terrence for a moment, before turning his gaze to the fresh lime soda before him. 'How are things going?' he said.

'The same, really,' I shrugged. 'You have the updates.'

'And?'

'And what?'

'I am still not forgiven?'

'There is nothing to forgive. You simply don't trust my abilities.'

'I thought I'd made it amply clear that is not the issue here.'

'So spell it out for me. What am I missing?'

'I think I've told you everything.'

'Everything? I feel like I know nothing about you, not to mention this company of yours.'

'I haven't held back anything you need to know.'

'Still on a need-to-know basis, am I?' It stung, because I was fighting for the survival of this company, even as I was still being frozen out.

'You know there is so much I just can't share, Reema. I have a history in black ops. How much more could I tell you without breaking secrecy?'

'This mysteriousness. It's insufferable.'

'You are the first woman to ever say that to me. Or to any man, I'd think. Mysteriousness is usually considered a very attractive trait.'

His poker face didn't slip, but I heard the smirk in his tone.

'Self-satisfied. Smug,' I said.

'Scared. Nitpicky,' he shot back. He was smiling, I was not.

'Bossy.'

'Impulsive. Adrenaline junkie.'

'Hah!'

'That all you got?'

My back was up once again. 'What else can I say when you are being so insulting?'

'Ever ask yourself what kind of a person becomes a private detective in the first place?'

'You are one to talk. Commando-black-ops-top-secret superhero. Who does that outside of a thriller?'

'So, I get no love for keeping country, and well, you know – you – safe?'

'Don't go all jingoistic on me! Is my lack of gratitude really the issue here? I don't see you asking Terrence why he is a private detective.'

'No, you don't,' he said.

'And why is that?'

'Forget it. This is a conversation for another time.'

'No surprise there, boss. Again with your ridiculous –'

'Mysteriousness? Do you really think I am doing all this for effect?'

'Evasions. If I counted how many times you answered my

questions with more questions, you'd quickly see what I meant.'

'One day, I'll tell you my version of the truth. My scars are old, Reema. If I am mysterious, maybe it's because I realize how ill-equipped I am to describe what happened to me without giving too much away. It's beyond any lexicon I have mastered.'

'But that doesn't explain why you are perfectly happy leaving Terrence's safety to him, and yet you can't think past mine.'

'No, Reema, it doesn't. And while I can tell you that I am also concerned with Terrence's welfare and have spoken to him about it on several occasions, if I still have to spell out in words why I would like to keep you safe, I have seriously overestimated your powers of deduction.'

So we were back to us.

'But before you accuse me of some sort of sexism, don't doubt for a second that I think you are capable of this. If you weren't, you wouldn't be here.'

Terrence walked back in. I stared at Shayak for a moment, looking for a reply that would capture the curious mix of exasperation, sadness and longing I felt despite my every effort to tell myself I didn't care, but he left before I could say anything more.

'What did I miss?' asked Terrence.

'Nothing. He got a call. He needed to go.'

It was with silent dread that Terrence and I drove back to the ashram. If we hadn't been afraid to begin with, we certainly were now. The body count was mounting, and if these people could kill a powerful man in jail, there was no telling how far they would go.

We parked and walked through the lobby where a few students were lingering over drinks. Since we had missed the dinner buffet by several hours, we decided to order room service. Opening the door, I welcomed the cool air-conditioned air and turned on the lights.

'Terrence, wait,' I whispered.

Perhaps because I was living in the skin of another; perhaps because the stakes in this situation had gone up several notches in the past few hours; perhaps because I had never been in a situation quite this fraught with danger in my years as a detective, whatever the reason, I had become highly attuned to my space. I knew exactly where Apu kept her hairbrush, and it wasn't on the left-hand side of the dressing table because she seldom used it any more. Her running shoes were also a couple of inches to the side of the closet, as if someone had moved them in order to open the door and had neglected to return them to their original spot. And while all of that could have been housekeeping being overzealous with a second visit in the day, my bath towel was still on the floor, where I had left it to be replaced.

We'd had an intruder.

EIGHT

I put up my hand to get Terrence's attention. Putting a finger to my lips, I pulled out my cellphone, and my fingers flew over the screen.

'I think someone has been in here,' I wrote.

His eyes widened as I showed him what I had typed, and I opened the door and went out. I kept walking till we were far away from the buildings.

'What the hell, Ray! What are you going on about?' said Terrence.

'Things are out of place. It wasn't housekeeping. I am sure of it.'

'Then why are we out here whispering, instead of in there trying to find out what's missing?'

'What happens if they didn't come to take anything? What happens if they wanted to leave something instead? Like listening devices?'

Terrence looked a little shell-shocked.

'Why don't you check the perimeter to see if you can find anything – or anyone?'

I didn't expect him to – who even knew when the intrusion had occurred – but it had to be done, and I wanted a few moments alone to check the room thoroughly.

Laptop, tablet, all were where we had left them, I would

have to spend more time to figure out whether any documents had been viewed or copied.

We had nothing on there that could be traced back to the investigation anyway. Almost everything was on a cloud somewhere, and encrypted.

Daanish's diary was the only physical thing I had linking me to the investigation in an oblique way, and I had been carrying that with me. I made it a point to have it on me at all times, to keep it away from unintended audiences as well as to sneak a few moments with it whenever I could. There were no valuables to speak of, and it didn't seem as though the intruder had taken anything of mine. Terrence came back. He began to go through his things, and soon became certain that nothing had been taken.

I looked around the room and closet once again. There was nothing there that could have given away our deception either. My baby bump, the dead giveaway, was safely on my person.

And then, as I opened the drawer of the bedside table on my side of the bed, I saw them. My birth control pills, sitting on top of everything, revealing loud and clear for anyone to see that I was not, in fact, pregnant.

I stared at them for a long while. I hadn't left them there, had I? I had been afraid housekeeping would find them, and it would seem odd that a pregnant woman would have them so readily at hand. So I had stashed them away at the bottom of the nightstand drawer, underneath my Kindle. I had made sure of it.

Someone had definitely taken a good look at the pills. Whether they considered them and realized their purpose and their oddness in a pregnant woman's room was something

I couldn't possibly know. The last thing we could afford after Savarkar's death was our cover being blown – and that seemed to be precisely what had happened.

★

The next morning, we were back in the Truth Temple. My mind was all over the place. We had barely gotten any sleep. After an emergency consultation with Shayak, we swept the room for surveillance devices, such as bugs or cameras. We decided not to report the break-in to George. After all, what could he do, and how did we even know he wasn't involved? I was suddenly overwhelmed by how insufferable the whole charade was becoming, and wanted nothing more than to raid the place and find out exactly what George was hiding.

Meanwhile, George had chosen one of his incendiary rants to get us started for the day.

'Mental health is all bollocks. You want to be unhealthy. Not too unhealthy, mind, just unhealthy enough. That's what defines you. If you were to look at any special person, anyone who has amounted to anything in this rotten, mediocre world, they are bound to turn out to have the crazies in someone's book.

'And if they don't today, they'll invent a new diagnosis for you tomorrow. They seem to be making this stuff up as they go along. Heard about the latest thing? Selfie addiction. Why not call it what it is: vanity. Why create a new name for it? Doesn't narcissism cover it well enough? Not when by inventing a new name they can get some funding to study it, maybe write a book about it and charge a bomb for advising people about it, and then sit back on their laurels for the rest of their lives.

'The key is staying in control of the crazy. If you let it spiral, it's all over. Depression is bad if it causes you to kill yourself, but pretty damn good if it only causes you to question your life. Yeah, someone will come along and tell you to get some help. So you'll find yourself a nice therapist. With some luck, that will go well. But if you pick a bad apple, you'll be left with someone shooting a bunch of ideas at you about how you can improve your life. And if you think these ideas are balls, that they don't work for you, then they turn the tables. You don't *want* your life to change, they'll say.

'So my advice is to save your money. If the answers are all within, look within. You don't need a stranger's advice; what you need is good attitude. And you can only have that if you embrace who you are, know yourself, forgive yourself, celebrate yourself.'

As far as spiels went, it was all crap. Save your money on a shrink and spend it on George? That's what it seemed to boil down to. 'Manage' your depression to question your life? He was beginning to sound like one of those anti-science, anti-vaccine, anti-everything nut jobs.

But what bothered me even more was that when the rant ended, we were thrown into meditation mode. I could think of nothing I liked less than the prospect of spending the next two hours inside my own head. Overnight I had been stewing, and not in a good way. Savarkar's death, Shayak's words and the break-in had not added up to a good night's sleep.

Who was I kidding? I was no soldier. I was no cop. The only real danger I had faced so far was staring down the barrel of a gun wielded by a killer a couple of months ago. I knew nothing of living in the shadow of death, and with the minister being killed – in prison, no less – and our room being searched, who was to say what was coming next?

It was easy to forget that real lives were at stake. Had we not visited Savarkar, would he be alive right now?

I suddenly felt the weight of it all sitting on my chest. I couldn't breathe. I opened my eyes and tried to calm myself, but it didn't help.

I almost ran out of the tent and to the beach. When I thought I was out of view, I ran into the water till it was up to my knees.

I tried to concentrate on a fishing boat, way out, a tiny spot on the horizon. I willed my lungs to do their job. When I felt the panic recede, I turned around. And there was George.

'Trouble meditating?'

'What gave you that idea?'

'It's not easy being with yourself, is it?'

'George, can you do me the courtesy of dropping the whole guru act when we are alone?'

'Don't you think I have learned something along the way to bringing enlightenment to the country's well heeled?'

'Okay, sage, what've you got for me?'

'Savarkar is dead. You're freaked out.'

So he knew. I supposed it must be all over the news by now. 'Thank you. I really feel as though I've got my money's worth now.'

'You are slamming into brick walls wherever you go, but you have all you need in that pretty, rather oversized, head of yours.'

Strange how his words echoed Savarkar's. *And that tells me you already have everything you need to find your man.*

'You know nothing about me,' I said. 'You see only Apu, and she is fake through and through.'

'It's not easy to change the way you think. You are new to the whole undercover life, so forgive me for saying so but your acting kind of sucks. I can't help but feel I am getting pretty well acquainted with Reema.'

'What does she look like to you?'

'You want a personality assessment? For that I usually charge extra.'

'You can add it to my tab.'

'You don't have one.'

'So you get my point.'

He grinned. 'What you are is a clutter cutter. It is your nature. You see things for what they are. It's a rare gift. Don't underestimate it: it should rank high on the list of any non-mutant's superpowers.'

'Therefore I see how full of shit you are?'

'Therefore you will soon see my true value.'

'What I see now is that you have an unnaturally healthy self-image.'

'Don't tell me that the inimitable Reema Ray believes in false modesty? I don't set much store by it, as you may have noticed.'

'If I am so fabulous, why do I feel so messed up?'

'Because you are putting yourself under too much pressure. You have decided this is the time to address your hubris. But let me tell you this: you are needed here. Savarkar had it coming to him, and you must separate yourself from your guilt if you are going to proceed.'

'Proceed where? We have nothing to go on!'

'It's just the beginning. Breathe. Watch. Think. Feel. Keep yourself open and the connections will be made.'

'I usually bake. It usually comes together then.'

'You could make use of the kitchen here, but I can think of more enjoyable ways to de-stress.'

'Do tell.'

'Back up a bit first. Tell me what upset you so much back there?'

'I began to question why I became a detective in the first place.' I was surprised to hear the words coming out of my mouth. Why hadn't I just lied, like I had intended to?

'And why did you?'

'It's a job like any other.'

'Bollocks. You don't become a detective because you didn't get into some business school filled with thick-necked buffoons. It's not a job for you at all, is it?'

'It's the adventure.'

'More bollocks. You aren't exactly Indiana Jones here.'

'How do you know? Maybe my suitcase is filled with treasure maps.'

He ignored me. Now he was thinking aloud. 'You don't seem to be after fame either. Not a single interview to the press after the Maaya Island murders.'

'Shayak would have had my job.'

'For what that's worth these days. You became a detective because you want to help people and getting paid for it is merely an excuse.'

'Plenty of people really want to help.'

'No, they *really* don't. And you know that. Deceiving yourself is a bad habit you are going to have to break. I thought we covered that in my session the other day.'

'I don't *have* to break anything. Wasn't I clear, George? I am not in the market for a spiritual guru or life coach or whatever other nonsense you consider yourself.'

'Maybe you should be. Maybe if you had your need for a teacher satisfied elsewhere, you could let Shayak . . . er, satisfy you in other ways.'

'Jesus, George, this conversation is over.'

'A prude. Should have guessed it. Fits right in with the stick-up-the-butt control thing you have going on. It doesn't take a detective to see you two would happily jump each other's bones before I could say "daddy complex".'

'Your wisdom lasted two minutes. After that, it's back to potty talk. Figures, George, figures.'

I had put sufficient distance between us so he wouldn't see the smile on my face. But then I turned around. 'Who knows about Terrence and me?'

'That your marriage is over? Only just about everyone here.'

'About the truth.'

'No one. Me. My assistant. Why?' he asked, giving me a sharp look.

'And your assistant. . .'

'I would trust her with my life. More than I can say for most people. Has someone said something?'

I thought for a moment about mentioning the break-in, but then changed direction.

'Why is it that you aren't more bothered about Savarkar's death?'

'Like I told you before, he isn't anything to me. If I'd had any real compunctions about a possible fallout, I would never have given you his name. I figured you were discreet about the fact that it was I who spilled the beans, otherwise whoever got to him would have come for me first, given that I am a free man and more of a flight risk than that poor sod was. So that puts me in the clear.'

George smiled his pirate's smile, but it didn't quite reach his eyes. I knew then that he was lying. George was deathly afraid. Of what and whom only time would tell.

★

'It's these Russians, I tell you.'

Terrence was at it again. How many times had I heard him rant about the Russian mafia taking over his beloved Goa? But this time he had even more fire in his belly. 'It's not just perception. It's fact. They have taken over large swathes of the state and are trafficking in drugs and women, and the local administration and police are in cahoots with them.'

'When you start using words like "cahoots", I think it's time to question your state of mind,' I said, taking a sip from the bottle of water that felt as sweaty and overheated as I did. We had just settled down after some pretty energetic yoga at the end of the day's session. Determined to relax, we had picked a beach away from the ashram. It was proving to be harder than I thought, even with the Goan sunset in HD. We were waiting for Shayak to give us instructions: Archana and he had been working overtime to get the war room ready, and he was supposed to send us a text telling us when and where to show.

Terrence took a swig of beer. 'You aren't Goan. You wouldn't understand.'

'Actually, I think I do. I come from Calcutta, remember? Every Bengali is certain that the city has gone to the dogs because of some minority or the other. When we don't have a specific community to blame, we throw the blanket over all the non-Bengalis we can find.' Though it was true, I was just playing devil's advocate. I didn't agree with Terrence's generalized condemnation, but was it suspicious that a place so Indian had signs everywhere in Russian? Of course. And was I secretly looking for an ex-KGB, foreign hand in all of this? I'd never admit it to him, but how could I help it?

'Ray, this is completely different! The Marwaris, the Biharis, the Punjabis have perfectly valid reasons to live in Calcutta.'

'If you were a true Calcuttan, you would call them Hindustanis. And I am sure the Russians have valid reasons to live in Goa –'

Terrence interjected. 'Yeah – if you consider trafficking in drugs and women valid.'

I continued. 'Most of them are only here for the season anyway. They must get here by charter, no?'

'Yes, and can you imagine a means of travel better designed for smuggling than a chartered plane?' asked Terrence.

'Yes, actually, I can,' I said. 'Even charters have to clear security. Over sea and land have been traditionally more effective ways of international smuggling.'

He just shook his head.

'You are telling me that every Russian in Goa is up to no good? That every pensioner is secretly a drug dealer?'

'No, that would be absurd. Just enough of them to make me want to see the back of them all forever.'

'That is the very essence of racial profiling. Not to mention a death sentence for the tourism industry here.'

'Then so be it.'

'Fine, then. From which countries would you like to allow visitors entry into Goa? What about the Nigerians? There has been quite a ruckus about the African mafia too. And the British? Our esteemed George is doing his bit to rob Goa of her virtue, isn't he?'

Terrence rolled his eyes.

'It's a serious question. If the Russians here are all ganglords, and the Nigerians and British too, then it is our foreign service's fault for giving any old criminal a visa, and our police's fault for letting them continue to break the law with impunity.'

He was silent.

I dropped my volume and continued. 'And what of home-grown plunderers like Savarkar? Has any member of the foreign mafia raped this land more than him?'

It looked like this point might sway Terrence, but it would have to wait till later: both our phones beeped. Our instructions were in.

We paid, and left the shack by the back way and got into the car. We drove for fifteen minutes till we found ourselves before a beautiful villa tucked off the main road. It was a delightful old one-storey Portuguese home in sky blue with white trim. The door wasn't locked and we entered to find Archana, Vinod and Shayak, and a complete office. Three computers, router, whiteboard, stacks of files. I was amazed how they had got this together almost overnight.

Vinod gave me his customary grin and cheeky salute. Archana was grimmer.

'So this is it,' said Terrence.

Shayak nodded. 'You have everything you need. And if you find anything missing, it will be arranged. There is surveillance equipment and other material on the way. The two of you now enjoy carte blanche. Your only restriction is the need for complete discretion, and safety.'

The makeshift office could not have come at a better time. After the break-in, it was impossible to do any real work in the hotel room without serious paranoia. And there was much to be done.

I sat down in one of the chairs and fingered the keyboard absent-mindedly.

'We've amassed a huge amount of data on Savarkar,' said Shayak. 'Too much, I would say. His activities, criminal and legitimate, are legion and we'll all need to get cracking on this now. Any trail we can find would help. Any word from your cousin, Terrence? We need to establish the connection between Daanish and Daaku.'

'He is free to meet when we are.'

'Set that up sometime soon. But for now, let's get started on those files.'

Vinod was dispatched to fetch dinner. Shayak gave detailed instructions to a hole in the wall nearby which, according to him, served the best Goan food around. He gave me a tiny wink.

We divvied up the files. Terrence, who was most updated on his home state's affairs, took one half of the mining scandal documents; Shayak took the other half. I was handed Savarkar's jail records, and Archana, who had a background in finance, took up the books.

'Is there coffee?' I asked.

'Of course,' said Shayak

We went into the kitchen and I was surprised by how beautiful and modern it was – much like Shayak's own kitchen in Mumbai. Then it dawned on me.

'This is your home?'

'What tipped you off?' Shayak asked with a smile.

'All the same kitchen gadgets.'

He laughed. 'Why does it not surprise me that you noticed

that? It's been used as a holiday home of sorts for Titanium employees, so I try to not leave too much of myself behind.'

'Do you spend much time here?'

'Not nearly as much as I'd like. But that might change soon.'

'Thinking of taking a holiday?'

'I am seriously contemplating selling my flat in Mumbai and heading here.'

'Are you considering retirement?'

Shayak shook his head. 'Can't afford it any more.'

'Yeah, right.'

'Seriously. But if I am completely practical about it, I won't have to worry about money for a while if I do sell. And who knows, perhaps I am ready to retire.'

Overall, Shayak seemed to be taking the ruin of his company and the erasing of a decade of hard work a little too easily in his stride. I wondered how much of it was sheer bravado, how much sheer exhaustion. But I wasn't going to probe, now that we were finally talking without the conversation degenerating into a fight.

As I turned to see what else was at hand, I bumped into Shayak turning away from the fridge with the milk.

'Sorry,' I said, reaching out to steady him, before realizing he hadn't budged an inch.

He held the stainless steel jug a safe distance away from me and took a deep breath.

For what felt like the first time that evening, I didn't avoid his gaze.

'I'm sorry, Reema,' he said, almost a whisper.

'You were only being honest. No need to apologize for that.'

'No, I wasn't. I was being an idiot. You are the right person for this job, no matter the circumstances.'

'And you should be here too,' I said.

I caught the sadness in his eyes and felt my breath catch.

'I think I like it better when we aren't talking,' he said.

Flushing, I took my coffee and fled to the safety of the living room.

*

With the new brief, my plans of getting to the diary would have to wait. I flipped through the jail records, starting with the dossier that had been compiled on the murderer.

Chetan Sharma, a small-time pimp. He was serving a sentence of about a year for robbery of a client at knifepoint. He had cooked in roadside dhabas for a number of years, between Ludhiana and Panjim, and had gotten involved with prostitution somewhere along the way. There was nothing in his file that approached the violence of cold-blooded murder; nothing that indicated any serious mental illness that would cause him to snap because of having to cook bhindi, as had been most ludicrously suggested.

If there was a line, however tenuous, connecting this man and Titanium, I couldn't see it. Anyhow, I doubted he would have killed Savarkar of his own volition: he was a lowly criminal who had probably been paid money – and probably not very much either, relatively speaking – to kill the man he cooked for. If Savarkar was as nasty as some of the other reports suggested, perhaps he may even have been happy to do it. Was it possible that one of Savarkar's other, myriad enemies had put Sharma up to the murder, and that it had nothing to do with us? The timing was just too convenient to make that a likely scenario in my book. I knew Shayak had already activated his contacts to try and get more information about him, but as of now, Chetan Sharma was out of bounds for us. He would just have to wait.

I continued to flip through the documents. There were no visitor logs or records of a more personal nature. There was some paperwork regarding his special arrangements and movements to court. But from what I had seen and heard of the way Savarkar was living, most of his privileges had been kept off the books.

It was frustratingly hard to create a narrative of any kind when the trail of evidence was constantly sidetracked by greased palms withholding information or distorting it. As I delved deeper into the file, the only things I could see beyond the early paperwork of his internment and routine documents were several complaints made to the authorities about Savarkar's behaviour.

Instigating fights among inmates. Sexual assault. Even one about stealing food.

Of all the facts I read, this one seemed most bizzare. What sort of person would want to steal jail food?

Just when I was about to dismiss it as standard bureaucratic noise, I noticed that all the complaints seemed to have been logged by the same man, John Gomez. If the superintendent had taken any action, none was recorded.

Surprise, surprise.

Perhaps we could use Savarkar's special status to our advantage?

*

The next morning, I stood on the cliff in Anjuna, waiting. In front of me was a rocky cliff, and I could see no easy way to get to the beach, with the water breaking on the craggy red rocks down below.

Behind me was a curious sort of bustle. Stalls, touts, tourists. When I had imagined one of Goa's famous party beaches in my head, it was not this. I had expected loud music and raves, lights and action. Instead, it was like an affluent village, with white people milling around and eager vendors hawking T-shirts, junk jewellery, sunglasses. No one approached me with offers of anything even slightly scandalous, and I was starting to wonder where this party haven really was.

Gomez had refused to meet me anywhere conspicuous. I had thought he had chosen this beach because of its distance from the jail, but it must also have been because of the crowd.

He was late. So late that I began to wonder if he was coming at all. But then I saw him: so clearly my man, so clearly out of place here. Sagging cloth bag on one arm, tiffin carrier in the other, brown pants, brown sandals and greying cream bush shirt. Not your average beach bum.

'Thank you for coming all this way,' I said, walking forward as he approached me.

He didn't respond. His eyes flitted across my face before he looked away again.

'Where would you like to go?'

'Go?' he asked.

He may have been seeking anonymity in the crowd, but he was a potentially skittish source. Plus, there was no place to sit and it was just too noisy for any kind of finesse on my part.

'This place is a little . . . busy,' I said. 'A restaurant, perhaps?'

'No.'

'The car?'

He thought about it for a moment before nodding.

We walked back to the parking lot and settled down in my car. I took the driver's seat and he sat beside me.

'As I mentioned on the phone, I saw your complaints against Savarkar in his file.'

'They were not my complaints, you see. I was simply reporting. It is my job, you see.' His gaze was fixed ahead.

'Where did the complaints originate?'

'Some were from fellow prisoners. Some from junior guards.'

'And yet, nothing was done in follow-up by the authorities?'

'Nothing. Absolutely nothing.'

'Why was that?'

'It is all the corruption, you see. The superintendent, the prisoners with money, the ringleaders amongst the guards – it's all a big scam. Gangs have taken control of the jail premises and government servants simply do their bidding. Big, big houses my colleagues have all built for themselves. How, when I barely have money to paint my two-room home once in ten years?'

I nodded sympathetically, but I needed more than the standard recriminations. What I needed were leads.

'Savarkar had the superintendent in his pocket?'

'Yes, as does any inmate who can afford his price. But from everything I have heard and seen over the past six months, Savarkar was the worst. Whatever he wanted, he got, you see.'

'But it wasn't enough to protect him?'

'How could the superintendent, or anyone else, stop that cook from using his knife? It was his karma, wasn't it?'

'You must have heard something about why the murder was committed.'

'Why does it matter? God finally gave him his due.'

A less righteous man might have wondered how those words sounded before saying them out loud. 'I wouldn't want the wrong man to be punished for any crime,' I said.

'Wrong man? How can that be? Sharma ran from the jail cell covered in blood, holding the murder weapon! I saw him with my own eyes when the guards chased him down.'

As upright as Assistant Superintendent John Gomez was, his dislike for Savarkar was too strong for him to look beyond the obvious. I would have to appeal to his sense of justice, and for that I would have to show my hand just a little. 'Sharma may have just been the instrument of larger forces.'

'What makes you think that?'

'I wish I could tell you more, but this is all I have as of now. But I would request you to make unofficial enquiries. I know you are the only person who can help us, the only person who has not been bought by Savarkar in that jail, and therefore the only person with nothing to fear.'

I waited for a response, and when he didn't say anything I continued. 'We are looking for someone who may have been conspiring against Savarkar. It could be a prison inmate or an official, who was passing messages to someone outside on his comings and goings, visitors and such. You know the status of corruption in the police and jail administration. I think you are our only chance of learning the truth.'

For some moments we sat in silence. Then John Gomez sighed, deep and long. 'Give me a few days. Let me talk to some people and see what I can find.'

'Mr Gomez,' I said, 'please be careful. Make sure no one

knows what your intentions are. I hope I am wrong about this, but if I am right, letting these suspicions be known might prove to be a very dangerous thing for you.'

'Danger is not my concern, Ms Ray. I will do my best.'

★

When I left, my mood was grim. I could only hope that I hadn't put John Gomez in harm's way. I was in no position to offer him support or even a clue as to who we were looking for.

I drove to the house, the long, winding roads through dense green doing their best to chase away my worries. Shayak and Archana had returned to Mumbai and Terrence was out with Vinod. We were both playing hooky from ashram duty today. The murder had forced us to change pace from watch and observe to all-out investigation, and I was taking full advantage to bunk as many sessions as I could.

I made myself a cup of coffee and sat down with the files once again. There was a distressing lack of real material to work with. It all felt like ancillary data that would not get us anywhere in a hurry.

If this had been the Titanium of old, by now we would have had a stack of solid evidence to sift through, including Savarkar's phone records – something I very much wanted to see. But without official backing, Shayak had come up dry with the phone operator concerned, so the vital window into what Savarkar had been doing from the time we asked to meet with him and his death was closed to us.

But there *was* a window into another dead man's world that I was developing an obsession for: Daanish's diary entries after the scribbled licence plate number of the truck bearing the drugs and Daaku Singh's case number. And finally, I began to see why Daanish's shorthand was so confusing. Not only was it a Vigenere cipher, as I had previously suspected, it now seemed the keyword was changed at random.

Though it was a toughie, at least it was a problem I could solve. I opened a document and typed the first sentence. Then I found an online code-breaking software that came highly recommended by a couple of experts I had found via an Internet chat room. Simple enough.

It worked. But only just. The gibberish was translated into slightly less confusing text.

Inspt Sngh. Vhcle rck.

BDRE PRS RD – what was that?

My early excitement fuelled me to continue. But an hour of this, and I realized that I could spend all month working on the diary and still not get very far. It took so much time just to transcribe and run through the software, and that was before you had to make sense of it. Given how thin my attention would have to be spread right now, I just didn't have the time to spare.

The more I thought about the masses of work lying in wait for me, the more I felt the panic build.

I put the diary down, leaned back in the seat and closed my eyes. What with the ashram and everything else, I hadn't had time to process Savarkar's death and what it meant. It was our investigation that cost that man his life. What information did Savarkar have that needed to be guarded so fiercely?

I turned to the computer to read through the latest coverage of Savarkar's murder. The local media was hardly the most diligent, and while there was national interest in the case, it wasn't very large at the moment. So there was nothing we didn't already know to be learned from there.

Thankfully, Terrence soon returned from his errand and saved me from sinking further into the funk in which I found myself. We were scheduled to meet his cousin Joseph, the lawyer.

We got in the car, and this time I found the roads, congested with office commuters, less than therapeutic. But as we entered the outskirts of Panjim, the graceful town by the river worked its charm on me once again.

Joseph had not been told about our cover story or where we were staying, and had been sworn to secrecy regarding Terrence's presence in Goa to the extended family.

His office was in a lovely old villa in Panjim. It was close to Altinho, where the High Court of Bombay at Goa was located in a beautiful ninety-year-old bright yellow and white Portuguese building.

The high walls of Joseph's office were lined with shelves of books, creating a cosy space of impressive proportions. His large desk was stacked with files and more books.

He had Terrence's easy smile, curly hair and dark skin, and was dressed in a very lawyerly and immaculate white shirt and crisp black trousers.

'Terrence, I have to say, all of this secrecy is quite strange,' he said after greeting us. 'And very much unlike you. So far I'd say you were the least private of all private eyes I've met.'

'And you've met many?'

'Only if you count those in books.'

'Well, I am finally on a top-secret mission, brother,' said Terrence. I could see him swell with pride: it was actually quite cute.

'That sounds exciting! And you think I can be of some help?' asked Joseph, leaning forward in his large black swivel chair.

'I'm sure of it. We need information about a court case: Daaku Singh vs State of Goa.'

Joseph's eyes narrowed at the very mention of it. 'This is something to do with Savarkar?'

Terrence paused, and I tried to contain my enthusiasm. 'Whatever it is, Joe, we need to know about it.'

'It was a particularly ham-handed affair, even by the incredible porcine standards of our law enforcement.'

'Stop. You're making me hungry.'

'You should both come home for a meal.' Apparently there was only so long you could go in Goa without mention of food. I loved this place more every second.

'I can't, Joe. Not this time. Tell me more.'

'I don't remember all the details offhand,' he said, crossing the massive room to the bookshelves on the far end. He climbed a ladder on wheels and pulled out a thick volume from one of the higher shelves. Case records. He returned with it and flipped through the pages, finally finding the entry he was looking for.

'What I am about to tell you is equal parts rumour, local lore and fact as ascertained by the courts. For more detail or fact checking, you need to give me time, understood?'

'Understood,' said Terrence.

'Daaku Singh earned his name many years ago when he came from Haryana to Goa as a mining mafia agent. He worked for a number of different companies as a government liaison, or fixer to be more accurate. Then, as avarice gripped our state, he specialized in striking deals for off-contract pillaging with ministers. He was very well connected, and every company looking to mine more than their permits allowed wanted to have him on the rolls. It is inestimable how many crores worth of minerals he has helped steal. He kept both the corporations and the government happy, and at one point, he was considered invincible.'

Joe's knowledge on this subject clearly did not come out of the book he had hunted for. He shared, it seemed, his cousin's deep concern about the twisted state of affairs in Goa.

'Then, a few years ago, he crossed the wrong man: mining minister Satish Savarkar, famous for taking the heftiest cuts for illicit contracts. They called him the 70:30 man. Seventy per cent of all profits from underhand dealings would go to him, or to a constellation of relatives that formed his coterie. I don't need to tell you this is all hearsay, I am sure. Facts of this nature are difficult to come by.'

He continued. 'And then Daaku Singh found a way around Savarkar, even as Savarkar was directly controlling the mining portfolio. He managed to get his friends the contracts they sought on the cheap by going above Savarkar's head.'

'Who could be above his head in this regard?'

'Not many people. The chief minister. A union minister, perhaps.'

'Not long after he tried to outsmart Savarkar, about two years ago, he was arrested for a gamut of white-collar crimes.'

'And then he ratted out Savarkar?'

'Surprisingly, no. That didn't happen till about a year later. It wasn't like Savarkar's activities were a secret. But when Daaku went to town in the media during his own trial, the CBI stepped in to save face. They couldn't possibly look the other way any longer. The investigation into Daaku's claims finally led to Savarkar's arrest.'

'Do you know why he waited for so long to talk about

Savarkar's involvement instead of using it to his advantage earlier on?'

'No, I can't say that I do. It is always possible that they had arrived at some private agreement. But that is pure speculation.'

What I heard was fascinating, though hardly a surprise. But it still didn't clarify why Daanish would have written Daaku's case number in his diary. And even stranger, the case number appeared the day before the drug haul, and Daaku ratted Savarkar out soon after the second drug haul. A coincidence? I didn't think so.

'Do you know of any connections to the Mumbai Police in either case?' I asked.

'I can't say that I do. Though it is not unusual for collaborations to occur in investigations of this scale.'

It was like looking for a needle in a haystack of crime. We hadn't been able to find any clear connections between Savarkar and Mumbai – at least none that could have tied him to Daanish. Looking closely into Daaku Singh's affairs would be problematic. A highly sophisticated white-collar criminal like him would have been very careful. And I didn't fancy making another prison visit. The last time we did that, it didn't end well for the inmate in question.

Perhaps the Mumbai Police would be able to provide details of their contributions, if any, to either the Daaku or Savarkar case.

We got up to leave. Joseph wouldn't let us go without a drink, and so we proceeded to a local bar for dinner. Terrence and Joseph introduced me to feni and arrack, neither of which I much liked. The cousins held forth on how feni making was a dying art and only those who made it at home, or had 'source' with skilled home brewers, had a chance of enjoying the spirit.

Unburdened of my baby belly, I happily switched to King's beer and discovered that Joseph was good company, full of long, hilarious stories about the Goan judiciary. At home, in every sense, Terrence seemed gentler and more genuine too. It was my first true taste of Goa, and spilled blood and conspiracy theories aside, it was beginning to beguile me into willing submission.

NINE

I woke up early the next morning and pulled out my laptop. Our conversation with Joseph the night before had helped abate my growing sense of panic, and spurred me into action. I had several tantalizing theories regarding why Daanish would have an interest in Daaku, but to find out more, I would have to test my hypothesis about the diary.

Vigenere ciphers were hard enough to crack with just one keyword, but a series of keywords with no clear demarcation of where one ended and the other began was incredibly tedious. There was only one way to handle this, and that was the old-fashioned way, with lots of grunt work. Every single word would have to be transcribed and then entered into a programme. I had quickly realized the previous day that I wouldn't be able to do it alone. I would have to run it by Shayak though, before I outsourced the task, particularly as the information contained within was potentially explosive.

I headed out of the room, down the beautifully landscaped pathway with its canopy of trees. It felt like a rainforest, with the smell of the soil wafting up and the moisture hanging thick in the air. Keen to prolong the rare minute of solitude, I took the long route to the coffee shop for breakfast. Walking down the wide hallway that separated the service area and the kitchen from the dining space, I turned the corner and came upon George engaged in a heated discussion with a woman I had never seen before. I could not see her face, but she had a beautiful black and red tattoo stretching from her wrist to her neck.

'What are you playing at, George?' I heard her say in an icy tone.

They were so engrossed in their tête-à-tête that they didn't spot me. I retreated behind the corner to eavesdrop.

'You are jumping to conclusions on the back of baseless speculation,' he replied.

'What is she doing at the ashram then? Is there some kind of investigation?'

'Haven't you trusted me for this long? Have I ever led you astray?'

'Then talk to me, George! I am not a child, nor am I one of your lost basket cases.'

'Where did you hear this half-baked information, anyway?'

'This is Goa, George. News travels fast when you know the right people.'

'It's just one more week. Then she'll be gone. And trust me, she won't be any the wiser.'

The woman turned on her heel and headed for the service exit. I waited for George to go back to the coffee shop before I left my spot.

Who was that woman? And how did she know about the investigation? And why did it scare her so much?

*

There was no further sign of the woman, but that didn't stop her from dominating my thoughts as I sat through George's session. Over the past couple of days, it had become harder to feign interest even for the couple of hours a day we had agreed on as the bare minimum to keep up appearances. The rest of the time we were producing a number of excuses: morning sickness, doctor's appointments, couple's work. Beyond a point, I couldn't care less about causing disruption in George's ranks. Murder made such concerns seem almost absurd.

As were most of George's sessions in any case. It wasn't as though he didn't make sense; it was just that his appeal was really to the lowest common denominator of self-awareness, to people so desperate for direction that every piece of common sense or insight was received as wisdom.

On that morning, he sped in and began to pace up and down. It was as though he had a bus to catch. 'Today, we talk about relationships.' George's swift movements, from one side of the tent to the other, were designed either to distract from his words or keep us on our toes.

'They say beauty fades. But that is a load of horseshit. The most brilliant person in the world might lose his marbles one day, become the worst blubbering mess you'd ever met. But no one ever advises you not to marry someone for their brains because they might go senile, do they?'

I had chosen a spot beside Olivia Stein today. She sat on the mat, legs crossed and folded up against her chest, in the compact, slightly awkward way of one not accustomed to sitting on the floor for extended periods. I could tell she wasn't listening to a word of what George was saying.

He droned on. 'So marry for beauty, I say, if you like. If you must marry. It is as good a bet as any. But if you are really clever, don't count on marriage for much. Get to know yourself better than you know any other person alive, and learn to love what you find, no matter how disgusting you think it is. And then find those parts of you that you kind of like, the ones that don't make you sick when you are drunk and it is 3.45 a.m. and your buzz has turned into a pool of self-loathing there on the bedroom floor. Because that is the part of you that you can turn into something great, something special. With or without a partner. With or without marriage.'

He stopped, stared out at the sea, and then turned back around and gave me a wink.

'And that, my friends, is how you find your way to the truth.'

His selling point. His mantra. The words which first led me to him.

'For those of you joining us for the first time, that is what we are all about. Relationships, marriage or otherwise, aren't our priority. But they are what most of us struggle with, and for that reason alone, we address it. Everything we have done till now has been focused on helping you get to a place where you can think about your true self with some honesty. Because without that primary understanding, how can we talk about anything else?'

He was met by plenty of nods and some soulfully closed eyes. And then he turned around and looked at me. 'With that, I would like to invite Aparna and Vishal to share.'

As all eyes turned to us, I cringed. I looked at Terrence, and I could see that he was also caught off guard. I would have to get the ball rolling.

'Much as I have . . . gained from the past few days, I still can't believe we are doing this,' I said softly.

Terrence gave my arm a squeeze of encouragement, a private gesture to assure me that I had done well, even as he turned to me with a frown. 'I can't believe you are saying that still, after all we've been through.'

'Why? Did you think that just because I've been playing along, all my doubts had suddenly disappeared? That I am willing to share my problems with this room full of strangers?'

Terrence turned to the others with an eye roll. 'It's been uphill, but I for one am happy we came.'

I shook my head, then patted my bump, as if to say our future child was the only reason I was going through with it.

George circled around us. 'Good. We are expressing the anger. Now try to push past it. Apu, is that baby really all you see in your future?'

'What do you mean?'

'Is Vishal any part of what you see ahead of you?'

'I don't see anything ahead of me.'

'Ah. Now we are getting somewhere.'

'Yes. How can I imagine our future when the present is so bleak? It's hard to stay together, despite everything, when you don't have anything holding you back. I am not a person of faith, I do not believe marriage is a superior state of existence, or inherently the moral choice. I do not believe there is something wrong in admitting things haven't worked out – even if there is a child involved. I would ensure my baby had a healthy relationship with its father. I am not cruel.'

'So that might be the future,' George egged on. 'You, alone, with a child who has an independent relationship with its father.'

'It might be.'

'But it's not so simple, is it? You are here, Apu. You haven't asked for a divorce. Can you try to remember why you wanted this relationship in the first place, if you are so down on the institution of marriage, particularly this one?' asked George.

'We had fun. We laughed. I liked him. I respected his work ethic.'

'All past tense?'

'It feels that way. The fun has been replaced by stress and laughter by arguments.'

'And the respect?'

'I think my cheating on him answers that question.'

'Ah. So you think that just because you had sex outside the relationship, you must not respect him?'

I shrugged. It was an issue close to my heart. Not only had my only serious relationship ended in some sort of betrayal, I had also cut my detective teeth on cheats, my Calcutta practice kept alive by my investigation of a stream of them. I had seen the hurt it inflicted. Is infidelity ever innocuous? In the scale of lies, perhaps. But in the scale of a lifetime of hurt, it is devastating.

'I am not given to polyamorous instincts in general. That might be the only reason why I chose marriage in the first place. But what that also tells me is that we are seriously damaged to have landed in this predicament.'

George nodded enthusiastically, but I could see the smile in his eyes as he looked at me. The bastard – he was trying to exorcise Apu's fictitious pain to enjoy Reema's very real discomfort. 'That is something we'll come back to during our contemplation of the physical art of love,' said George. 'And as you may have heard, that is not a subject we shy away from.' Smiles all around.

'For now, I want you to leave sex out of the conversation.

Do you respect your husband? If your answer is no, remember it doesn't mean he isn't deserving of it; it might only mean you aren't seeing him for who he is. And you don't value what he has to offer you at this point. If that is the case, you might be correct in your assessment that the relationship has run its course. It is up to you to opt out of this relationship, and seek new values that are relevant to the Apu of today. Or perhaps, if you are so inclined and the foundation is strong, you can reinvent your existing relationship, to make it more in line with your present needs. We shall have to see whether the two of you can get there or not.'

He turned to Terrence, who was bracing himself for what was coming next. 'Don't think I have forgotten about you, Vishal. But what I get from you is more denial and less self-awareness. Yes, you want to save your marriage, but why? I think you both need a break from us, to thrash these issues out. I want you to work with my assistant Shyama to tackle some of the issues we just discussed. Go where you need to. Shyama's role will be to mediate. She is trained in talk therapy, and though I know I have been down on shrinks in general, I embrace the principles when needed.'

George, George, George. What was going on in that head of his?

'We'll bend the rules of the communal meal this evening so the two of you can go on a date. Act like you've never met before. Romance each other if you feel like it. Don't, if you don't. Come back tomorrow and we'll hear how it went.'

As the group dispersed, George came to us, held both of our hands in his. 'I just gave you a get-out-of-jail-free card, my darlings.'

'Sounds like a passport to hell to me,' I mumbled.

'That is what you get for playing hooky,' he said, his blue eyes twinkling at me. 'Shayak wants to see you at Intersection Cafe today.'

So that's what George's latest power play was about. 'Where's that?' I asked.

'Hastings here will know.'

'What about all that stuff about Shyama?'

'She needs to head into town for the day. I just thought it would be a better way to mess with you.' And with that, he was off.

But damn George for his infernal methods: his lie just made tomorrow sure to be ripe with all the sharing. Even before this, though we'd managed to avoid most of the sessions, we were regularly accosted in the resort by fellow participants curious to know how we were faring; now they would be more so.

'Where is this Intersection Cafe, and why doesn't Shayak want to meet at the house? Why on earth couldn't he give us the message himself?' I said to Terrence as we walked to the car, accompanied by Shyama.

'Aren't you in a foul mood today? George finally getting to you too?'

'It has nothing to do with George,' I snapped.

'Relax, okay? Intersection Cafe is a small place near the airport. My guess is he wants to meet us there because he is keeping this trip as short as possible. As to why he couldn't give us the message himself, with these new rules about not using cellphones for anything useful, there aren't a lot of options to get an actual message across, are there?'

I turned to Shyama. 'What are your real plans?'

'There is a car waiting for me at the main road. You can drop me off there.'

'Where are you off to?' I asked, trying to sound casual.

'Just some errands in Margao,' she said.

As we set out, I tried to shake off the mood. Tomorrow, I would find a way to cheat George out of the sadistic pleasure he was anticipating. For now, I would focus on the next few hours. Another meeting in another restaurant. Though he had apologized at our last meeting, I had not been able to let go of the lack of trust he had displayed in my abilities. But this time, I would not let Shayak's doubts infect me.

I was decidedly casual when we reached the white-tented cafe, as I took in the hippie chic vibe, clenched fists lying discreetly by my sides.

I saw him seated and chatting quietly. If I had been all psyched to meet Shayak, it was his companion who made me jump this time.

DCP Ajay Shankaran.

I took a seat. 'Ajay,' I said.

'Reema.' He smiled back.

'You didn't tell me you were coming here.'

'You didn't ask.'

The surprise on Shayak's face didn't escape me. He had no idea I had been in touch with Ajay about the Daaku–Savarkar case.

'Sorry to spring this on you,' said Shayak, directing his attention to Terrence, 'but there was little choice. You'll understand why in a moment, but first of all, I would like to thank Ajay for coming.'

What a contrast it was! The first time I had been with Ajay and Shayak in a room together the atmosphere was one of complete cooperation, with Titanium and the police working together. But by the time we closed the investigation into the Maaya Island murders together, something had changed fundamentally.

Aside from all the professional drama that had occurred, there was the personal element. Ajay had asked me out at some point during the course of the investigation, and I wasn't quite sure how we had left things. He hadn't asked me out again, so I supposed that was my answer. I had been conflicted enough about pursuing a relationship with a man, no matter how interesting he was, whom I had a professional relationship with. If that made Shayak forever out of reach, it applied to Ajay as well.

'Thanks for letting us in on it,' said Ajay. There was a time when such cooperation would be the usual scheme of things. But things had moved well past 'usual' where Titanium was concerned.

'There is another reason I asked you to come now. I am scheduled to fly out shortly. The situation in Kyrgyzstan has become volatile. We've been working with an Indian company there, in security, and the insurgents have captured three of our men. Without any cooperation from the ministry of external affairs, things are at risk of spiralling out of control, and it is imperative that I get there as soon as possible. Reema and Terrence are running the show here, and I wanted to brief them while I still could.'

Hostages! Shayak leaned back, giving Ajay the floor, not once looking at me. In that moment I felt so petty to be holding on to my resentment when he was in the midst of a hostage crisis.

'To be perfectly honest,' said Ajay, 'it was becoming critical that I come here anyway. There are several case files on my table that cannot be closed till we get to the bottom of this.'

'But you aren't in uniform,' I said.

'No. Not only is it expedient not to be identified as law enforcement at the moment, I am here strictly off the books. This is well out of my jurisdiction.'

As far as I was concerned, this was a hindrance to progress. Ajay the policeman brought with him critical access and resources. In his private capacity, he was merely one of us. Admittedly with heaps more experience that might be invaluable in Shayak's absence, but inherently crippled.

Ajay seemed to gauge the reason for my question. 'A few key members of my team are aware of this visit and they are prepared to give me whatever institutional support they can, but my superiors have to be kept in the dark.'

This could not be without personal risk for Ajay. If the commissioner of police knew he was here with Shayak, his job might be on the line.

'The Goa Police also have no idea I am here, at least officially. In fact, one of the reasons I thought it necessary to come here was because they are doing nothing – and seem likely to continue to do nothing – even after we passed a couple of tips their way. The CBI is conducting an investigation into the death of Savarkar, but as far as I can see, they are viewing it as open and shut: a prisoner being exploited and abused, and snapping. As for the drug cases, forget about it: they are buried so deep it would take another bomb to blast any evidence out of wherever it is.'

'How is that possible?' I asked.

'I wish I could stun you with some insight, but I am afraid the answer is probably exactly what you would expect it to be,' said Ajay.

'Have you learned anything new?' asked Shayak.

'Odds and ends, here and there,' said Ajay. 'I'll send you a document on those. The purpose of this trip is quite specific at the moment: I am hoping to glean some information from another ongoing case. A case of theft at the ordnance factory is being currently investigated, and we have been cooperating with the Goa Police on that front. They are bringing in a man today who is involved, and I am hoping to have a shot at questioning him off the record. I think it is not far-fetched to assume he has a hand in the munitions used in the Mumbai blast.'

'Where is he now?'

'The police are in the process of picking him up. He'll probably be taken to the Cuncolim thana. I've worked with Ramesh Dhavalkar, OC in question, in the past, which is how I got to know of these developments at all. We need to be there in an hour.'

'Anything else you need to run by me?' Shayak asked us.

Terrence shook his head. 'Nothing new to report.'

'Reema?'

'A number of things, but all so preliminary it does not necessarily bear mentioning. There is some connection between Daaku Singh and Satish Savarkar, and given that the Daaku case was mentioned in Daanish's diary, I reached out to Ajay to find out if there was some Mumbai Police involvement.'

Ajay took up the thread. 'And as far as I have seen, nothing so far. Though it is not uncommon in big prosecutions for policemen to provide information or leads off the record. There is no way of knowing if Daanish himself had, though his team did not and they say he had nothing to do with it. I reached out to the prosecutor in Daaku's case and so far have heard nothing back.'

'You are collaborating already? Excellent. Any more headway on the diary?' asked Shayak.

'I think I need some help at this point,' I said. I explained to him how sections of it had different keywords. 'Breaking the whole thing down is a very tedious process, but it can be done by someone with time.'

'The diary can't leave Goa, so the best solution is to hand it over to Vinod for scanning. He will be here as of today and stay till we resolve this. Have him send the files over to Neeraj' – the tech maverick we worked with from time to time – 'who shouldn't have too much trouble decrypting it, from what you say, and can send it back over a secure connection to a secure machine.'

Shayak then handed us both new phones and gave us his own number. 'Every few days, you'll be getting new numbers and new devices. Still, use your phones sparingly, and never to pass on critical information.'

'How do we get in touch with you?' asked Terrence.

'For the next few days, I am off the grid. After that, if it's something urgent, contact only Archana, and she'll know how to reach me.'

'Why the sudden increase in secrecy?' I asked.

'The team has been reporting increased efforts at hacking Titanium's secure files. These attacks are coming from the outside, and are apparently so flawless as to be undetectable. It was only because Neeraj witnessed an unauthorized incursion in progress that he was able to figure it out – and stop it. As of now we are offline till further notice.'

'It'll slow us down,' I said.

'Rushing will get us nowhere.' He stood up. 'Savarkar is dead,' he continued. 'There was no way we could prevent that. But the goal from here on is harm minimization.'

'What about Titanium?'

'What about it? It's only a company.' He looked as though he meant it. 'No more blood.' Shayak checked his watch. 'I really must get going now. Ajay will take it from here.'

I watched as he left the restaurant; no time for goodbyes.

'We'd better get going as well,' said Ajay.

'Would it be possible for one of us to go back to the ashram?' I asked.

'Sure, if you need to,' said Ajay.

'Terrence, I am positive George is up to something,' I said. I had already told him about the exchange I had witnessed between him and the mystery woman. 'The more I think of it, his behaviour today seemed suspicious. He only wanted it to look like he was jerking us around. Now I think us being gone is an end in itself.'

'Preaching to the choir, Ray. You know I think everything that man does is slimy. I'll head back and see what I can find.'

'And keep a lookout for the mystery woman.'

*

It was just a little awkward to be seated beside Ajay as he raced through the roads Terrence and I had trundled down just a short while ago. Not only was he not in uniform, he was wearing a bright printed blue and yellow Hawaiian shirt that would have made Devika cringe, olive cargoes and leather chappals, as well as the aviators he always seemed to have on. He was taking the out-of-uniform thing way too far, but damn, did goofy Goa look good on him.

I had taken off the baby bump in the car on the way over, an undertaking that marked a great leap forward in my abilities

as a contortionist. What was a disguise in the ashram was a
giveaway on the job. Ajay had shot more than one curious
look in its direction when I had dumped it in the back of his
rented sedan.

'Whose idea was the disguise?' he asked.

'Mine, if you can believe it.'

'I think I can.'

'I shall choose to take that as a compliment. Any
expectations from this meeting?'

'A clue as to who may have acquired the explosives and
ammunition we have been seeing in Mumbai, in these two
drug hauls.'

Which was just the kind of break we needed. 'You said
you thought the same guys are involved in our case and this
theft. Why?'

'I think either they are involved or they know who was
responsible. It's like the popular kids in high school might
not all hang out together, but they are intensely aware of the
competition.'

'All social groups act in similar ways, even if they are anti-
socials?'

'Yup. The theft was a two-man scam. One fellow in
inventory, and one fellow in administration. We are going to
meet our man in inventory. If I were him, I'd make it a point
to know if anyone else was trying to steal things in my care
that I might choose to steal another day.'

'Fair enough. What about the tips you mentioned to the
Goa Police, the ones you said they did not act on? Anything
for us to follow up there?'

'One of them Shayak has already checked, and it turned
out to be a dead end. We've recently arrested the people

involved in the shoot-out over the second drug bust, and one of them said the people who had hired them were possibly involved with a group of Russians operating inland, near Quepem.'

Close to the cafe where we had met Shayak once. I had wondered what he had been doing all the way out there. 'And what did he find?'

'Nothing. There was some sort of an operation there, but there was no evidence of any drugs, and there was no one matching the names mentioned by the two men arrested.'

'Who were these guys?'

'Guns for hire, regulars on the Mumbai scene. They were in the dark about the operation. Had no idea what was in the crates.'

'Had they been paid?'

'Up front, in cash. Not surprisingly, no trail.'

Ajay pulled over a few hundred feet away from the thana.

'I am going to leave you here for a few minutes,' he said.

'Why?'

'I am here unofficially, and taking you into the police station will attract too much attention.'

'Huh?'

'I know it'll make me sound like a caveman, but you know how badly productivity is shot every time a woman who is not a cop and not a criminal enters my thana. And that is Mumbai. I can only imagine how much worse it will be here.'

'You are right. You do sound like a caveman. And that's the most ridiculous thing I've ever heard.'

'Reema, you wouldn't think I was being sexist if you heard the boys frantically gossiping like old women every time you left. They would crane their necks to see what you were doing the whole time you were around. If it wasn't so pathetic it would have been hilarious. The fact that you missed it all does you no credit as a detective.'

'Great! So now it's my fault?'

'Not your fault at all. I tried to talk to them, but it seemed to only make it worse.'

I didn't even know what to say any more.

'But this is not misplaced chivalry – or chauvinism,' said Ajay. 'It is simply operational necessity. It is important that I fly under the radar here. You too.'

'You could have told me. I would have brought my old spinster disguise.'

Ajay looked at me, imploring and apologetic all at once.

'So why bring me here at all?'

'I want you to meet the suspect. That is the important bit here, and I'll make it happen. You'll only have to wait till I have a chat with my friend Ramesh and find a way for us both to discreetly interview this guy.'

I agreed reluctantly, not that I had much choice in the matter. I stood around or paced in the unpleasantly sunny spot in which we had parked. There was absolutely no shade to be had at that hour, and by the time I finally saw Ajay strolling towards me, I was soaked through and more than a little unhappy.

'They are coming here,' he said, apparently oblivious of, or ignoring quite effectively, the daggers I was shooting him. 'They'll pull up in a jeep. Ramesh will be driving. You get into the passenger seat, I'll get into the back with the other guy.'

I waited as Ajay spent some quality time with his phone.

A few minutes later, a police van trundled down the dusty road and stopped just short of us.

★

Once in the vehicle, there were no introductions; we simply proceeded as if this was nothing more than routine. I folded a leg under me to be able to turn around sufficiently to have a look at the accused, Hemant VS. He was a scrawny man, late forties, and looked absolutely terrified. Though, to be fair, if I were a criminal who had been fed a steady stream of reports about police brutality and encounter killings, I would be frightened senseless by this unscheduled and unwarranted day trip from the lock-up.

'At the moment, I have absolutely no interest in you,' said Ajay. I had seen him in this role before: cold, spare, unyielding. 'All I want to know is who bought your goods.'

'I don't know who or what they were for. I was only delivering them.'

'You didn't think to ask?' He seemed calm enough, but I could see Ajay seethe with a very real, very quiet rage.

'I was not allowed to ask.'

'By whom? Who were you working with?'

'Melvin Gomez, assistant manager.'

'We've heard that before. Who else was there?'

'No one!'

'What did he tell you?'

'Nothing, most of the time. He needed me to move stock out of the warehouse. If it was a small amount, I wasn't even there to deliver it to the final party. I would drop the stuff off at his house after office hours. Only if he couldn't manage it himself did he ask me to come along for the actual delivery.'

'How often did this happen?'

'Maybe eight–nine times total.'

'How long has this been going on?'

'Five, six years, perhaps.'

'How often have you delivered C-4?'

'Only once,' he said.

'Don't lie!' barked the OC.

'Twice, twice, sir, that's all!'

'When?'

'Once two years ago. Once last week.'

I could feel the frisson of fear that pulsed through the car.

'Details. Now.'

'Both times it was the same. Sir wanted me to come because it was such a delicate shipment and we couldn't just lug it around. We put it in the back of a van and drove to Mapusa. We dropped it off there.'

'And you know nothing else about the buyer?'

'I never met anyone, I swear! There was a deserted field in the middle of which was a little shed. Sir had a key. We opened the door, left the stuff, and took another bag away, with the money.'

I looked at Ajay. His face reflected my excitement.

'Can you take us there?' I asked.

He nodded.

'Let's do it,' said Ramesh, hitting the brakes and doing a three-point turn on the deserted road. It was quite a way off. Mainly there was silence in the car, but occasionally a question would be thrown at the man in handcuffs.

'Who else was involved in the theft?' Ajay asked.

'I told you! No one!'

Hard as it was to believe, it made a certain kind of sense.

A little hush money here and there, but the smaller you kept this sort of operation, the more efficient it was. Hemant was in charge of inventory, Melvin Gomez in charge of orders. A few cleverly forged documents, a guard in your pocket and you were home clear.

How much was siphoned? Who really knew? I did not believe this man's claim that there were only eight or nine consignments. After years of theft, who knows how many guns and bullets had landed in the wrong hands.

'Were there other employees also stealing?'

'No. It was my job to ensure it was all in order. It was only these few times that I took anything.'

'You don't think that was enough? It's not like you were stealing ball bearings. Those were bullets, explosives for bombs that killed people!' yelled Ramesh.

'The explosives were only taken twice, sir. Else, it was just guns, sometimes only bullets!'

'Only bullets! That is your defence?'

'No, sir, not my defence, sir. But believe me, I had no choice! My mother. She's in hospital, sir, with cancer. I am an only child, sir! How could I afford to pay for her treatment on my salary otherwise?'

There was a period of silence, during which I ran through his story in my head. Of course, it was possible that he was lying, but his fear felt terribly real. Even if the particulars were bent to suit his narrative of being a lowly pawn, it was probable that in essence it was true.

'There was no one at the delivery point?'

'No.'

'When you went to this shed,' I asked, 'you didn't consider taking the money and not leaving the explosives?'

'No.'

Strange where he chose to draw the line on his dishonesty – when it came to honouring his deal with a killer.

Hemant said we were now close by. He was watching the road, giving Ramesh directions.

'Stop, stop,' he cried.

'If you tell me we are in the wrong place now, I'll wring your skinny little neck,' snarled Ramesh.

I saw nothing but an expanse of green field, with brown patches where the grass and other vegetation had died.

'There must be some mistake.'

'What do you mean?' said Ajay.

'It was here. Right here.'

'What was here?' asked Ajay, looking around.

'The shed. It's gone!'

We all got out of the car. Hemant led us to where the shed once was, and sure enough, there was a small clearing where sand had been poured over and raked across evenly.

'This is where we delivered the C-4.'

'Are you sure?'

'Yes! It was the third lamp post after the turning.'

'I'll send a team to look for evidence,' said the OC.

And I was sure they wouldn't find any. Whoever this man was, he operated like no other criminal I had ever encountered, mostly solitary and choosing temporary partners who were able, like him, to work in the shadows. Every person we found – the shooters, drivers, potential witnesses – had so little to offer. This man had no face, no history, no trace. In a criminal conspiracy of this magnitude spanning years, including murders and bomb blasts, it was a rare thing to keep things so utterly contained. The only crack had been

Rishi, who turned out to be an uncontrollable element. But even he may have known little to nothing about his boss – and had, at any rate, stayed completely mum. The best way to never be caught is to never be seen.

Like a mirage, the vision of a man rose before me, shimmering, elusive, unworldly, amorphous.

TEN

Terrence and I made a courtesy appearance for an hour at George's morning session. Then, evading for the moment the need to share the dreaded fictitious progress on our fictitious couplehood, we headed to the office and began work on the reams of information we had to process. The munition man's records, obtained from Ramesh, were the latest addition to the lot.

I was still sifting through the most recent excavations about Satish Savarkar's old life, which Archana's Mumbai team had gathered. It was, predictably perhaps, filled with drama of the dirtiest kind.

Nowhere were there drugs. Not even in jail, apparently. But what did catch my attention was movement. Savarkar's work – mining, ports, transport in an earlier stint – all involved getting things, often illegal things, I was sure, from one place to another.

'What if Satish was the logistics arm of the operation?' I said.

'What do you mean?' asked Terrence.

'There is nothing to point to a link between Satish and drugs. But what I do see is plenty of capacity in the transportation sector. What if he was moving the stuff?'

'What did we learn about the trucks that were caught in both the hauls?'

'The first haul was actually a convoy of trucks with drugs hidden in spices. The second was in a consignment of furniture. The drivers were all hired for the jobs one-off.'

'Just because he has no reported connection to drugs, doesn't mean he didn't have any. What if he was behind the whole drug thing, and his death was unrelated, and that we have nothing left to investigate?'

'That would be convenient, wouldn't it?'

'No one said the truth was necessarily inconvenient, did they?' Terrence retorted.

'There are so many things that don't fit with that.'

'Only according to George – and Savarkar himself.'

'Well, we don't have anything connecting him to the crimes, not really,' I remarked.

'We might still find something.'

I could only shrug. Did I think it was Savarkar? No. I was beginning to agree with George's assessment – the man we met in jail, the man whose life was spilled across our desks in a paper trail of crookedness, did not have the diabolical precision of the man we were looking for.

What does a dead man have to be most afraid of? Those were Savarkar's parting words to us. Was he referring to himself? Was he the dead man whose goose was cooked in prison? Or was it someone else, who Savarkar chose not to rat out? Either way, what was the answer to his question?

For a change of pace, I turned my attention to the first batch of jail-broken material from the diary. Vinod had been spending all his free time at the scanner. Neeraj was sending us back files that, though decrypted, were filled with what essentially amounted to another kind of code.

I stared at the documents, red pen in hand. It required a

slow, careful read to make sense of it. There were no spaces between words, which was bad enough. But combined with the fact that Daanish wrote mainly in abbreviations, it was horribly time-consuming, and I couldn't make sense of certain passages at all.

As I had suspected, each keyword only held good for a few pages. So Neeraj was running chunks of text through the programme, checking the output to locate where it stopped working, then running the whole lot again to find the second keyword, and so on. So I was getting only three or four pages at a time. I had five sets of data now, and it was up to us to translate it into English.

What had become apparent was that Daanish had been keeping records of investigations, some of which had legs in both Mumbai and Goa.

What it was all about was still beyond my comprehension. I would need a bucket of patience, coffee and time I just didn't have, to work it out.

My mind began to wander. I scanned news sites for updates on the Kyrgyzstan situation, but it seemed it had been kept on the down-low.

I went back to the papers, cross-checking names and dates online, and was making absolutely no headway when the bell rang. Terrence went to answer and came back with Ajay.

'Any news from the police station?' I asked.

'Ramesh has booked the guy. The administrator too, but he isn't talking at all at this point. I've just come from there, in fact. As you predicted, there is almost zero trace evidence at the shed site. Turns out it belongs to Sussegado Pharma, which has a bunch of land in the area, and our man seems to have been a squatter.'

'So what next?'

'I am trying to decide on the next course of action. What are you two up to today?'

I explained what I was doing with the diary data, and Ajay didn't look overly interested. He had been through the papers and work of his predecessor enough times and had had no luck in learning anything pertinent.

'What have you two uncovered about George so far?' asked Ajay.

'So little it is actually shocking,' I said.

'Any chance he is clean?'

Terrence guffawed. 'I am not entirely sure,' I said.

'What makes you doubt his involvement?'

'His personality aside, his stray connection with the Maaya Island murders aside, the only thing we have found on him that might be dodgy is connected to Santa Maria Travels, an agency he supposedly runs but seems to have very little association with.'

'What do you know about it?' Ajay asked.

'We have ... obtained some data and documents, but have so far seen little of use. The team in Mumbai is still going through it. In fact, we are expecting updates soon.'

'There is a piece of information I have received,' said Ajay. 'I am not sure of its origins, so I have treated it with scepticism so far. British consular officials have allegedly made several unauthorized visits to Goa, which has ticked off the authorities.'

'Why?'

'I don't know, to be honest.'

'And why aren't these visits meeting with approval?'

'No government appreciates outside meddling, even from

foreign missions of friendly countries. And who knows what they are digging around for.'

'Where exactly have they been hanging out?'

'Exact location unknown, but in the vicinity of Margao.'

'What was the source of this information? The local thana?'

'It was a Mumbai journalist, who apparently had it from his sources. Given the journalist's history of stories, I would say the information was coming from the US consulate.'

'Why would he call you?'

'I don't know. I do not deal with these things, and that's precisely what makes me suspicious.'

'And you can't come out and ask?'

'I did. He gave some gyan about how I was the centre of the universe and knew everything.'

I smiled. 'Aren't you? Don't you?'

'The shady dealings of the intelligence community are well beyond me,' he said with a shrug.

'I bet not.'

'Are you claiming I am withholding information from you?'

'You and everyone else. Give me one reason you feel this has something to do with George.'

'Because this same journalist's colleague had, just a week before, called me up and happened to ask why George Santos was never charged with any crimes despite several rounds of questioning in the aftermath of the Maaya Island case. I could be off the mark, but they may be making a stab at some sort of story regarding George.'

'You know what has been my favourite theory since we started investigating George? That he is intelligence,' I said.

'MI5?' Ajay asked.

'Go one better.'

'MI6? James Bond himself?' Terrence whistled.

'It's hardly a stretch, is it? A shadowy British male, adept at keeping secrets.'

'But intelligence operatives are supposed to fly under the radar, not be sluts for photo-ops with the who's who of Bollywood.'

'George, I think, is capable of anything. But sadly, the theory doesn't hold water – we've tested it. Quite a while ago, I had asked Shayak to check with his connections about George's status as some sort of operative.'

'And?'

'They claim not. They assert that he is a private individual and whatever he is doing, legal or not, is purely his business.'

'But they would say exactly that, wouldn't they, if he were a spy?' said Terrence. 'Ajay, do you have any other source of information in the intelligence community?'

'I'm afraid I don't. And at the end of the day, does it really matter? It's not pertinent, is it? You seem to have ruled out George of serious involvement.'

I shrugged. It didn't sit right, of course, that there could be a serious spy mission happening in the backyard of our investigation and that it was wholly unrelated. But Ajay was right.

We went back to our documents. After tucking into the lunch Vinod brought us, Ajay left.

A couple of hours later, our forensic accountant, Nayana Thapar, called.

'We've been making some headway in the Santa Maria Travels records,' she said. 'Its legitimate activities seem to include routing all ashram-related travel and tourism expenses. This accounts for much of its billing. On paper, it pays the resort rent for each of the sessions George runs there. He also organizes travel for those overseas guests who request it.'

Much of this we already knew, so I was waiting for the punchline.

'The irregularities start at about this point. There are several payments that have been made, for instance, for private yacht rental when such a boat doesn't exist. And payments made to a crew and repairman for care and upkeep of the vessel.'

'Do we know who actually received this cash?'

'No. But when we got a look at the bank statements you obtained and compared these records with that, we could see a pattern begin to form on and off. Sometimes, following a bank transfer from an overseas participant, we would see tickets being booked or hotels being arranged over the next few days. Then we began to see that pattern continue in certain cases even when the names did not match up. Payments were being made by one party, and the tickets purchased in the name of someone completely different.'

'Couldn't that be explained by something quite innocuous? Such as a loved one paying for the course at the ashram?'

'Yes, it could have been that. So we checked the IDs that were used for the booking, and none of the names turned up anything.'

'Why would that be?'

'That, I think, is as far as I can take you.'

'Anything else?'

'Nothing for now. But we are still working on it.'

'I know this might seem a strange question to ask, but have you seen anything to suggest possible ties to government agencies?'

'As in payments from or to them?'

'Yes, I suppose.'

'None at all.'

I hung up and considered what this new information meant.

My mind went back to something Terrence had been crying himself hoarse about since the beginning of this business: that George Santos was a trafficker. Was he creating false identities for a human smuggling operation? That would also explain the presence of intelligence officers in the vicinity. Was it everything to do with George, and nothing to do with us?

There was only one way to be certain. I had to get across a message to Shayak. I called Archana and explained the task to her.

'It is extremely sensitive,' I said. 'There are names. And another thing.'

'Don't tell me over the phone. Use our usual channels.' We had taken to using a secure email on the Tor network.

'Then should I mark it to Shayak as well?'

'As far as I know, as of yesterday, he is without connectivity.'

'How are things going there?'

'It is tense. But between Shayak and the insurance negotiator, resolution is expected soon.'

'How will you get the message to him?'

'We've set up a communication system which is slow but effective.'

'How soon can you relay it to him?'

'In an hour or so. When he'll respond is another matter. But I'll ask.'

'Shayak is okay?'

'Like he'd ever tell me otherwise?' said Archana with a sad laugh.

I put the phone down and wondered what on earth the two of them were up to. I knew Archana was Shayak's most trusted resource, and they had worked together for years. As far as I could see, she was one of the few people with access to every part of Titanium.

I loved Archana. Which made admitting I was more than a little jealous even harder.

★

About half an hour later, Ajay popped in again. 'What are you two doing for dinner?' he asked.

Terrence and I looked at each other. 'Nothing, really. Planning to head back to the ashram,' said Terrence.

'Let's go out instead.'

Terrence looked hesitant.

'Let me guess: you don't eat?' Ajay said to him.

'Yeah, that is the only explanation for this double chin. George won't be happy. We've been gone for most of the day.'

'What is he, your mother?'

'More like a strict headmistress with devious methods of torture, such as uncomfortable amounts of sharing and public humiliation.'

Though Terrence was right, I couldn't be bothered any more. 'Let's go. Might as well have one proper Goan night out after being here for so long.'

'From what I have heard of George, his workshops never lack for parties,' said Ajay as we shut down and packed up.

'Yeah,' I said, 'but with every auntie in sight worrying about my unborn child I can't properly enjoy myself.'

'If a party is what you are in the mood for, I know just the place.'

We enlisted Vinod to drive and piled into the car. Ajay directed him to Cavelossim, and then asked him to pull over on a suddenly busy stretch, one of those departures from the miles of nothingness that made south Goa such a miracle. We walked a few feet to the restaurant Ajay had his sights on, Lucy's Lair.

'I suspect the great gourmand Reema Ray might find the food wanting, but there'll be enough fun to make up for it.'

But Ajay was wrong. We entered the packed restaurant, with a live band playing soft rock covers. We stood by the bar as we waited for a table, and unencumbered by baby belly or ashram familiars, I had a drink. Then I had another one. By the time the food came, I was pleasantly buzzed. And it tasted delicious. Partly because it was, in fact, delicious, and partly because I was having such a good time.

★

Over the next two days, Ajay developed a habit of dropping into the office whenever he had the time. We'd exchange notes, put him to work and keep the dialogue going to disguise the fact that we were still getting nowhere. It was early days yet, and Ajay, who was far more experienced in these matters, didn't seem to sweat about what was to me a frustrating lack of progress. And I still hadn't heard from Shayak.

But then, I received a fresh batch of notes from Daanish's diary. A few letters jumped out at me as familiar. SSGDO FRM.

'The land where the ammunition drop took place – who owned it, again?' I asked Ajay.

'Sussegado Pharma,' he said.

'It's a favourite Goan word. Means don't take tension,' said Terrence.

But I was no longer listening. I was rifling through older notes from the diary, comparing them with what I had just read. The same series of letters had popped up a couple of times now; it had been in the very first few pages that I had decrypted, and again now.

'If the diary actually mentions Sussegado Pharmaceuticals, and it was the scene of the explosives delivery, it is way too close to home to be a coincidence. He must have been on to something,' I pointed out.

'What does he say about it?' asked Ajay.

'The first instance is part of a list, I think, of companies.' I passed the relevant sheet around to Terrence and Ajay.

'GoGreen Agro. Centaur Nutriceuticals. The second, I have not yet made sense of. Could these companies be fronts for illegal drug manufacture? He was investigating something for sure. We haven't decoded enough of the diary yet to figure out exactly what.'

Ajay was silent as he pored over the transcripts.

I hit the Internet again. There wasn't much of anything on Sussegado, but there was mention of a factory opening in a local news blog dated four years ago. But when I typed in the other company names, they all came back with the same registered address as Sussegado, all apparently part of RLK Holdings.

'Let me contact my friends in the police here and try to rustle up some information about these companies,' said Ajay.

'Sure,' I said. 'I think we'll head out to see what we can find.' I looked at Terrence. 'Ready for a stakeout?'

*

After spending all our time staring at our computers and chin-wagging with tight-lipped, uncooperative non-sources like George, a stakeout seemed like a return to proper detective work.

We found an outpost of Sussegado Pharma that roughly corresponded to something we had found in Daanish's notes. It was about an hour's drive away, inland. Not far from Quepem, I noted when I checked the map.

'This no phone nonsense really blows,' said Terrence, with a yawn.

'I don't know. I think it restores some of the charm of this job,' I said. 'And equally useful – old-school detective methods are so much harder to hack.'

'Charm? Ray, if I didn't know better, I'd say Goa has turned you into a simpering romantic.'

'When it comes to the cloak-and-dagger stuff I am more of a romantic than you think,' I said. Strange to talk about romance when, at the moment, I was fake-married with a fake baby bump at a fake ashram.

Thankfully, as always in the field, the bump was now

tucked away in what could only be described as a body bag on the back seat. I was happy to get rid of the dead weight. But just because I didn't want to be recognizably Apu didn't mean I wanted to be revealed as Reema. So I had covered my head with a hat and put on a pair of sunglasses. Thankfully it was Goa, and such accessories would not attract undue attention.

We got to the address of the factory. The place screamed disuse. It was little more than a shed – large but quite basic. Even the sign for Sussegado Pharma was covered in dust. Weeds had taken over the small open area around the factory, light bulbs had gone missing from holders, the rusty metal gate was hanging on its last hinge.

'This place looks like it has been abandoned for years,' I said.

'Yes, but even quite new places can look like this after a couple of Goa monsoons,' replied Terrence.

'We'll find out which it is soon enough.'

So we waited, settling into the old, familiar kind of detective work. This was how I had made my start, how every private eye makes her start: on her ass, in a cheap car, hopefully with chips or a sandwich to tide her over at mealtime, imbibing the least possible fluids to ensure her bladder holds its peace.

'Have you ever peed in a bottle during a stakeout?' I asked Terrence.

'What?' He looked appalled. 'Where did that come from?'

'That's what seemed to be implied in the books I grew up on. Seemed a little unfair that I don't have that option.'

'Jeez, Ray, I never knew you had such aspirations. But if that is what you want, I can hook you up with some kit that will make it possible. There is a gizmo that –'

'Spare me the details. Anyway, now it's too late. I've trained myself to do without,' I said.

Terrence didn't even have to carry an empty bottle. He chugged away at an obscene amount of cola. Then, he got out of the car and sauntered around the boundary wall of the factory, ostensibly to take a look around – but, I guessed, really to take a piss.

'So?' I asked, when he came back.

'No sign of life. Pretty sure it is abandoned. I had a peek inside through a gap in the metal sheeting and it seems empty.'

'Of people or things?'

'Both.'

We could break in, but I needed to run such extreme steps by Shayak first since there was no pressing cause for it. Extended surveillance was our best bet, but even if we could get a man on it around the clock there were too many concerns.

I turned to Terrence. 'The problem is that this car will get pretty suspicious pretty fast. There isn't anything else for miles. How do we explain what we are doing here if someone starts asking questions? Let's move on. Maybe come back in a bit and do a drive-by to see if we can find a less conspicuous place to park.'

'Maybe we can ask Ajay to have his police buddies take a closer look.'

I nodded. Without more information, there wasn't much else we could do. We drove down the road, circled back and checked out the surroundings, but still found nothing. I checked Google maps, and there were virtually no pins for miles around us. After hanging about for a while longer, we decided to head back for the day. Terrence would be going to the ashram to continue his vigil on George, while I went to our office.

I was alone when I got there. I collapsed on the chair and for a moment just took it all in. Every day the graceful Portuguese villa looked more and more like a war room. Cables everywhere, laptops, desktops, printers, copiers – Archana had arranged for it all.

I continued to read Daanish's notes, and the deeper we got, the more perplexed I was. I had no idea what half of it meant. And what I could make some sense of left me all the more confused. There were details about cases across the country, far and wide, with no apparent link.

But of one thing I was growing sure: this information was being hoarded with a very specific design. I was looking at it from too close, catching a whorl here, a line there. Till I had more information, and took a step back, I wouldn't be able to see the whole picture.

*

The next day was a series of sessions, and Terrence suggested we stay in.

'Something feels different here,' he said softly at breakfast, attacking a plate of crisp bacon and eggs over easy.

'What?'

'It's almost as though we are cruising through sessions, and then all of a sudden, George's head isn't in the game any more.'

'What do you mean?'

'I guess I am not sure. But you'll see.'

'I thought we had dropped our interest in George,' I said.

'I'd find it hard to imagine a time where George wasn't at least a little interesting.'

I still wasn't convinced when George immediately turned the spotlight on us as we entered.

'Nice to have you both back today. I trust you are feeling better?'

My fictitious morning sickness had reached epic proportions by this point.

'I am. Thank you.'

'Would you care to share how the two of you are going at this stage?'

Met by blank stares from both of us, he continued. 'All of the others here have been sharing during closing sessions at the end of each day. It would be nice to know where the two of you are, as well.'

'We're working on it.'

Ordinarily, George would not have let it go at that. But it was just like Terrence said: he seemed distracted, and moved on to something else.

We coasted along till lunch. That was when I got the mail from Archana. I was to go to the house by 5 p.m., no later, and await instructions. About what, she didn't say.

*

Trust Shayak to go old-school. For people like us, this might actually count as foreplay.

In our Goa office, also Shayak's home, there was a hidden compartment in the cupboard, behind which was, of all things, a radio. And not just any radio: a short-wave radio. A big black box, with an astonishing number of dials and switches, that looked like something one of my parents' collector friends would guard with his life.

I had never operated a short-wave radio before, so Archana was at hand with very detailed instructions about how to tune in. She had, I presumed from her flat, precise tone, a list of steps which she was merely relaying without judgement, as was her fashion. She gave me plenty of time to figure it out – the real business of the evening would not commence till about 6 p.m.

And what was that business, precisely? I wasn't altogether sure. So I did as I was told, fiddling with dials, hearing several obscure channels in foreign tongues pass by till I landed upon the frequency in question.

'This is a test, 1, 2, 3. This is a test, 1, 2, 3. This is a test, 1, 2, 3.' After about five minutes of listening to a strange voice intoning these words over and over again, I decided that I couldn't take it any more. I had my appointed time, and till then, I turned the volume down so it was only a murmur in the background, and set the alarm on my phone for five minutes to six. And then I waited.

The alarm went off and I turned up the volume. At exactly 6 p.m., there was a slight pause. My ears perked up with anticipation.

'Hello?' It was Shayak's voice.

'Hello?' I responded, and then immediately felt foolish. He couldn't hear me.

'Sorry for the excess of melodrama. But there was no other way. The following is the information you sought.'

I was ready with a pen and paper, as well as an audio recorder, as per Archana's instructions.

It was code, and it was quick. My hand flew across the page for a good ten minutes. I was grateful for the recording, as I couldn't be sure of my accuracy. Then, another pause.

'And that's it. Goodnight.'

It was as abrupt as that.

My phone rang almost instantly.

'You got it all?' asked Archana.

'I think so.'

'I am mailing you the decryption data,' she said.

'Shayak is safe?' I asked.

'Yes, he is out of email range. And phone for information this sensitive is always out of the question for him.'

In my spy craft fixation, I had heard about number stations: mysterious short-wave radio frequencies on which random numbers were broadcast. The most reasonable conspiracy theorists believed it was the method used by intelligence agencies to communicate safely with agents in the field. Several had even admitted to it.

It was likely that Shayak had just made use of a numbers station.

Opening my mail, I saw Archana's message. 'The name of your agency.'

Steele Securities? I could only assume this was a keyword, and since we had spent so much time on Daanish's diary, it would make sense to stick to the Vigenere cipher. It was the logical choice, as Shayak knew I was familiar with it.

I transcribed the first few lines of the message. Then I opened the software Neeraj had souped up for us. I entered the keyword 'Steele' and waited.

It was legible.

And then I got down to the business of typing it all in, which seemed to take forever, given my level of impatience.

As it came together, I worked faster and faster. Though in essence, I had expected this information, to actually have a confirmation left my mouth hanging just a little bit open.

*

Back at the ashram, I entered the room, baby bump back on, and collapsed on the bed. 'You know Olivia Stein?' I said.

'Sure. Dark-haired, keeps to herself? I think I spoke to her once,' replied Terrence.

'That is one more time than I have. She never opens her mouth in any of the sessions either. Now I know why. Shayak sent a message: she is British intelligence.'

'What? How does he know?'

'I asked him to check up on that information Ajay brought us, about there being intelligence operatives about. This is all he managed to get. He doesn't know what she's doing here, but she is definitely a working agent. A good one too. I had also asked him to check those names we got from the Santa Maria logs, but he hasn't had any success yet.'

'Olivia is investigating George?'

'I suppose she must be. A little strange that he's allowing her to hang about at his ashram, in that case.'

'Everything about George is strange. But this might explain what I saw earlier today.'

'What is that?'

'After the afternoon session of crap, I saw her talking with George.'

'What about?'

'They were too far away for me to hear, but it all looked very odd. George was angry, and Olivia was responding with a perfectly straight face. After about two minutes of this exchange, just as I had sort of drifted over within earshot, he stormed off.'

'And that's it?'

'That's it. Olivia hardly opened her mouth.'

'Did you ask George about it?'

'In passing. At that point I didn't know she was intelligence, else I would have tried harder to listen in, or something. He said it was nothing. Not that I expected any different.'

'You need to be persistent with him, Terrence. Don't let him slither away so easily.'

'Hey, cut me some slack! It's not like I'm not trying. With you around he at least gives us the time of day. When I am alone, it's a different matter.'

'Why do you think that is?'

'Let's just call it the Ray Effect.'

I rolled my eyes. 'It's because I don't let him get away with as much crap. Come with me,' I said, taking him by the hand. 'George is just the guy I wanted to meet now, anyway.'

'What about?'

'Just some thoughts I've been having. And this Olivia business, of course.'

*

'As an old Goa hand, tell me how the drug trade here works.'

It might have been a soft question, but it was a necessary one. We were back on George's terrace, and I chose politeness as the strategy for the evening.

'What makes you think I know?' George was not very good at playing the clueless innocent, but I had expected nothing less than outright denial.

'There are scores of white tourists traipsing through your facility for enlightenment every year. Are you trying to tell me that drugs are never a part of it?'

'I never buy for them.'

'What sort of New Age guru are you?'

'The self-appointed kind,' he said, flashing me his cheekiest grin. 'But I am quite earnest about this: I'm quite tough on drugs. If I catch any of my students using anything harder than marijuana, I ask them to clear out.'

'Is that why you fired Arti?'

Now I had George's attention. After a brief narrowing of the eyes, his face became a mask.

'I didn't fire Arti. She is clean. You have received bad information.'

'Really? I was told there was some mess involving a guest with a troubled past and a sexual harassment charge?'

'Yes, there was. The guest was a user. I kicked him out. And then I promoted Arti to manager of my bar. I wouldn't call that firing.'

'Who was the guest? I heard he was a film person.'

'That's just Chinese whispers at work. He was some low-life scum from Gurgaon. Johnny Brar.'

'The arms dealer?'

'Alleged.'

'Who was just shot?'

'Yes.'

'And he hit on Arti.'

'Yes. Years ago. Why is this relevant?'

'Maybe it's not. Back to my original question. Tell me what you know about the drug business here. Think of this as a purely academic exercise.'

'I can tell you that Russians, British, Nigerians, Israelis are all involved. Heavily.'

'Now tell me something I don't already know.'

'Like?'

'How do the drugs come in?'

'Any way, anyhow. Over land. Charter. Ships. The key to success in such endeavours is to keep mixing things up, keep things fluid. Best way to avoid detection.'

'But plenty of people are not avoiding detection. So what is going on there?' asked Terrence.

'Double-crossing. Trying to bypass the cops in the chain of pay-offs. Fatal stupidity. Your guess is as good as mine.'

'What about manufacture?' I asked.

'What do you mean?'

'Goa is club drug central. Ecstasy, ketamine, MDMA. Don't tell me no one is making them here.' There had been busts in Mumbai, Hyderabad, Himachal. Why not here? If I were a criminal, I wouldn't be able to think of a better place to operate than Goa: relative anonymity, vast empty spaces that were far enough from civilization to avoid suspicion, a ready market for drugs. A legitimate pharmaceutical industry would make such things pretty easy to hide.

Sussegado Pharma. The name itself should have been a dead giveaway.

'And what if they are?' said George. 'How does that connect to anything?'

'If Savarkar is the end point of our information trail, the start is the 2010 blast and shoot-out in Mumbai. Our focus has been on anything that connects the two.'

'How do you think Savarkar ties into it?'

'Savarkar was mining minister, with additional charge of ports. So far, with the limited information we had, my working hypothesis has been that Savarkar was somehow involved with moving drugs, with his ready access to ports, transport authorities and the right greasable palms amongst the police. The drugs from the haul, chemical in nature, could have

come in from just about any source country. Sell some here,
ship the rest to other parts of the country.'

'And now? How have things changed?' asked George.

'I am not saying they have.'

'But now you are looking at manufacturers here? Why?'

'There are some things even I can't tell you, George.'

'That familiar feeling,' he said with a wink. 'I'm assuming
this theory too still has something to do with Savarkar.'

He hadn't shut me down. Which told me that despite his
evasions, George did not really have anything to do with
drugs. He was chatty only on subjects where he had no
exposure.

He continued. 'There are rumours, of course, about
factories here. But I know nothing concrete. Though you
refuse to take my word for it, I don't really run in those
circles.'

'Say for the moment that I do take you at face value.
What can you tell me?'

'It's the foreigners who keep getting caught. Nigerians.
Britons. Russians. But as you know, nothing happens in Goa
without the collusion of Indians.'

'Really?'

'Don't be naïve. You know how hard it is to set up a
legitimate business in India as a foreigner? As a criminal,
things are no different. You need someone to help you work
the system. You need to know a guy for everything. You
need to be able to buy off the right people, at the right time,
and ensure you are getting what you paid for. Luckily for
them, and unluckily for Goa, most criminals – at least the
good ones – already possess these skills.'

'Okay. Now for specifics.'

'From what I *hear*,' he said, 'most of this sort of activity is happening in the north.'

No surprises there.

'But I can't tell you where, simply because I haven't bothered to find out.'

'I am sure you know someone who has.'

'That may be true. But they won't talk.'

'They will if you tell them to.'

'And why would I go and do that?'

'Fair enough. Do you know anything about a Savarkar connection to any of this?'

'No, but I have no trouble believing it. The man's corruption was epic. In Goa, that means two things: mining and drugs. Real estate is a natural extension thereof. So even if I haven't heard specifics, I am sure you can do the math.'

'Have you heard of Sussegado Pharma?'

'Can't say I have.'

'Okay. One more thing: who is Olivia Stein?'

A pause to drain his whisky. 'One of my returning students.'

'Why were you arguing with her earlier today?'

'Three of her friends were supposed to come for this workshop. Since she was such a good client, I had reserved their seats without taking an advance payment. Then they cancelled at the last moment, too late for me to find replacements. So I am three students short this batch. Five, if I count you two insincere ones who aren't even bothering to pay for this beautiful experience I am providing you. And there is nothing more dreadful than not being able to help those in need, is there?'

'George, here I thought you were finally opening up to me.'

'Believe it or not, it's the truth.'

'Doesn't it matter to you that people are continuing to die?'

'That's not on me.'

'You are standing in our way, George. Which is worse than not helping.'

'Reema, even if I am not telling you the truth, not every lie is connected to your case!'

'Are you sure about that?'

'The harder I try to convince you the more you'll disbelieve me. But believe me on this one.'

'What a load of bollocks,' said Terrence as we walked out.

'We need to find out what Olivia is up to here. Let's keep a watch. Tomorrow, unless absolutely necessary, you stay put here. If she's around now, let me see if I can engage her.'

But she was nowhere to be seen. I found a dark corner and from my handbag took out a map of the premises, which marked who was occupying each room. We found Olivia's: the lights were on, and when I walked by, I could hear voices. The resort was just too open in its layout to allow me to put an ear to the door, so I satisfied myself by finding a bench from where I could see it. In about ten minutes, two leggy blondes exited. Skimpily dressed, heavily made up.

I returned to the room and told Terrence what I had seen.

'Do you think George and Olivia are running some sort of trafficking scam?' he asked again.

'Just because the women were not wearing much? This is Goa, isn't it? And Olivia is legit – we know that now.'

'Ray, this is your first visit to Goa. For once I am going to agree with George that you are naïve. Conspiracy theories aside, just like every big Indian city, Goa is crawling with women who sell sex, and many of them just happen to be white. Where do you think they come from? If someone is trafficking them, why not George? Why not Olivia? Wouldn't a contact in intelligence be extremely useful if you dabbled in recreating identities?'

'Show me something more solid than a short skirt to back up your theory.'

Terrence shook his head. 'You know what goes with trafficking better than bread does with butter?' he said. 'Drug smuggling.'

*

Archana finally hit gold with the Savarkar family financial records. Sussegado Pharmaceuticals had, over the course of two years, paid upwards of ₹2 crores to Savarkar's wife, their alleged director. The next day, I received Archana's mail with the entire scoop. Sussegado was registered as a nutriceuticals manufacturer, but its products had gone off the market, and they had seemingly shut shop. Except for ongoing payments to Savarkar's wife till about ten months ago.

I called Ajay and told him what we had seen at the abandoned factory, and the information we had received that morning.

'Not a lot to go on,' he said.

'I know. We need to find some more facilities.'

'I'll get on it. We also need to look at the whole company in more depth.'

'I've asked Archana to put more people on it.'

'Great.'

After that I had no choice but to move on; there was just too much to do.

There was an entire piece to the George puzzle we hadn't had the time to explore, with all the post-Savarkar murder mayhem that had erupted, and that was the Sundown Bar. I decided it was at last time to check out the place where it all began, in a sense. It was also Arti's workplace. If my timeline was correct, she had been here when the murderer spent months hanging about the beach as he worked for George.

It was quite something to see Arti working the bar. Everyone seemed to know her, and as she went about her business of mixing drinks, serving them and chatting with the guests, her energy repelled unwanted attention like some mysterious force field. Not that men didn't try their luck – Arti was extremely attractive and, after all, this was Goa – but she left them in no doubt as to how much they could hope to get away with.

I took my seat at the circular bar with its high stools, feet barely grazing the sand.

She gave me a smile, and I saw the tattoo that rose up from her left arm stopping just short of her left jaw. Black and deep red tendrils, like branches of a tree, delicate, climbing up her arm. Just like the one on the arm of the woman I saw speaking to George at the ashram. Was it our presence she had been so angry about that day?

'Mojito, please,' I said. 'Hold the rum.'

Arti got busy, the eyebrow ring glistening, bangles clinking. She was wearing a singlet the colour of sand and short shorts with a 1960s' Mickey Mouse on them. She was so fast I could barely keep up with what was going in.

When my drink was before me, I took a greedy sip. With her eyes on me, I spat it back out into the glass.

'Virgin,' I said. 'There is rum in this.' As good as it tasted, my fake baby could not be publicly subjected to the possibility of birth defects.

'Oops! My mistake. I am so used to making mojitos, muscle memory kicks in.'

In a minute, she made me a new one.

'How far along?' she asked.

'About four months now.'

'You have amazing self-control,' she said with a wink.

Her laughing eyes gave me pause, though I wasn't quite sure why. 'When the incentive is right! What about you? How long have you been doing this?'

'Feels like forever.'

'You seem to know everyone here.'

'Sure I do. That's Sammy over there. He's from Lithuania, and comes here to escape the cold and look up my skirt. That's Brenda, and her partner Susan, from Florida. Apparently the sun and beach are completely different here from back home,' she said with a little eye roll and wave. 'And there is the Kapoor khandan, which comes every year for the patriarch's birthday. They don't chat much, but they drink loads, so who cares!'

'You have been here a couple of years now, right?'

'Right,' she said, wiping down the bar.

'So you knew the guy who killed all those people on that island?'

'As a matter of fact, I did,' she said.

'What was he doing here?' I asked.

'Drinking, mostly.'

'Strange how things worked out for him.'

'You mean, ending up in jail and all?'

'I guess,' I said with a shrug.

'I wouldn't know anything about that,' she said.

And with that, she switched off. 'Cheers,' she said to me, as she strode off to take orders from a group that had just walked in. I was there for about an hour or more, but apart from asking a question – whether I wanted anything else – she kept her distance.

Eleven

Ajay had tracked down another Sussegado factory and came to pick me up from Sundown. The cops had confirmed that the last one was deserted. They had broken in to poke around, found plenty of chemical residue, but it was too early to tell any more than that. This one was functional, Ajay had already confirmed, and he insisted on coming with me in place of Terrence.

'No point in wasting more time on this. My friend has given me a clean chit to investigate if I see fit, and I thought you might want to come along.'

I bristled. Sussegado had been our lead, not his. But I wasn't going to start a turf war that I couldn't win. I wanted to go along for this, and we needed him if we wanted to get a foot in the door somewhat legally.

'So this is another Sussegado drugs factory?' I asked.

'Well, no. It's one of the group companies, a food factory actually. But about six months ago, the pollution control board apparently received complaints from an environmental group about chemicals being dumped in the area.'

'What kind of chemicals?'

'It seems they haven't taken it up as yet, but it is suspicious in this context. Then, one of the beat cops, when I asked around, said he had noticed a changing fleet of expensive cars, which, in this part of south Goa, is cause for raised eyebrows.'

'Really? That seems odd to me, that a police officer would notice the cars.'

'It seems perfectly in character to me. Just think about it: if you are looking to call on an office to enhance your side income a little, what better place to hit up than one with disproportionately expensive cars?'

I dismissed it with a quick shake of the head. If I stopped to think about the corruption, I would never get any work done.

'In context, the cars make perfect sense,' said Ajay. 'The proprietor of Sussegado Pharma is a man named Joaquim Fernandes. His main businesses even I have heard of – he has a ton of mining concerns under the Fernandes Group. He is one of the richest men in Goa, and cars are his passion. RLK Holdings is just one of the companies he owns. Hotels, educational and medical institutes – you name it, he's got it.'

'Why would a man like that be involved with drugs?'

'Because his mining licences are on the verge of being cancelled? Because his hotels are being sold off one by one? This is clearly a man in need of cash. He still sponsors the football team, but things are looking bad for him now with Goan iron ore at risk of being shut down.'

As we neared our destination, I kept my eyes peeled. And I began to see why overt displays of extreme wealth might be more conspicuous here than elsewhere in Goa. There was no palatial villa, nightclub or starry hotel in these parts. It was farmland and dry, dusty roads.

When we reached the factory, there were signs outside for all the quintessentially Goan processed foods – bebinca, sorpotel, sausages, balchao.

Just then, a Ferrari pulled out of the gate of the factory. We craned our necks to see who was behind the wheel, but all we could see in the fading light of dusk was a pair of sunglasses and what appeared to be a young man.

'Does Fernandes have a son?' I asked.

'Not that I know of.'

'Can't imagine giving a car like that to a driver to drive.'

'That is one sexy machine,' said Ajay.

'Really?'

'You are above all such pleasures, I suppose,' said Ajay, eyebrow raised.

'No, it's just that my turn-ons are a little different.'

'And I don't think I could ever figure them out.'

An awkward silence followed.

'So what piece of technology gets you hot under the collar?' he asked after a while.

'Oh, I don't know. I am pretty old-fashioned. A gleaming espresso maker? Not so different from that car. Both are red hot and chrome.'

Ajay looked at me as though I were mad. 'At least the Ferrari can take you places.'

'On roads such as these, you aren't likely to get very far. And if we are talking about going places, without coffee, I would never even leave bed in the morning.'

We were parked close to the factory. For around thirty minutes, we didn't see any other activity. I could smell the spices and vinegar, ghee and flour. It was making me feel hungry and queasy at the same time.

'What we know for certain is that this is a fully operational foods factory,' said Ajay.

'And possibly nothing else?'

'Possibly.'

'But look at the guards. They are armed.'

Ajay pulled on to the road again, and we circled the facility. It was fairly large, but it was only one building. There was another gate at the back.

'Look at that,' I said. 'There is CCTV coverage in the front, but at the back there is nothing, though there are two armed guards there as well.'

'The question is, how do we get inside? I can't charge in without a warrant. We could ask the police to look into it, but everything is just taking so much time, and they are already up to their necks in this stuff.'

Such were the problems of working off the books. 'How do you feel about some subtle subterfuge?' I asked.

'How subtle?'

'Very, if you consider the scale of subterfuge that might be going on inside there.'

'Let's see what you've got.'

★

The words 'weights and measures' had the power to open every factory door, and usher in an era of scraping and bowing which was wholly foreign to me.

The manager was sitting before us, ashen-faced as an errant schoolboy.

'We have received a complaint about one of your products,' I said. 'The sorpotel. It was shipped to Maharashtra, which is why the Mumbai Police is here. This is Ajay Shankaran, and as a courtesy to his friends in Goa he has come to speak to you before seeking a warrant.'

'Warrant, sir?'

'I don't have to tell you how serious a transgression this is. Discrepancies about weights, possibility of adulteration – these are not minor offences,' said Ajay.

'Yes, sir, yes, sir. How can I help you, sir? I am sure there is a mistake somewhere. If you allow me to call my superiors –'

'That will not be necessary,' interjected Ajay. 'I would like to see your measuring equipment and will do a random check of your packaged products to ensure the weights are matching up.'

'Of course, of course. Tea, sir?'

'No, thank you,' said Ajay, standing up. I followed suit.

The manager and three lackeys scampered after us as we helped ourselves to a tour of the facility. We started in the main room, which had two production lines, one wall of ovens, and men and women operating fairly low-tech packaging units.

'As you see,' said the manager, 'the dosing of all our finished products is automated. But then we also check the weight of each one here.' He led us to a weighing station.

'I will tell you when I am ready for that. Let me finish my inspection,' Ajay said.

'Of course, sir. Of course,' said the manager. His ashen face was accompanied by an increasingly shrill voice. He repeatedly cast glances at a door in the middle of the back wall. Would that lead us to the section we saw being guarded from the outside? Because there was no way the room we were currently standing in stretched the whole length of the building. There was something substantial on the other side of that wall.

I closely trailed Ajay, the manager quick on our heels, towards the first closed door to the left of the factory. Inside, there were rows and rows of shelves filled with sacks, canisters and jars of all kinds.

'What are these?' I asked.

'Our dry provisions are stored here. Flour, rice, sugar, etc.'

We moved on to the next door, and as it opened, I was hit by the smell of vinegar and spices. Men and women in aprons and hairnets stood at vast cauldrons, stirring with ladles the size of my head. 'Sausage, sorpotel, all our pork products are made here,' explained the manager.

When we reached the next door, we were greeted by a stony-faced guard who hadn't been there even minutes before.

'What's this?' said Ajay with a haughty look at the manager.

'Sir, I am sorry, but even I do not have access to this room.'

'What is behind here?' he demanded.

'It is not part of the factory.'

'Of course it is. It is part of your premises.'

'I don't know, sir. You will have to meet the management.'

'You are the management!'

'I mean my bosses. I have nothing to do with what happens in that room!'

His state of panic, his choice of words made me even more certain that all was not as it should be on the other side of that door.

'You are the manager of this facility, and you say you have no business with what is happening behind here? You are in the food industry! What if this is contaminating your products!' Ajay snapped.

The manager was so worked up by this point, he could only blabber.

'Either you are a fool or you think I am one,' said Ajay.

'No, sir, no sir.'

'Open it now!'

'But I don't have the key. As far as I know it is just empty space.'

'And you always have an armed security person at hand to guard nothing.'

He gulped so loud I could almost hear it. 'Sir, to go in there, I request you to come back with a warrant.' He was almost cowering now.

'How about I arrest you now and then we can make it a two-in-one trip to court?'

The manager was sweating bullets, but had run out of protestations.

'Open this door right now.'

'I don't have the key, sir, God promise, sir.'

'What about this guard here?'

We turned our attention to the man wearing the uniform of a private security firm named Leo.

'I cannot let you pass,' he said.

'I'd like to see your licence for carrying that gun,' said Ajay.

'Sir?' he said, bravado dropping in an instant.

'You need a special permit to carry one of those.'

The guard spluttered for a while, but by then, Ajay had grabbed the gun from him. I doubt he even knew how to fire the thing.

'I am sorry,' Ajay said to the manager, 'but I am going to have to arrest this man.' He slapped a pair of cuffs on the protesting guard. The manager had slunk away to the corner, and was on his walkie-talkie. The other members of the staff looked on, bewildered. I anticipated no resistance from them.

I wasted no time. I kicked the door with all my strength. It did not budge.

But between me and Ajay, in the end, it gave way.

In an instant, the smell of meat and freshly baked bread was replaced by an acrid cloud that rolled over us. As I started to cough, Ajay, holding the gun, rushed ahead of me. He passed me a handkerchief on the way. I covered my mouth and nose, but it was too late – the fumes had filled my lungs. When I stopped hacking, it didn't take me long to realize we were inside a chemical lab. A drug lab.

It was empty, but a second later, the door to the outside opened, and the guard we had seen patrolling rushed in.

Ajay stood his ground, cocking the gun he had confiscated from the guard's colleague. This fellow too had no idea what to do with his firearm, and rather than take guard, he dropped it on the cement floor and threw his arms up in surrender. Ajay motioned for me to pick up the gun. He quickly checked to see if there was any other source of resistance on the way, corralled the second guard into the main factory, and ordered the doors sealed. He called Ramesh, the OC, and then we waited in the manager's room, with a trembling manager and two very confused guards.

*

When Ramesh arrived, he had his men lead the guards and manager away, while we checked out the lab. It looked like your standard school chemistry lab, with burners, pipettes and flasks. One counter seemed to be delegated to packaging, with pill presses and the like.

This was clearly an active lab, and everything would have to be tested individually. Finally, it felt like we had a real break.

'We need to pay Joaquim Fernandes a visit,' said Ajay.

'Yes, but wouldn't it be best to have a look at what comes out of that factory first?' I said.

'We can't afford the delay. We can't give him a chance to run.'

'I'll bring him in,' said Ramesh.

'Do you have enough?'

'For the moment. But we will need to process the lab quickly to be able to get anything to stick.'

'I think we can help with that,' I said. 'We can send the samples to Titanium in Mumbai, which has the best lab in the country.'

'We don't have the budget for that.'

'Make two sets. Send one through the usual channels. I'll have the other one dispatched as soon as you can give it to us. It will be processed free of charge.'

Ajay assured his friend that Titanium forensics had been regularly used by the Mumbai Police to close cases. He neglected to mention the current impasse.

'Why would you do that?' Ramesh asked.

'Because we will need a favour from you, too. Let me and Ajay have a crack at Fernandes before you arrest him,' I said.

Ramesh shook his head. 'That is not possible. It is one thing to help you, and let you help out, and another to delay an arrest for a guaranteed flight risk.'

'We just need thirty minutes. Your men can wait outside the whole time.'

'Why?'

'He won't talk once you have him arrested. And I can't afford to have another person go silent.' Or be killed by a jail visit.

'You think he will talk to you?'

'It's the best chance we have.'

We called in Vinod and Terrence, and while they stayed with the team awaiting a full forensics sweep, Ajay and I drove to Fernandes's house in Reis Magos followed by a police van at a distance.

The industrialist's residence was a sprawling mansion – any more opulent and it would have to be described as a palace. It was heralded by Corinthian columns and a massive gate off a lane that snaked downhill towards the bay. On the other side of the river were more hills dotted with buildings, and on the water beneath plied tourist and commuter boats.

A guard at the gate took our names, and made a call before opening it for us.

'We aren't far from Aguada jail, are we?' I asked Ajay as we pulled into the driveway.

'No. I think it should be about fifteen minutes away.'

'And it overlooks the water too? He'll have the same view, at least.'

We approached the house where a man was waiting for us in front of a grand double-panelled doorway.

He took our names, asked to see Ajay's ID, and disappeared inside the house.

He emerged with Fernandes himself. Tall and slender, the industrialist had salt-and-pepper hair and was wearing an impeccable white linen shirt and grey trousers.

'We have just come from your foods factory. I am sure you have had news from there,' said Ajay.

'Why am I talking to you and not the Goa Police?'

'Because of the two shipments of your drugs intercepted in my jurisdiction, one in August 2010 and the other in September 2012.'

Fernandes's face was a carefully composed mask, but he couldn't stop his jaw from clenching the tiniest bit.

'But the Goa Police are also on their way,' Ajay added, 'if that makes you feel better.'

'I'll wait for them, then.'

'I had a feeling you might prefer a Goan jail, Mr Fernandes, such as the very accommodating one just down the street, where your influence can make life easy for you. But don't forget what happened to Satish Savarkar. If you cooperate with me now, we could arrange to have you moved to Mumbai, which might be a safer bet.'

'I'll take my chances.'

He turned around and went back into the house.

'It was always a long shot. We can talk to him in jail,' said Ajay.

'And risk another life?' I said.

'Well, if he is your guy, he's safe, isn't he?'

We met the police van that had waited at the head of the road. In it was Ramesh.

'He's not talking.'

'And we can't arrest him yet.'

'Why?' asked Ajay.

'Message from above. Rock-solid case or no arrest. Not surprising given how well connected this guy is.'

'But I thought you said he was a flight risk?' I said.

'I'll keep an eye on him.'

★

Back at the office, I waited for Terrence and Vinod to return.

'How did it go?' I asked.

'There should definitely be enough to nail the bastard,' said Terrence.

'We need everything we can find about Joaquim Fernandes, and any connection he may have to Titanium and Satish Savarkar,' I said. 'And we need it as fast as possible.'

'What are we looking for?'

'Evidence, of any kind. Even if it isn't definitive enough to take to the police, we need something to use as leverage to get him to talk.'

As they started to go through the records, I made some calls. Archana, to ask her to do the same. And then George.

'To what do I owe the pleasure, Ms Shenoy?' he said.

'Joaquim Fernandes. What do you know about him?'

'Old Goan aristocracy. Why?'

'Any links to our case, George? It's critical.'

'Last time I helped you in a similar situation, a man ended up dead.'

'George, are you really blaming that on me?'

A pause. 'No, of course not.'

'Then talk to me. Whatever you've got.'

'Connected with your case? I can't say I know anything.'

'What else?' Threatening Fernandes with exposure on a completely different front might be effective as well.

'Joaquim Fernandes has been working quite hard to run his business into the ground. It started with Cotigao wildlife sanctuary, inside the 3 km fringe that is supposed to be protected. He was quietly backing efforts to start mining there. He tried to keep it out of the news because of his family's reputation as being rooted in the community.'

'And the mine?'

'What do you think?'

'They went ahead with it.'

'I will leave it to you to discover just how pear-shaped it all went.'

'How do you know this?'

'I make it a point to stay informed, Ms Shenoy. The source isn't important. It is a good one, though, that much I'll tell you.'

I lost no time looking up the contentious mine. It wasn't on the edge of a wildlife sanctuary; according to activists, it was inside it. I called Terrence over.

'Tell me everything you know about Cotigao.'

'It has been raped. No other word for it. For years, they did it secretly. Then it was just blatant, out in the open. Finally the court put an end to it earlier this year. But I am sure they'll be at it again soon enough.'

'How long ago would you say it started?'

'Under the watchful eye of the dearly departed minister, during his term. So about five years ago or so?'

I found more sordid details about the piece of land that used to be home to gazelles and bears, and now had been reduced to a canyon of mud and waste – and that, after a decent amount of time had passed, was sure to be converted into some godforsaken resort no one would ever want to visit.

'We need something more solid to link Fernandes to the site, because there is absolutely nothing official as far as I can see,' I said, after a good hour of reading.

'Let me check with my cousin,' suggested Terrence.

He got back to me pretty quickly with a short list of names. 'These are the companies that were listed in a PIL brought by an NGO. It sought not only to ban the companies from this site but also to get their licences revoked. They succeeded in the first part of the motion, and the companies were all issued heavy fines.'

We looked up the names of the executives of all the companies. No link to Fernandes. 'One of these has to be a front for the Fernandes Group,' I said. 'We don't have time to look through their financials.'

'What about the date of incorporation?'

'Worth a shot.'

Of the five, it turned out that only one was formed in the past ten years – Goa Mining Company Ltd. The others were either multinationals or had a track record.

'But the CEO of this company is legit. He is from the trade.'

'That doesn't mean anything, does it? Do we have a list of board members?'

Terrence pulled it up.

I picked up the phone again. 'George.'

'I trust you have spent the past two hours productively?'

'I have some names for you. Tell me if any of them ring a bell. Priya Sharan. Anthony Menezes. Preet Bardhan. Vijay Patel.'

'Preet Bardhan.'

'Who is she?'

'Not a she. A he. Joaquim Fernandes's lover.'

                    ★

Word was sent to Fernandes about what we had learned. More accurately, four words – Goa Mining Company Ltd.

It was what we needed to open the door to his home for us.

He met Ajay and me in the foyer this time.

'I want this off the record. I have checked with my lawyers, and they assure me your jurisdiction here is limited. I am only speaking to you now as a courtesy in the hope of some discretion from you in return.'

'About your lover?' asked Ajay.

'No, about my involvement in Goa Mining Company. My mother is ill. She devoted her life to Goa, and I don't want to upset her now.'

We followed him through the house to his study. It seemed he had been there when we arrived; Bach played softly in the background and a half-full cup of tea sat on the desk, which faced vast windows overlooking the water.

He took a seat, as did we.

'About yesterday, I am fairly certain we will be able to prove your search was illegal,' he began.

'You can try,' said Ajay, with a shrug, 'but the door is now wide open on your entire operation, and I don't think it will help very much to waste time fighting this charge when several more weighty ones are sure to follow.'

Joaquim Fernandes looked like a man not generally given to bluster. He looked at both of us unflinchingly. 'How can I help you?'

'What we will be investigating over the next few days is whether it was your drugs that were intercepted by the Mumbai Police, and if you had a hand in the blast that killed three people and the shoot-out that killed three more.'

'I didn't steal anything, and we didn't hurt anyone. But I can tell you what you are bound to find out soon enough. The drugs you intercepted were produced in my facility.'

'What was their final destination?'

'North India. They were hidden in spice and food packets, and would have made it there safely too, had it not been for the Mumbai Police.'

'The spice and food would mask their scent?' I asked.

'In case there were any stops on the way.'

'And yet you must have ensured that the police looked the other way?'

'Yes.'

'You used your connections? Or did you have some help?'

'I guess there is no harm in revealing it, since the man is dead after all. Satish Savarkar.'

'He did more than just make some phone calls for you, didn't he?'

'No, not really. He smoothed the way for the shipment through his contacts. He would call the relevant people to make sure the trucks weren't searched.'

'You were already in business with him for your illegal mining contracts,' I said.

'No comment,' he said.

'Your shipments were meant for domestic consumption?'

'No comment,' he said again.

'Was that the only route you employed?'

'No comment.'

'I can imagine,' I said, 'some consignments sneaking in with your illegally mined ores that were headed overseas. How better to hide something illegal than inside something else that is far more valuable and just as illegal. No one will look for any hidden stuff because people have been instructed to look the other way, also by Savarkar, who was, quite conveniently, minister-in-charge of ports. It was a stroke of genius. And it all only fell apart when Savarkar was jailed.'

'Very clever, Ms Ray. But I would remind you there has been a ban on iron ore mining in Goa of late.'

'That is such a shame. Is that why you are using the once-compromised Mumbai route once again?'

'I am no longer involved in that particular activity, Ms Ray. I don't remember saying I was involved in the second intercepted consignment.'

'You said they were your drugs.'

'Yes. And, I think I could go as far as to say that they were exactly the same drugs from the first time around.'

'I don't follow.'

'You do remember what happened to the first consignment, right?'

'It disappeared.'

'Yes. And then two years ago, it was loaded onto a truck and, on the outskirts of Mumbai, discovered once again.'

'So what? You got sloppy,' said Ajay.

'I am not one to make the same mistake twice. After the first incident, I scaled back. What you saw yesterday was our only manufacturing unit, and you will see that there are no more recreational drugs being made there.'

'What are they then?' asked Ajay.

'It is not relevant to the current discussion. But what I can tell you is that Goa is a small place. News travels fast. So when a shipment of drugs that looked a lot like our old product was loaded onto a truck, a call was made to me.'

'Why?'

'An old associate thought I might be interested in a shipment that looked very much like mine, being sold by someone else. He even had a sample of the shipment. He called to ask if I had got back in the game and was using another transport company. I assured him I had not. I called Savarkar to check whether he knew anything about it. He claimed he didn't.'

'You expect us to believe that someone was foolish enough to steal your drugs, bring them to Goa, and use the same trucks you used, and they got caught in the same place, again!'

'I didn't say that, did I? The truck was not the same company I'd used – the information simply got back to my transporter.'

'You are covering for him?'

'No. The scale of my legitimate operations commands a certain loyalty. That's all. And the route for the second batch of drugs and the point of interception were not the same, as far as I know. They were taken to Mumbai for holding and processing, but they were actually discovered outside city limits.'

'Do you know what the intended destination of the shipment was?'

'No, but I would guess they were destined for transportation by sea. That quantity would be extremely hard to smuggle through an airport. And I am pretty sure Savarkar was lying to me, and his preferred channel of late has been the water. And I can give you a very good reason why it was caught.'

'Why?' I took over the questioning.

'Because I tipped off the police commissioner.'

'So you had been double-crossed.'

'Yes.'

'By Savarkar?'

'Possibly. But I don't think he stole those drugs. He was running scared after the bomb blast, terrified of being implicated in the death of two cops.'

'How do we know you are telling us the truth?'

'You can call the commissioner and ask how he heard about the second consignment. Why would I have had him confiscate my own shipment?'

★

In a few minutes, the OC, Ramesh, was at the door to lead Fernandes away. They had their warrant.

Ajay and I returned to the car. I slumped into the seat and stared out of the window for the first five minutes of the drive.

'I can't believe you look disappointed at this outcome,' said Ajay.

'We are no closer to finding our killer, and Titanium's saboteur.'

'Now you are just getting greedy. Bringing down a major drug manufacturer is not enough for you today?' said Ajay with a smile. 'Let's go celebrate.'

We headed for a shack on Benaulim beach and sat side by side on two cane chairs, looking out at the water. There was a long table full of loud students drinking beer and passing around cigarettes and plates of food. Their volume was loud enough to drown out our voices.

'I can't call the commissioner, since he doesn't know I am here. But I will activate some contacts and see if I can verify Fernandes's tale. But let's assume for the moment that it's the truth.'

'It would be a rather audacious lie.' I shrugged.

'What's on your mind, Reema?'

'I am thinking aloud here, but isn't it beginning to look like the two drug hauls were actually bookends to this entire operation?'

'Yes.'

'What about the time in between?'

'Fernandes claims he got out of the drug game after the first mess-up.'

'And they had just got unlucky when the tip reached Daanish the first time?'

'Yes,' said Ajay. 'Something is bothering you about this, isn't it?'

'Maybe it's just the circularity, with the same drugs coming back and being seized. What are the odds?'

'You heard Fernandes. It wasn't chance: it was design – he made the interception happen.'

'If Fernandes is in the clear on the conspiracy and murders, we still don't know who stole the drugs. Doesn't it sound like an inside job to you?'

'The cops with access were all investigated. They all came back clean – at least for this crime.'

'Then who?'

'You think Fernandes is lying.'

I shook my head and took a sip of beer. 'He is a white-collar criminal. I don't see him orchestrating a bomb blast and a heist like that.'

'He could have been motivated by a fear of detection. I still don't trust his story. He is rose-tinting his role in the whole thing. Did he stop making recreational drugs after the deaths in Mumbai, or because Savarkar had landed in jail and he could no longer help move them?'

'It's possible. Savarkar was a crucial component in the logistics arm. And it is he who was killed. I would put money on Savarkar knowing who our man was. Possibly the only one to have known.'

'So then let's wait and see what the Goan team come up with when they investigate the factory.'

'And till then?'

'I don't know. But let's see.'

As our dinner arrived, conversation slowed. I looked out at the darkness, unable to shake the feeling we had overlooked something fundamental. I tried to take my mind off it, and succeeded through the dinner itself, but as we walked towards the car, I stopped in my tracks. 'It just doesn't seem right.'

'I have had that feeling stay with me for entire investigations,' said Ajay. 'Sometimes, even when you get to the truth it doesn't feel right.'

It wasn't a long drive to the hotel, and the silence we fell into lasted the duration of it. He stopped 100 feet or so away from the entrance and turned to me.

'Look, I know this is not a good time. And I know you have reservations about the whole thing. And I know you didn't return my call after our last dinner. But I'm going to be stubborn and not let it slide.'

He was waiting for a reaction, but I found myself unable to speak. He leaned forward. There was plenty of time to move away, and I didn't. As his lips met mine, I felt myself wanting to respond. But I couldn't.

He ended the kiss and pulled away.

'It's Shayak, isn't it?' he asked. I could see a touch of disappointment, and a little anger.

'It's not anybody, Ajay. I really am sorry, I really do like you.'

He clutched the steering wheel. 'Then I wish you'd do me the courtesy of honesty,' he said quietly.

'There is nothing between me and Shayak. If there was, I

wouldn't be sitting here having this conversation with you. That's not who I am.'

'But you want there to be?'

'It's more complicated than that.'

'At least that sounds like the truth.'

I bit my lip. 'I really am sorry.'

'I am too.'

★

The next day, as I waited for the investigation into the factory to produce some leads, I took my notes, my tab and a pen and paper, and parked myself at Sundown Bar. Arti wasn't there. I ate copious quantities of fish grilled in spicy rechado masala and chugged fresh lime soda. When Terrence came around, I surreptitiously stole sips of his beer.

We were being met everywhere by dead ends. The Goa Police searched the factory premises and confirmed what Fernandes had said: recreational drugs were no longer being made at that facility. A raid was on to check others. What we had seen were mainly spurious cancer drugs, being smuggled out to China where the demand for Indian cancer medication was extremely high, given local alternatives were twice the price. They had not been able to confirm this, but preliminary investigations revealed that my hunch had been correct: the drugs had once been smuggled out in illegal ore shipments, which were also much in demand in China. Now, they were going out with whatever else Fernandes could piggyback on. Pork product, spices, even baby formula. While despicable in itself, all this had no connection with our ongoing case.

And then there was a piece of news that promised to

break the deadlock, and it came by way of John Gomez of Aguada Jail. I had been calling him every few days in the hope that he would have found something to shed light on who had ordered the hit on Savarkar. So far, he had come up with nothing. But finally, he called me.

'I think I have something.'

'What is it?'

'I am not sure. But you told me to let you know if I found something unusual.'

'Yes. Anything.'

'I think it is best that we meet so I can show you myself.'

And so we set up a meeting for the evening, this time in a small restaurant near Baga frequented mostly by locals. I started out the moment the appointment was fixed, but it was a long way and Gomez was already waiting for me when I got there.

He seemed more relaxed this time when I took a seat across the table from him.

'What do you have for me?' I asked.

He slid an envelope across the table. 'See for yourself.'

I took out two pieces of paper. It was a photocopy of Daaku Singh's summons for an appearance in Savarkar's trial, and another document that seemed like it was a photocopy of a photocopy, it was so grey and marked. I glanced through it.

'Where did you find this?' I asked. What I had before me was a letter Daaku had sent Savarkar while he was still minister, on behalf of Goa Mining Company Ltd, asking for permission to mine in Cotigao. There was a clear handwritten note – Savarkar's writing, by the looks of it – in the corner stating that permission was being denied.

'Savarkar's belongings were handed over to the police and then the family, so I don't have access to those, you see. Though as far as I learned from the jail register, there was nothing of note. But I found this tucked into a slit in his mattress when I searched it yesterday.'

The paper had been folded, but it was otherwise crisp. It couldn't have been in the mattress for long. 'How did he usually bring documents into jail? Aren't there any restrictions?'

'For Savarkar, getting everything he needed was no problem. Either a family member or his lawyer would bring it in.'

'And how would he move things out?'

'What do you mean?'

'You said there was nothing suspicious amongst his belongings. I am assuming that doesn't mean he never had anything to hide.'

'Savarkar, for all his crimes, seemed to be clean of drugs and addictions.'

'That is not the sort of thing I mean. Cellphones, documents, that sort of thing is what I am looking for.'

'His belongings, as I said, went to the police.'

'Then why would he hide this?' I asked.

'I don't know that. But I did check the visitor log for recent entries, and his lawyer had not come in for a few days. But Savarkar did receive another visitor apart from his family members.'

'Who?'

'The name given was Karan Johar.'

I closed my eyes. There was no doubt that name was made up. 'Any other details?'

'We have started a new system whereby jail visitors have to present an ID. This Karan Johar gave a driver's licence. While we don't keep copies, I have the number. You can check it.'

None of Gomez's other efforts had borne fruit. He had found plenty of enemies of Savarkar behind the ancient walls of Aguada, but no one with the sort of clout necessary to orchestrate a jail murder of such bravado.

'What does the superintendent have to say about all of this?' I asked.

'Ha!' he scoffed. 'What will he say? He must be scared that his turn is next!'

I left, firm in the knowledge that the driver's licence would turn up nothing. I would send it, of course, for verification, but I wouldn't be holding my breath. It was a shame they didn't keep scanned copies, because the photograph would have been something to hold on to. For, I had at last caught a scent. Karan Johar, whoever he was, was lurking amongst us. Wherever he was, he must and would be found. It was only a matter of time.

TWELVE

It slowly crept up on me through the course of a fitful night that the letter was the first straight line in our mess of evidence. And where it pointed to was increasingly disturbing.

Fernandes–Savarkar–Daaku–Daanish.

First thing in the morning, I pulled up the rest of the diary notes I had received and had had little time for in the past few days. I turned to the sections immediately before and after the Daaku entry.

It all seemed so innocuous. There was an entry about a traffic case in Vashi. Another about a factory raid in Goregaon. I could find no thread to connect them, nor could I connect them to our current case. I also found no connection to any of the cases Daanish had been officially looking into during the same time frame.

I then skipped straight to the section after the licence plates. I was back to my two-day window between the interception of the drugs and Daanish's death.

I had skimmed through it previously, made a quick stab at unravelling it. But had made no headway. Now, however, I had new information that might help.

Still no connection.

And then I checked the pages prior.

Amongst several other police cases, I found one stray

entry. Dr KQ. BKC. That struck no chords. But a few lines down, another jumble of letters did: Vny Srma.

Vinay Sharma. Daaku's lawyer.

And the line became just a little clearer.

I didn't share my diary theories with Terrence. But I did show him the letter from Savarkar's cell.

'We need to take a look at what happened after Savarkar denied permission to the mining lobby, because the companies named here were amongst those just fined a couple of hundred crores for mining in the exact same area,' he said.

We cross-checked the data from the PIL and reports, and Terrence was right. It wasn't just Fernandes's front company; all of the companies listed in the letter were later given the green signal.

I passed on copies of the copies I had to Ajay, to see if he could find out more.

Karan Johar was our man – this was almost certain to me, while his identity was only one of many mysteries. That he was the one who brought Savarkar these documents was the most logical possibility given what we knew of Savarkar's comings and goings; and that he was using them as some sort of threat or inducement also seemed to be in keeping with how our man in the shadows functioned.

One good thing that came of all this was that Terrence finally stopped seeing the Russian hand in everything. Little consolation when I felt my brain running circles around itself. I tried not to think of the case at all – and it really was an effort. But I thought by putting some distance between myself and it, while we waited for the information about the documents, I would be able to look at it with less jaded eyes and find an elusive angle amongst the multitude of components we were processing.

Sundown Bar looked like a good place for this. I could see why Rishi had made this place home. Perhaps that was the real reason I chose it as my refuge – it made me feel like I was back to where it all started.

There, on the lounge chair with a front-row view of the sea, Rishi may have sat, hitting on some girl, drinking a beer. There, sitting on the bar stool, he may have met our man Karan Johar, and they may have shared a plate of food, and over a third drink, talked about what Rishi really wanted to do with his hacking, what it all meant to him. And then, casually, the stranger may have mentioned this job in Titanium, which would give him access to secrets, important secrets.

Or maybe nothing like that happened.

Of course, Arti may not be hiding anything. Even if she had seen anything suspicious, she may not really remember. She would have met thousands of beach bums since. I watched her mingle when she wanted to, sit in a corner with a book or her computer when the workload was light, having a drink of her own. I never caught her at it, but I knew she had an eye on me. She wasn't as good as she thought she was at this cloak-and-dagger stuff.

There I was, thinking about the case again! There was just no getting away from it. Suddenly, I just wanted to stop pretending, tear off the baby bump in public view and down a tray of tequila shots. I'd had enough of the lies. They had obscured the view for too long now.

George, now – was I any closer to figuring him out? I had tried my best to keep an eye on him whenever I could, in my own little operation. I hadn't felt the need to tell Shayak, or even Terrence.

I didn't even have to leave the premises for this exercise. Between sessions, or after returning from the office, I had been hanging out near his room whenever I could. I was usually concealed, though in plain sight, on a beautiful wrought iron bench, amidst the thick vegetation of the resort. He had many visitors, many of them white, looking like tourists – all with sunglasses on, even in the middle of the night. Though they looked like they could be, they were not part of the workshop. Sometimes, when they were there, an Indian visitor or two would also come in.

None of this was unusual, of course: George was white himself, and foreigners did tend to herd together. He had lived in Goa for a while now, off and on, and must know busloads of people. But something about it felt off. Why did he and his guests never leave the room? Why did I always feel like it was business and not pleasure? Why did they only come after dark?

Mostly, it was pretty hard to see or hear anything. But finally, three nights ago, when one of the girls had taken off her sunglasses, I was struck by the notion that I had seen her before. She was very blonde, very blue-eyed, though both of those things could well have been faked. She was in her late thirties or early forties, perhaps. I couldn't place her then, but the conversation I overheard helped me do so.

She was on her way out of George's room, and didn't look happy. Her voice was raised as she stepped over the threshold but before she could get another word out, I heard a soft voice – George, at his most menacing. 'Leia, watch yourself,' he said.

'Now you are threatening me?' she had responded.

'No. Just think of it as a reminder that you are a very long way from Wales, and I am your best – no, your only – bet for getting what you want.'

As soon as she left, I had raced back to my room and turned on the computer.

Leia. Leia. Leia. Thankfully, not a common name outside of Star Wars fan clubs. Even fewer in Wales. It wasn't hard to find what I needed online.

It had been a grotesque crime. It happened a couple of years ago, which is the only reason the details didn't come back to me immediately.

Leia Atherton. Her child had been kidnapped on her way back from school. The ending was not a happy one. The girl was finally found, dead. The investigation had led to the arrest of a paedophile who had claimed other victims, but not before the tabloids tore apart every aspect of Leia's life.

And here she was now. What did she have to do with George Santos? What did she want from him? And why did it seem as though they were not at all pleased with each other?

It was as though the George Santos of today was an even greater mystery than when we arrived. Everything about him seemed most improbable, unless he was perpetrating a very elaborate con. But, between Arti and Leia, I was finally beginning to catch a glimmer of the truth.

I drained my fresh lime soda and looked up to see Arti strolling on the beach with a man I had seen her with before. They walked, not quite hand in hand, but somehow never losing physical contact of some sort. A flirty half touch of the fingers. He said something that made her laugh. She replied with a twitter and a light slap on the arm – so light it was almost a caress.

Arti looked at him, her lover without a doubt, and then at me out of the corner of her eye. She knew I was watching.

I felt a sudden pang of longing. Had I ever experienced that careless intimacy in a relationship? My last serious boyfriend had been way back in college, so young and intense that nothing was careless. Why couldn't I just let myself have fun?

Just then, a bag hurtled into the chair beside me. Terrence.

'Letting me do all the heavy lifting, eh?'

'I sense you have some information to share.'

'Ajay called about the documents from the prison cell.'

'And?'

'He checked with Vinay Sharma, Daaku's lawyer, and found nothing. But then he called the prosecutor and it turned out the documents were straight from her file in Savarkar's case. Daaku was going to hammer the final nail in Savarkar's coffin, and this was the evidence he was relying on. Showing records of his Swiss bank account which prove he wired about $2 million the next day to another numbered account that he claims is Savarkar's, he was going to tell a story of how to buy a national reserve forest, via a corrupt public official.'

'Who would have access to that file?'

'Not clear, but you know what's plenty suspicious? Among the Mumbai cops working on Savarkar's case was Girish Kamat.'

'Wasn't he one of the cops involved in the Worli shoot-out over these drugs?'

'Yup.'

'That seems like too much of a coincidence to me.'

'Yup.'

'I need to talk to Ajay.'

'He had called to talk to you,' said Terrence, a little sheepishly. 'He seemed to have mixed up our numbers.'

Somehow I doubted it. I hadn't thought Ajay would let personal awkwardness interfere now, when it hadn't so far, but perhaps our latest encounter had left him feeling bitter.

I scanned the beach. There was a red-headed, thick-waisted woman feeding a beach dog. An Indian man was having an energetic head massage, while two women were selling junk anklets to unsuspecting foreigners at approximately nine times the price she would have sold one to me. Two women removed their bikini tops with a nonchalance I envied.

'I continue to be surprised you don't spend all your time in Goa,' I said to Terrence.

'If you are talking about those old women, you've got to be kidding.'

'Why?' I asked. They were older women but still attractive.

'Those shrivelled-up mounds do nothing for me. I've got my eye on higher things.'

I snapped around, ready to threaten bodily harm if I caught him with an eye anywhere south of my clavicles. Instead I saw him staring inland, past the beach and into the distance, where red-earthed hills rose gently towards the sky.

'There,' he said. 'Home. How I wish we could visit.'

'Miss your mother's cooking?'

'Of course. Don't you?'

'You haven't tasted my mother's cooking.'

He laughed, but his wistful gaze told me that near home was also where *she* was, the woman he had been talking to on the phone.

'Why don't you go up to see her?'

'What, now? Impossible, remember?'

'Hmmm.'

'Let's finish the job, Ray. Then we'll see.'

★

It was the last day of the workshop, and I must have been the happiest person at the resort about the fact that it was ending. While our work was far from done, and Apu might still be needed, it meant less time with the bump on and less time pretending when we could be working.

Between sessions, I had received a message from Archana. As I had expected, the Karan Johar licence was fake. The address on it was an abandoned old house that Vinod had been asked to check out, just to be sure.

And then, in an only slightly stilted conversation with Ajay, he confirmed what Terrence had reported, adding that they were still trying to see who else had access to Daaku's evidence. The prosecutor, however, seemed clueless about the leak – as far as she was concerned, no one should have seen the papers apart from her legal team. But then, it got a whole lot more awkward when I asked about the policemen involved, now Ajay's subordinates, previously Daanish Alam's. Would they have access to the documents as well? Weren't they appearing as witnesses for the prosecution?

'What are you suggesting, Reema?'

'Unpleasant though it may be, I think it is pretty clear, Ajay. And hardly surprising, given the circumstances.'

There was a long pause on the line. 'No, you are right, of course. We had investigated the officers already after the theft of the drugs. But with so many new areas to consider, we'll have to look into the possibility once again. I'll be in touch.'

Then it was time for the closing session, and George had told us attendance was compulsory for this one.

Thankfully, George seemed to be more in a mood to talk than to listen. 'I think we have talked more than any of us would like, shared more than we'd ever thought we would, and are eager to hit the party. Which will be a sensational one, I can assure you. Whether you choose to continue on this journey we have started or return to your old ways, whether I see any of you again or not, I would like to leave you with a thought tonight.

'Remember, you are the centre of your own world. That means you are the locus of its pain, but also of its joy. You can choose to ignore it, to embrace it for yourself, or cast it out through the ripples you create in the world. There are those people who aim to go through life without leaving the merest footprint. Their aim is to exist pleasantly, quietly, peacefully, without offending or drawing attention to themselves. And there are those people who look at everything around them only to see what can be changed – bettered, but also sometimes made worse. Because causing an impact often has unintended consequences. If you want to be noticed in this life, to love fiercely, to give generously, be prepared to cause hurt and heartache because even the sun that shines brightest casts shadows.

'When I started on this journey myself, I had no idea where to start. After all, if you have known only unhappiness your whole life, would you recognize joy if it happened to you? How do you open the door for joy if you can't even see it? I hope, over the past two weeks, you have succeeding in unloading some of the guilt, anger and shame to get a little closer to who you dream of being. Now it is time for you to go back to the real world and see if you can hold on to even a fraction of the progress you have made here. Good luck.'

He shot me one of the looks I had come to expect from him, like he was sharing an inside joke with me. But this time, he seemed almost embarrassed. And it hit me like a ton of bricks. George Santos, whoever he was, was a bleeding-heart romantic. Whatever his game, his words were, approximately, what he believed. The man truly was full of surprises.

*

If there was one thing about George that did not surprise me at all, it was that he knew how to throw a riot of a party. Half an hour after his rousing finale, complete with waterworks from several participants, promises to stay in touch forever, two participants (fortunately formerly single) announcing – to no one's surprise – they had found true love in each other, the beach was aglow. The smell of barbecue infused the air. The bar had been thrown open, and by the time we got there, there was a reckless amount of revelry and champagne. The men were taking turns posing with fresh fish on a slight detour from the grill. George was working the room with the confidence of a man in charge. One of the participants did the rounds with a tray laden with shots, challenging everyone to a game of Truth or Dare. Whichever they chose, the reward was a bottoms up.

The newly declared lovebirds were surrounded by a circle of people who wanted to know every detail, and I heard them say they were taking an extra two weeks off to travel

India together before she went back to Delhi and he returned to the States. I couldn't work up the enthusiasm to join them, so I stood back and took in the scene.

Soon, Malvika came up to me.

'You'll be back?' I asked.

'Like clockwork. Next year. Every time I leave full of hope, and with a mission. I see it through, and when I am done with it all and low on fuel, I come back for more.'

'So what do you have in mind now?'

'Everest base camp, I think.'

'Wow!'

'Think I'm too old?'

'I think there is no such thing and you are in fantastic shape.'

'You know, Apu, I meet a lot of people here. It has made me something of an expert, I think. You are special. Too special to waste your life in an unhappy marriage.'

'You don't see us making it?' I felt like such a fraud in that moment, lying to this lovely woman who took this process so seriously.

'That's not relevant. But I can see that you don't see yourself making it. And isn't that what counts?'

I stretched my arms out for a hug. It was much easier than finding another lie, and perhaps the evening was getting to me too, just a little bit.

Within half an hour, the beach was packed. I realized it was not just a party for George's students, it was for all of his staff. Spotting Arti, her boyfriend by her side, I walked over.

'Nice to see you here,' I said with a smile.

She smiled back. 'I don't think you have met Sid.'

'No, I haven't. Apu,' I said, putting out my hand.

He gave it a firm shake, and behind the well-groomed beard, I saw a smile. Like Arti, he too had several tattoos on his arms. His were less intricate, less original. Barcode, barbed wire, some Chinese script.

'What are you doing in Goa, Apu?' he asked.

'Finishing up today with this workshop,' I said with a shrug.

'Did you find it useful?'

I nodded. 'George is something, isn't he?'

'That he is,' said Arti.

'And what are you doing in Goa?' I asked Sid.

'I am an adopted native.'

'Here full time? Lucky. I wish I could live here. But I am told jobs are scarce.'

'Depends on your line of business.'

'And what is yours?'

'I am currently unemployed.'

From Arti's laugh, I guessed this was not the truth. 'No, really, he is an entrepreneur,' she said.

'And what about you?' he asked me.

'I am a boring old techie,' I said. 'My husband too.'

'Is that right?' he asked. 'Why is it boring?'

'Strapped to a desk and staring at a screen isn't half as glamorous as being a spiritual guru, is it? Ah look, there's George.'

George had come over to find us, casually draping an arm around my shoulders.

'I hope the party is up to your standards, Arti,' he said.

'Not as good as ours down at Sundown, but not too shabby.'

'I was told you worked here once, Arti?' I said.

There was an awkward exchange of glances all around. Finally, Arti spoke. 'That feels like a lifetime ago.'

Sid squeezed her hand. 'Nice meeting you, Apu,' he said as he led Arti away.

We watched them go. 'My, my, Reema. You sure know how to clear a room.'

'Why was her reaction so drastic?'

'Arti is cagey.'

'And it seems as though Sid is even more secretive than she is.'

'Not surprising.'

'Why?'

'If he knew the question would bother her, it would bother him more. I've never seen a man quite as much in love as Sid.'

'Really? But why did she leave here? Not because of sexual harassment.'

'Reema, will you believe me if I told you it has nothing to do with you?'

'I might believe you and still not be able to leave it alone. You gave her the job at Sundown when she left here. Why? What connects you?'

'Arti doesn't believe in dwelling on the past.'

'You mean she is on the run. As is Leia Atherton.'

George shot me a look. 'Good lord, nothing as extreme as that.'

'You are lying.'

He laughed. 'Reema, your honesty is truly refreshing.'

'As a blatant departure from your own pack of BS?'

'My world is not as clear-cut as yours.'

'But you know you can trust me.'

'No, and I'll tell you why: I am not sure your concept of

justice and mine would overlap at all times, which makes it a dangerous proposition.'

'Ethical relativism?'

He gave me his cheekiest grin. 'You do know how to talk dirty to a man. Enjoy the rest of the party.'

I finally found Terrence again. He was regaling people with stories of college in Mumbai, buying weed and drinking toddy. I wonder whose memories he was stealing, as I knew he had gone to college in Calcutta.

My phone rang then, which took me by surprise. So few people had the number. The caller ID was blocked. I moved away to take it.

'Hello?' I said.

'Good instincts.' It was Shayak; back in civilization it would seem.

'I know. But what in particular are we talking about?'

'George. You were right.'

'Confirmed?'

'Yes. From the horse's mouth.'

'Now what?'

'Corner him. Get him to talk.'

'Easier said than done. I just tried and failed once again.'

'He's a slippery one. But you can do it. You cracked this and you have what you need now.' And then a pause. 'I need to go.'

Just that hint of hesitation.

'Shayak?'

'I'll be home soon, Reema.'

And with that, the line went dead.

I stared at my phone, willing him back on the line.

When I looked up, I saw Terrence had come to stand by

my side. There was a smile on his lips unaccompanied by mockery, for once. 'It looks like I'm not the only one in love,' he said softly.

'Oh shut up,' I said, hitting him on the arm.

'Better be careful with that sort of assault. We are supposed to be married, not brother and sister,' he said, bending down to whisper in my ear.

'Well, that's over now, isn't it?'

'Tell me you'll miss me,' he said as I walked away. 'Come on,' he called out, 'just once!'

I put my phone in my pocket and walked into the shack. I was going to throw caution to the winds and procure myself a tall, cold one.

There were people all around, and I wove my way towards the bar.

'Where do you think you're going?' Terrence said, at my tail once more.

'I need to talk to someone.'

'Not without me.'

'Come along, then,' I said.

There sat Olivia, beside the bar, manning the laptop. She had volunteered to be DJ for the evening. I wanted to talk to her, especially in light of what Shayak had just told me. But I needed to get her away from this place.

'Hi, Olivia. Can we talk?'

She looked up, surprised at first, and then gave me a measured look. 'Can it wait?'

'Not really.'

'Just a minute.' A young woman was hanging about the bar and Olivia installed her at the console. 'I'll be right back,' she promised.

A few feet away were Arti and Sid. Sid took her by the hand and led her towards the water. Arti had her back to me, and was talking fast in hushed tones, but Sid looked over her shoulder and saw me. I saw a flash of alarm on his face. He took Arti's arm and pulled her in close.

And then it was as if the earth was being torn apart. I reached for Terrence just as we were thrown to the ground. And then – nothing.

*

I opened my eyes. Light. Screaming. Darkness.

And then pain. And light, brighter than it should be. The smell of burning. Chemical. Coughing. George. Darkness.

A harsh fluorescent beam hit my face. I could hear metal against metal. I was shouting. For Terrence. Where was he? What was that horrible noise? Why couldn't they hear me? A strange face closed in on mine. And then a pinprick. Darkness.

THIRTEEN

I awoke. In the darkness of the room, I could not tell where I was. I tried to sit up but couldn't.

I forced myself to breathe. Where was I? Under my fingertips was a papery bed sheet. I could see light in the hallway. A cheap hotel? And then I registered the smell.

It was a hospital. I turned my head slowly, and saw that I wasn't connected to any wires or drips. Then why hadn't I been able to sit up? I couldn't be sure how badly I was hurt.

I found the call button, and pressed. In a matter of seconds, a light went on and a nurse was by my side. 'You are awake,' she said, cheerfully.

'Can you tell me where I am?'

'You don't know?' she asked. Her face was a mask, but I could see the flash of concern in her eye. 'Let me call the doctor.'

A woman, mid-forties perhaps, entered the room and picked up my file, never breaking eye contact with me. The nurse was back as well.

'Good to see you awake,' said the doctor.

'How long have I been out?'

'Not long.'

'What's wrong with me?'

'Mild concussion.'

'So I can move around?'

'I'd advise caution on that front, at least for tonight. Keep your movements to a minimum.'

'Am I alone here? Where's Terrence? Where is everyone else from the beach?'

The doctor looked unsure. 'You should contact your people.'

'Who brought me in?'

'I'd rather you got the full picture from your office.'

Office? 'Can I make a call?'

The nurse brought me a tray with my phone, wallet and the jewellery I had been wearing. My personal effects.

All of a sudden I felt my tummy. Where had my silicone baby gone? I felt awkward about asking them.

I picked up my phone and turned it on. And then I dialled the only person I could think of. Thankfully, his phone rang. 'Shayak,' I said.

'You are up!' he replied, sounding relieved.

'Still in Kyrgyzstan?'

'No. Five minutes away from you.'

'What is going on here?'

'I'll explain everything when I see you.'

'When?'

'I'm already out the door.'

Flashes came back. The screaming. The pain. Terrence. Blood.

There had been an explosion of some sort, but I could be sure of little else. I thought I remembered being loaded on to an ambulance, and then, it all became increasingly hazy. A medivac team. Doctors on board some sort of aircraft – a helicopter? George. Odd. What was he doing holding my hand? But that was it. I must have been drugged.

Ignoring the doctor's advice, I slowly got up, stumbled to the curtain and drew it open.

The Mumbai skyline. What were we doing here?

Walking over to the door, I turned the knob and swung it open, only to have my path blocked by a steely arm.

'Madam, I cannot let you pass,' said a guard as I peered out.

'Why?' Was he armed? I didn't know if I should be relieved or appalled.

'I have my orders, madam.'

I took in what I could of the black, unmarked uniform. Titanium, of course. 'I would like to see the person who issued these orders.'

He looked at me, steely-eyed. 'Forget it,' I said. Only one person could be behind this. I'd ask him soon enough.

I went back to the bed and sat down, closing my eyes and opening them again. I felt no pain, but was woozy. I had no idea what medicine they had given me. I could feel scratches and bruises all down my right side – I wasn't sure how I got them. Hadn't I fallen on sand? The doctor had said I'd sustained a concussion. I remember hitting wooden planks hard as I went down. The deck of the beach shack?

But where was Terrence?

Shayak walked in. If I'd expected any kind of greeting, I was mistaken. He stood in the doorway, stormy, his hands balled into fists at his side.

'I thought you were still away,' I said.

'I just returned.'

For us? Because of the explosion? 'How long have I been out?'

'Little over ten hours.'

'Really?'

'You were given a minor sedative on the trip over. Nothing major. But you were probably groggy from the painkillers and the injury. You were sleeping it off. Anyway, you didn't miss much. It is still only 10 a.m.'

I was completely disoriented – I had thought it was afternoon. 'So I am okay.'

'You are.'

'Terrence – how is he? Where is he? And everyone else?'

'Terrence has been injured quite badly. His left arm has severe burns and caught shrapnel from the explosion. He is in surgery now. We'll find out more soon.'

'Is he –'

'He should pull through without a problem, according to the doctors. But they haven't told me the extent of his injuries yet. You, on the other hand, only have a mild concussion. Miraculous, given how close you were to the blast. You were possibly cushioned from the worst of the impact by your baby bump.'

'Imagine that!' I said. 'Where *is* that damn thing?'

'Safe and sound. I am treating it with new respect.'

'What about everyone else at the party?'

'One casualty. Half a dozen more injured.'

'Who?'

'Victoria Price.'

'Should I know that name?'

'No. She wasn't one of George's students. She was a friend of one of the staff. Just nineteen years old.'

'Where is she from?'

'Australia. Which also means the attention from the media about the blast has quadrupled.'

'Where was she?'

'At the DJ console.'

I closed my eyes. The girl Olivia had asked to play the music? She was there because of me. Because I had called Olivia away.

'Are you okay?' asked Shayak. When I finally opened my eyes, he was by my side.

'What about Olivia? I had been with her.'

'She is quite bruised up. She was closer to the blast, but seems to have been protected by a table or something from the explosion.

'And George? I remember him by my side.'

'Yes,' he said softly. 'He is fine.'

'Why was I sedated?'

'They thought it was worse than it actually turned out to be, so as a precaution till you reached a hospital and could be examined, they kept you under. Also, you were resisting so much, George said the doctors did it to keep you safe as well as quiet.'

'I remember a helicopter.'

'Yes. It brought you to Mumbai.'

'Why not somewhere closer, in Goa?'

'Terrence and Olivia both needed medical help greater than what the facilities there could provide.'

'Olivia too?'

'Yes, she has a couple of fractured ribs, and there were fears of spinal damage that have luckily proved unwarranted.'

'Who called the chopper?'

'George. He had the presence of mind to call me within seconds of the blast, and told me there was a medivac team he had worked with before. The chopper took you to Dabolim, and from there, once the doctors determined Mumbai was the best bet, they brought you to Mumbai by a medically equipped private aircraft and then to the hospital.'

Even hours ago, George coming to the rescue would have seemed an unlikely scenario. But now I thought I knew who he was.

'I've never been on a helicopter before. Shame I can't remember it.'

Finally a smile. 'Get better and I'll see what I can do,' said Shayak.

'When can I leave?'

He shook his head. 'You are under observation for the next forty-eight hours.'

'Are you and George working together now? Why did he call you?'

'I don't have to tell you how shrewd George is. After the explosion, he acted fast. He told me what had happened, to ask what to do next,' said Shayak, running a tired hand across what looked like four days' worth of beard. 'He is not a man to call the police. Though of course he finally did, it wasn't his first reaction.'

I was still confused. 'And you told him to shut us up?'

'Yes.'

'Why?'

'It was a volatile situation. You two are – were – under cover. We needed to maintain that at the time.'

'And now? Have we been outed? This must be all over the news.'

'We've managed to keep it out.'

'More of your usual paranoia?'

'It has a more specific purpose this time.'

'What?'

'If you agree, and that is an important "if", we need the world to think that Apu and Vishal were killed in that explosion.'

I felt my jaw slack a little as I gaped.

'There is no doubt in my mind,' continued Shayak, 'that the bomb was intended to do just that.'

'You think we were the target?'

'It makes sense. Why choose that spot in Goa, on that night, right before you were to leave the ashram? Any other scenario is just too much of a coincidence. You are getting close.'

'With what we know now, what if it was meant for George? Or Arti?' I asked.

'Why now? Who would want to kill either of them?'

'Who knows what the pair of them are messed up in?'

'I think we know more about George now than before, don't you?'

He was right about that. George as the money-laundering guru with gangster links, as I had thought of him till quite recently, would be a logical target. But our new information made that a much less likely scenario, particularly in a public attack of this nature.

'But for the moment, it is almost irrelevant to our course of action,' Shayak said. 'Right now, you have some pretty serious decisions to make.'

'So Apu plays dead, and Reema continues the investigation?'

'Yes.'

'Or I leave and bid it adieu.'

'Yes.'

'But Apu's picture, meaning my picture, will be released to the world as a fatality?'

'Yes,' said Shayak again, voice flat.

'What about my parents?'

'You'll speak to them and tell them the broad strokes. No one else.'

'I have a grandmother too. It'll kill her to see my picture in the paper. I'll need to warn her.'

'Does she gossip?'

'She's as tight-lipped as a spy. Smarter than most people I know.'

'You take after her, then?'

'Some say.'

'Fine, her too.'

'And Devika.'

He started shaking his head.

'Please?' I couldn't give up the chance to see this through, but I couldn't do it at the expense of my closest friends. I thought of Sunaina, Santosh da. Terrence's family. The logistics – a fake funeral? So much pain for so many people out there who would be seeing my face with every article and every clip on the twenty-four-hour news cycle.

'Okay,' he said. He seemed unable to look me in the eye. 'Everyone else, those who don't know you were going undercover at all, you can just lie to outright. If they contact you, tell them it is a bizarre coincidence that has nothing to do with you.'

'What does this thing entail, exactly?'

'I wish I knew. All I can say right now is that if Apu and Vishal were the targets, it is because the killer wanted Reema and Terrence dead. Giving him what he wants will buy us some time. It will create some difficulties as well, because anyone you have interacted with in the course of your stay at the ashram will be more or less off-limits to you. And bear in mind, we have no way of knowing how long this might go on.'

I bit the inside of my lip. It could be a couple of weeks. A month. Maybe even two?

'There'll be a lot of publicity surrounding this. So it's not exactly like you will go quietly away. Everyone who has ever known you will think you are gone. Give that some serious thought.'

And also to all the deaths that had occurred in the course of this crime, years in the making. Daanish and the other three policemen. Ashutosh Dhingre. Afreen. Bystanders, the latest being Victoria Price.

'What about Terrence?'

'We have to assume that Terrence will be benched for the foreseeable future.'

'I work alone?'

'No. You will have a new partner.'

'Who?'

'Me.'

'But all of your other work! What about Kyrgyzstan?'

'The hostages are home safe. The rest can wait, for now. The moment that bomb exploded, this became my top – my only – priority. I've let both of you down, big time. The only reason I am not pulling you off this case is that you know too much to be replaced. It's a bloody mess, Reema, and I am sorry you are in the middle of it.'

'I'll do it,' I said.

'You are sure?'

'The stakes are too high here. And if you are right, I very nearly did die. I would like very much to see this through.'

'Okay,' he said. 'Let's wait till Terrence is out of surgery. That gives you a couple more hours to change your mind. If you still think it is a good idea at the end of it, we'll start making calls to your families later tonight. The news will have to go out after that.'

★

I stared down at Terrence's somehow shrivelled form. It was as though his whole body had shrunk since I had seen him last.

I was wracked by guilt. The only reason Terrence was there on that beach was because of me. I had involved him in my investigations that had led to him joining the Titanium team just as it had begun to sink.

His mangled arm was covered in bandages. The doctors had determined there was no way to save it. It would have to be amputated. Terrence's parents, who had arrived from Goa, requested the doctors to give them a day to speak to Terrence, to prepare him for what had to be done.

His eyes fluttered open, slowly, painfully. I tried to put a smile on my face, but it failed me.

'Drugs, good,' he muttered. 'Water, please?'

I called the nurse, who came in and checked that everything was in order before adjusting the bed to a reclining position and holding a cup of water to his lips.

For a long while I just sat by his side, waiting for him to regain his bearings. He would have heard the news last night from his parents. Shayak must have been in to see him as well.

'Terrence, I don't know what to say.'

'At least you aren't telling me everything will be okay. So you are doing 100 per cent better than almost everyone else.'

'Have you decided what to do?'

'I'm back in surgery today. There isn't much of a choice, is there?'

'Afraid?'

'Like you wouldn't believe. But the doctor said the elbow can be saved, and this makes a huge difference to the range of motion later on. Shayak has offered me some sort of bionic arm, and of course, financial compensation generous enough that I wouldn't have to work again if I didn't want to. Titanium has lost everything except its employee insurance, lucky for me.'

'Sounds about right.' It was a grievous injury sustained on the job, after all. I'd expect nothing less. 'And what about the other stuff?'

'You mean the dying and what not?'

'Yes.' My family was different from Terrence's. My parents were divorced, they met relatives a couple of times a year, and though there would be plenty of people who would be extremely distraught on my account, I knew my parents had the breathing space to keep up the pretence of normalcy. Terrence's parents lived in the town in which they were born, where they had always lived, deeply rooted to their communities. His photograph being released as one of the deceased, whether or not he had a beard and hipster glasses and a different name, would be received completely differently.

But he just shrugged. 'As long as my parents and sister know the truth, the rest – who cares? How do you feel about it?'

'Unsure at first. But increasingly confident that it is the only thing to be done.'

'Good,' Terrence said. 'Remember, Ray, I don't want your pity. What I really, really want is for you to go out there and catch the bastard that did this.'

I nodded, a silly smile on my face as a tear escaped despite Terrence's orders.

'And, before I forget,' he continued, 'thanks for saving my life.'

'What are you talking about?'

'No need for false modesty, Ray.'

'Modesty? I honestly have no idea what you are talking about.'

'You leaped at me, pulling me down just in time. Then George dragged us both out of there. We were close, Ray. If you had landed on top of me, instead of the other way around, God knows what would have happened to you. You could be in my position, or worse.'

'Are you sure you are remembering right?'

'You must have taken a worse knock on the head than you realize, if you've blanked out about being a freakin' hero. For me, the whole thing is in slow motion. I can't forget even if I try. Told Shayak all about it, too,' he said with a wink. 'I think you should prepare to find yourself irresistible pretty soon. You can thank me later.'

*

When I left the room, the last person I expected to see was George holding two tall cups of coffee, but after everything I had learned, I shouldn't have been surprised.

We went back to my room, me greedily grabbing a

cup from him. 'You could have saved us a lot of trouble,' I said.

'Where's the fun in that?' There was a softness in his gaze I hadn't seen before, and I felt a surge of affection for this man.

'Terrence told me you pulled us back from the fire.'

'I hope he also told you I shouldn't have had to. Normal people hear an explosion and they run away. Not you. You plunge right in. Saving your friend with no thought for yourself. Next time, just duck, will you?'

But he knew I wouldn't, just as he wouldn't go quietly into the night.

'I have so much to ask you,' I said. How wrong I had been. George had never added up, and I couldn't let it go even as I persisted in looking in the wrong places to understand him.

'Just a few more minutes. Shayak asked me here today. I can only imagine it was to discuss just this. I will lay myself bare for all of you,' he said with a flourish.

'I know most of it anyway.'

'Do you now? Tell me.'

And so I did. I started with Arti, because that was how I had arrived at the truth. Her face had been plastered all over TV but I – and the rest of the world – had only ever seen old photos, from school yearbooks and the like. And she had changed a lot over the years. Without Leia, the pieces may never have fit. But when I stumbled on the truth about *her*, I started to get a sense of what George was up to.

The confirmation that Olivia Stein was British intelligence was enough to give me a strong suspicion about who Arti was. Her real name was Raya Mehta, one of the most wanted women in England. She had had a desk job at the MI5 and had leaked a bunch of documents about unauthorized monitoring of thirty South Asian individuals believed to have ties with a mosque in London, another in Pakistan and also believed to be sponsoring terrorists – a disastrous intelligence which had led to a bloodbath.

The information, revealed to a leading newspaper, had put three intelligence officers behind bars, led to the resignation of a minister and the head of the intelligence agency, and resulted in a parliamentary enquiry. She disappeared after handing over the information, which triggered an international manhunt once the British Parliament ruled her a traitor for divulging classified information, no matter what the ramifications of the contents. If she set foot back in the UK, she would be tried for treason.

And yet she was here, possibly because it was the one place she could disappear in without attracting attention, but most likely because of George. If you were planning a life on the indefinite run, you wanted allies.

At long last, I had uncovered what George Santos was doing: he was giving runaways a new life, a new identity. In Goa, where white people and foreign accents drew no attention. In Goa, where there were nooks and crannies where law enforcement, or the media, or international intelligence would not, could not, reach. In Goa where there were a thousand ways to disappear.

Leia Atherton was not a criminal. Far from it. But though some regarded Arti as a hero – hell, count me among them – she was a wanted woman.

That made George's activities highly illegal, and explained his efforts to keep us close and yet far enough to not really see anything. It is why he, though innocent of the conspiracy and murder we were currently probing, was running scared of investigation, and had repeatedly given us just enough information to point us in the right direction – which was conveniently away from his real agenda – and no further.

But that wasn't even touching upon who George *really* was.

'It's amazing. There is so much about you –'

George raised a finger to his lips in a silent shush. There was a smile for me in those electric blue eyes.

'The first person in twenty-five years, outside of my coterie, to have figured it out. It was always going to be tough to keep it under wraps when you came snooping around. I wasn't sure whether it would be you or Shayak, but I'd like to think my money was on you.'

'Do you regret what you did?' I couldn't help asking. He had lost everything in the process, and what good had it really done?

'I think it is time to ask why you talk so much about regret. What does that mean to you?'

'Really? Even now,' I said, pointing to where we were, 'can't you drop the whole Zen thing?'

'It's more important now than ever, Reema. Since they are fixing you up anyway,' he said, 'this would be just the right time to screw your head back on straight.'

'And since I know you aren't the fraud you pretend to be, I should listen?'

'Oh, I'm a fraud all right, just not the sort you initially thought I was. But I am not going to get distracted and forget the question.'

'Regret. I don't know, I don't think I have ever given it any thought.'

'I know you are lying, but I'll give you the benefit of the doubt and tell you to think about it. Fast.'

'It makes you look back and lie to yourself. It is the last refuge of the unhappy, I suppose.'

'Sounds deep. Continue.'

There was only one thing I currently regretted: Shayak. I so regretted pushing him away, and I didn't know how to fix it.

I thought about what I had said to Shayak, early on, and about that original disaster couple, my own parents. 'It makes you tell yourself that what happened didn't happen for a very good reason, when in actual fact, it doesn't really matter why it happened. All that matters is that it happened. And there can be no going back.'

'Good. And?'

'I suppose it's hard for me to separate the romance of that from the random chaos of reality.'

'I can always trust you, Reema, to pare it down to essentials. Before we talk about who I am, I want you to understand *why*. It is not for the faint of heart, this letting go. To do so, you have to rid yourself of the illusion of narrative. That our lives are a neat, linear story unfolding with the control of a master artist. You have to trust the moment, and the immediacy, that very random chaos you are talking of. I think this is the only real thing I have learned in my life. It is powerful, more powerful than most of the idiots who pass through my little ashram realize. More powerful than I allow it to be. But I've said it before, Reema, you are special.'

The door opened and Shayak came in. 'Thank God you're here,' I said. 'I think I have had more of George than I can take. Let's go see Terrence so we can do the grand reveal in front of him.'

When we got to Terrence's room, I didn't allow for any further distractions from what this meeting was really about. 'You were right all along. George is a trafficker,' I announced to Terrence.

'What are you saying!' Terrence was almost shouting.

'Guilty as charged, but not the kind of trafficking you were thinking of, I suspect,' said George.

'What other kind of trafficking is there?'

'He is taking in runaways.'

'What the hell does that mean?'

'Arti. Leia. They, amongst others, needed refuge.'

'From what?'

'Leia is on the right side of the law, tragic though her story may be. Arti is far more interesting. She is the Drone Strike Whistle-blower.'

'What!'

I told him the whole story. 'The mosque in Pakistan suspected of having terrorist ties was mainly legitimate. And the intelligence gathered resulted in two drone strikes in Pakistan that led to the death of over fifty civilians, including children, and only one lower-rung Lashkar operative. Arti is the one to have made that information public, at great risk to herself.'

As I looked at Terrence's bewildered face, I realized how remarkable the story was, and it hit me all of a sudden that, for all my efforts at living on my own terms, I was terribly mainstream. I was buttoned up, solidly middle class, wedded to the straight and narrow, inasmuch as a private detective, female, in India could be. But I didn't challenge any moral boundaries, personally or otherwise. I bucked the trend, but I could not imagine breaking free from my world and what it meant to me.

'Arti – or Raya – chose the higher path. She gave up everything for an idea. Whether or not you think of her as a hero, she is exceptional,' I said.

'She is,' agreed George.

'Okay, enough,' said Terrence. 'Who is this asshole?'

'I'll let him talk. He's good at it.'

But poor Terrence would still have to wait. 'First tell me how you figured it out,' George said.

'We first figured out who Arti was. Thanks to some inputs from British intelligence.'

'Olivia bloody Stein.'

'Sort of. Shayak's Foreign Office contacts include her handler. When we heard murmurs of an intelligence officer at your ashram, we grew suspicious. He confirmed when we asked, and it was he who let Shayak know that you were on the up and up without revealing anything else.'

'Gave me the all-clear, is it? That is a bit of a surprise.'

'Don't you think? So who else could she be after? It had to be Arti. And then I considered her connection to you. We had run your name, face and everything else we could rustle up through the system, and come up empty. Then I realized that Arti's boss at MI5, who had quit after the whole leak debacle under a cloud of possible collusion, had also been in charge of another high-profile whistle-blower several years ago. And the more I thought of it, that whistle-blower could well have become a fraudulent guru with a penchant for the ladies.'

'And why is that?'

'Because he wore his flamboyance like a badge of pride.'

'How do you know that? He was never even interviewed!' said George.

'Flamboyance of appearance is nothing compared to that of words.'

'Like handwriting.'

'Right. Those little flourishes that never go away.' I had used George's language to identify him once before. Now again, I used them to confirm a suspicion, and I was sure I was not wrong.

I pulled up the only interview he had given. 'What is life but memories? And not ours, but the ones we create in others. Our bodies, our minds, and with them our memories are destroyed, all at once. And yet, we can live on in others. We usually take this all too literally – seeking immortality through procreation, which lasts a couple of generations. But by changing the world, we can live on forever.'

'So said great statesmen. And serial killers,' completed Terrence. We had both heard it, more or less verbatim. It was part of one of George's more diverting sessions by the beach – and also his great parting shot from another life, a long, long, time ago.

'You live for fifty years and try to be original every time you open your mouth,' George said, sulking ever so slightly.

'Don't beat yourself up about it. If it hadn't been for the link between you and Arti, we would have never stumbled upon the truth.'

'Much harder nowadays, in our selfied world, to disappear without a trace.'

'Unless you are a genius like Arti.'

'Yes.'

'Back to the point. Who the hell are you, George?' asked Terrence.

'I was merely a witness.'

'A whistle-blower, just like Arti,' I clarified. 'It was the late '80s. A British munitions company was supplying arms to mujahideen in Afghanistan, led by Osama bin Laden.'

'Oh my God,' whispered Terrence.

George took over. 'I was a lowly marketing executive, but I was seen to be a rising star. Fast rising. I was barely four years old in the company, but I had proven myself early on and they took me for one of these "sales" trips. We met representatives in Dubai, and after one meeting and one night of women and drink in the company of an undersecretary in the ministry of defence, we returned on the private jet to London. And I knew that I had to speak.'

'And then?'

'There weren't so many protections in place for whistle-blowers then. I was threatened, accused, maligned and unemployable by the time we were through. It became almost certain that I would be tried for divulging classified information. So I recorded everything I knew, and left the country.'

'Just like Arti,' said Terrence. 'You are a fugitive?'

'I haven't set foot in England since 1996.'

'And they are still after you?'

'There are people high up who would not like to see me return. They know that the information I divulged could be the tip of the iceberg. But now they have bigger fish to fry.'

'Yes. And they have sent Olivia Stein here to investigate.'

'And you are cooperating with her? But you helped Arti escape!'

'Cooperate is a strong word.'

'She is staying at the ashram,' said Terrence.

'So are you. Would you say I was particularly cooperative? There is more than one way to skin a cat.'

'But still! She is the enemy, isn't she?'

'Don't worry about Arti. She doesn't need my help,' George said with a laugh. 'I don't think she ever did.'

'You'd give her up, though?'

George fell silent.

I had to believe there was more to it – with George there always seemed to be. But what did I know of his loyalties and his needs? There were so many ways in which a man could be worked upon to turn on his own. And now there was no time to pry. Especially since we finally knew that George was not involved in our case, that he was fighting his own wars, for reasons of his own, and we could count him as our ally.

George left, and Shayak and I lingered in Terrence's room. 'Maybe there are worse things in the world than starting from scratch,' mused Shayak.

'What would you do?' asked Terrence.

'Exactly what we are doing right now.'

'The three of us – a detective agency?'

'It's one way to make a living.' He got up. He was so serious that it seemed impossible that he might be joking. But he so rarely cracked a smile these days, and the proposition seemed so ludicrous, that I thought he must be.

Shayak and I left as well, to find a woman standing just outside the door. She was young, and pretty in a homespun sort of way. She seemed nervous.

'You must be Lucy,' I said. No doubt this was Terrence's girl.

She seemed startled at being spoken to, and then nodded. I imagined what she must be going through: the man she had fended off for so long lying in a hospital room with his arm hacked off.

'He'll be happy to see you,' I said.

'Can I go in?'

'Of course.'

She turned the handle and opened the door, and I could see a slow, shy smile touch her lips as she saw Terrence.

'Finally she comes,' I muttered as she shut the door behind her.

'Some women don't like their men whole,' said Shayak.

'Not funny,' I said. Inexplicably, tears threatened.

Shayak stretched his fingers out to give my hand a quick squeeze. It was the first time he had touched me since the explosion.

Fourteen

It would be at least a week before we could return to Goa. My injuries demanded some time off, and we needed to find a safe base from which to operate. Being dead demanded that we lie low. Terrence was still holed up in the hospital for recovery, after which he would be transferred, along with his parents, to one of Titanium's safe houses in the city. I was currently there myself, with nothing for company but Daanish's diary and hourly phone calls from my mother. My father was dealing only marginally better with the deluge of concern that had engulfed the Ray family, so he decided to seize the opportunity to travel abroad, something he was prone to in times of stress. I heard from him only once, first thing in the morning from wherever he was. I got innumerable messages and emails from friends, asking whether I was okay, and if Aparna Shenoy was somehow related to me. My standard reply: It was a very disturbing coincidence that the dead girl looked so much like me, but I am still very much alive and very much at work in Mumbai.

If I had previously thought my life choices were too safe, that was rapidly becoming a non-issue.

So I kept my head down and stuck to the diary. The whole thing had been transcribed now, and I went through all of it over and over again. The first round was slow going, designed to make the text readable, and then I had to decipher the cryptic text. There were names of people, dates, companies, deals.

I was surprised to find, in the later sections, an entry about George.

It started, apparently, with a complaint filed after one of his rock star performances in Mumbai. 'Sex is seldom about love, even when we have it with the person we love. So why romanticize it? Go out — have sex. Have a lot of sex!'

It was positively toothless compared to some of the things I had heard George say, but one viewer took exception and went ahead to the local police station — coincidentally Daanish's — and lodged a complaint for indecency.

Bizarre coincidence?

Where did that leave the rest of it?

So I started from the beginning of the diary again, to look for connections to our case. And I began to find them. There was nothing on Joaquim Fernandes, but an old 377 case had been brought and dismissed against his lover when he was a young man. And that is when I cracked it: Daanish Alam was collecting dirt on people in power.

Had the much-decorated, much-lauded Daanish Alam been a blackmailer? And was one of his associates in the Mumbai Police, with access to all of this information, an accomplice who had stolen the drugs and continued his work?

The suggestion that Daanish Alam was anything other than completely upright, practically a saint, had simply never been made. I knew I was far out in conspiracy theory territory, and for the moment, the effort to prove or disprove this would be wholly, solely mine. I went through the financials at my disposal, and there was nothing to suggest any kind of irregularities. Daanish's policeman's income was not much, but he had still managed to save a reasonable amount of money. His wife's accounts were also clean. She worked, and received money gifts from her father from time to time.

But I had hardly expected to find anything there. Daanish would have been smart enough to not keep money from illegal activities in his bank. There was no evidence of disproportionate assets in his publicly disclosed accounts either.

The only person who might be able to help me with answers was his wife, Faiza. I didn't relish the idea of speaking with her about this, but I had little choice. And I didn't want to say anything to Shayak just yet. He and Daanish had been friends, after all.

★

We met at a coffee shop. Faiza seemed far more composed this time, off her father's territory and with some time to prepare for a talk.

For me, however, in light of what I now suspected, this meeting was much more awkward than the first. 'How are you?' I asked, after she had settled down and ordered a mocha.

'Same. Getting on with things in my own way. How is the investigation going?' she asked.

'It is all much more complex than I thought it would be.'

'Are you any closer to learning who may have caused the blast that killed Daanish?'

'We are getting there. But honestly, right now it's difficult to say.'

'So what do you need from me?'

I had already made my request when I had called her. 'Have you found it?'

'I did. I knew I hadn't thrown it away.' She pulled the small blue booklet out of her bag: Daanish Alam's passport. 'I don't know why you'd want it, though.'

I stopped briefly at the formal, stiff, smile-less image of Daanish, colours faded ever so slightly. And then I quickly flipped through the pages. There weren't many stamps. A month-long trip to the US in 2008. If I remembered correctly, that was when he had gone for training. It was considered a big deal on the force and had been mentioned in every obituary.

A trip to Bali in 2010. 'Did you go as well? Was that a holiday?' I asked.

She nodded, sadness overwhelming her small face once again. 'It was when we were trying to work through our problems. The holiday was a disaster from the beginning. I think it was there that we realized we had nothing to say to each other any more.'

And then I found what I was looking for: a three-day trip to Mauritius. It was just four months before the bomb blast. 'What about this trip?'

'This was work.'

'Are you sure?'

'Yes. Why?'

'It sounds to me like you aren't sure at all, Faiza.'

'It's just that I could swear those dates coincide with when he told me he was going to Hubli for an investigation. When I was going through his belongings after he died, I found these entry and exit stamps on his passport. That was when I began to seriously consider that Daanish might have been having an affair. I even asked someone from his office about the trip, and they didn't seem to know what I was talking about.'

'And you found nothing else pertaining to this trip amongst his belongings?'

'Sorry. No. Do you think this is relevant somehow?'

'I don't know much at this point, to be honest. But anything unknown about Daanish's life is probably worth following up.' I couldn't help but feel my certainty grow. Mauritius. An island nation with a reputation for two things: being a lover's paradise and a tax haven.

Which had drawn Daanish there?

FIFTEEN

I was at Shayak's place a couple of days before we were scheduled to leave for Goa. I hadn't disclosed my suspicions yet, but had mentioned I wanted to share something to do with the diary.

'Shayak, I have a theory,' I said, surprised by how nervous I felt.

'Those might be the most frightening three words I have ever heard,' he said with a smile.

And I hadn't even started. 'You aren't going to like it.'

'I think I guessed that from your epic preamble.'

'I've thought about nothing else since spending so much time in that awful hospital bed and I can think of only one solution which fits all angles of this case.'

'Spit it out.'

'Daanish Alam,' I said, watching his face.

It went blank. 'What about him?'

'I think he is our man.'

'I don't understand.'

They had been friends, I reminded myself. Some kindness was in order.

'I know this will sound like a preposterous suggestion to you, but what if he didn't die? What if he stole the drugs and disappeared?'

'I was at his funeral, Reema.' I could hear the beginnings of anger in his voice.

'Was there a body?' I asked, though I already knew the answer.

A pause. 'No. He had been blown to bits so small it was given up as a lost cause.'

I paused. His face was stormy. 'Stay with me on this. Please. What if the explosion was a smokescreen? What if he orchestrated the theft of the drugs, and then blew the place up in order to make it look like he had died?'

'And then?'

'I don't know, Shayak. I haven't worked out all the details yet.'

'Reema, you haven't worked out the details because there aren't any details to work out. This is a figment of your imagination. I am going to cut you some slack for having been through a blast yourself and watching your friend suffer. But you need to shake it off, because we have a lot of work to do.'

'You won't even hear me out?'

'Hear this out first! How could he have possibly escaped detection while orchestrating several crimes subsequently? No matter how much he loves the shadows, he would have had to come out sometime! His face was all over the news for months!'

I had spent the past forty-eight hours thinking of nothing else. 'There is a lot you can do to disguise yourself. Just think of Apu. If you had a picture of Reema and held it up beside Apu's face, you'd instantly know they were the same person. But without context, no one would have looked at Apu and thought she was Reema.'

'But even without the long hair, with glasses and a baby bump, no one who knew you before would possibly mistake Apu for anyone but Reema.'

'What would have stopped him from getting plastic surgery? The best that money could buy?'

'This sounds more and more like fiction and less like fact,' he said, standing up. He left the room with a shake of his head to tell me he had heard more than enough.

But I wasn't about to give up. I followed him into the living room.

'Remember what Savarkar said to us in jail? "What does a dead man have to be most afraid of?" What if that dead man was Daanish? What if he was giving us the answer all along?'

'Hardly a smoking gun, Reema. Those words could mean almost anything.'

'Look at these diary entries,' I persisted. I had coded them all by colour, grouping his notes according to which politician, gangster or public official they had compromised. I had found links to Daaku and Savarkar, of course, as well as George, Joaquim Fernandes and several other police officers in both Mumbai and Goa.

'Look at this,' I said. 'He had an entry about your ex-wife. She had been named by a drug dealer as a customer.'

He stared long and hard at the entry I pointed out, but eventually shook his head.

'How else can you explain it?' I demanded.

'In a million ways. There are so many possible explanations for each of those entries that don't add up to your crazy theory!'

'There is the possibility he was part of a bigger conspiracy. That I am wrong about him being alive but right about him being involved. Perhaps he has accomplices who are carrying on the work.'

Shayak sighed. 'As far as working theories go, I can at least treat that as more of a possibility. Show me some evidence and then we'll talk.'

*

I gave it a rest that night. I knew I would need more, much more, in hand before I broached the subject again.

The next morning, the forensic report came in from the explosion, and Shayak and I regrouped. While the explosives used were not of the same composition as those in the blast that had killed Daanish, they were confirmed to be a match to the type of explosives we know were sourced illicitly from the Goan munitions factory.

'Pretty much everyone involved in this business could have acquired the ammunition,' he pointed out.

I knew I had to get my work done before we left Mumbai. Where Daanish had been a real person, with a real family and a real job. In Goa, if he was indeed there at the moment, he was a ghost to me. The only way to convince Shayak would be to produce evidence of the man himself, flesh and blood.

What did I know about him? He would have been hanging about at Sundown Bar, making friends with Rishi, hovering around the periphery of George. That was the assumption that had driven us undercover at the ashram, but – and we had always known it was a possibility – he wasn't one to stick around. If he was guarding a cache of drugs, he would also need a safe place to keep it. He would want to lie low, and if I was correct, he would have needed to change himself.

When pushed to the brink, he chose explosives as his tool of destruction. And yet what I was also seeing was a man who, like a small fish swimming in the wake of a shark, took the path of least resistance. He made no ripples of his own, he kept his footprint as faint as possible. His ammunition was acquired by greasing one person's palms. His sabotage plot was put in motion with one operative placed well to wreak maximum havoc.

He was not afraid of bloodshed, though he avoided hands-on combat – possibly for fear of exposure. After the botched attempt at stealing the drugs back after the second bust, he may have decided that to do something well, he'd have to do it himself. The story fit with the control freak super cop Daanish had been. But bombs were safer than bullets because they could be operated from his favourite spot: the shadows.

I didn't think he'd be squeamish about spilling a little of his own blood either. With so much to hide, he had possibly been observing George's methods of helping people disappear. In fact, I wouldn't have been surprised if Daanish had flirted with the idea of enlisting his help, having discovered George's purpose here. But he wouldn't have made any overt gestures – he was too clever not to realize, before long, that George's methods may be crooked, but his purpose was far from it.

So he would have weaselled his way through George's constellation in search of refuge, learning ways to mask his identity, to lie low without burrowing in a hole somewhere.

I had asked George several more times if he could remember whom Rishi had been friendly with while he had been hanging out in Goa, and he could not. He said he didn't spend that much time at Sundown. Remembering a stray face from two years ago when he met so many people on a day-to-day basis was simply not possible. 'You have to remember,' George had said, 'how little I really had to do with Rishi personally. I gave him a brief for the kind of network I needed for maximum security, and left him to his own devices.'

Now with Apu being dead, I couldn't even ask Arti again what she remembered about Rishi's time there.

Of all the aspects of this subterfuge I felt Daanish might lack experience with, physical transformation headed the list. What George had mastered for his stowaways was no mean feat. Sometimes it involved plastic surgery, as with Arti, sometimes it was more along the lines of the Apu–Reema switch, as with Leia. If you were going to be dead and reborn and not leave civilization as you knew it, and were engaging in some serious criminal activity, to attempt to avoid the surgeon's scalpel was insane. Having lived with a physical disguise, I was sure if you were serious about killing yourself and returning in another avatar, you would have no choice but to drastically alter your appearance.

I called George. 'Is there a plastic surgeon you generally work with?'

'Do you want a bit of nip and tuck? Will I be out of line if I say you don't need it?'

'Thank you for the pep talk, but it's not for me. If I was hanging out at the ashram, and I wanted a recommendation for a surgeon, is there someone you would send me to?'

'Who is this person?'

'George, I can't say any more than this.'

'There is a very special surgeon I recommend only for my best customers.'

'And by best you mean what, exactly?'

'Those calling for the highest expertise and the greatest discretion.'

'Sounds like it fits the bill.'

'Dr Qureshi, Bandra Kurla Complex.'

He was not in Goa, because, as George pointed out, no surgeon worth his salt would live there. For anything other than dental work, lasik surgery and rehab, apparently no tourists trusted the medical establishment there. So he and his protégés would drive down to the exclusive clinic on the outskirts of Mumbai. When the surgery was too rough, he would use the medivac team he had called in after the blast.

'It's where Bollywood's lesser stars go to have their work done,' he said.

'Why not the better-known ones, if this guy is so good?' I asked.

'Because an Indian doctor just won't cut it for them. London or LA is where they go.'

Sometimes I wasn't sure if George just made stuff up for effect. 'I need to meet him,' I said.

'As part of our new mantra of cooperation, I will set up an appointment for you, because quite frankly there is no way in without one.'

He hung up and called back in half an hour. 'Tomorrow, 4 p.m. BKC is far, and I warn you that tardiness will not be appreciated. Leave with time to spare.'

'BKC?'

'Bandra Kurla Complex.'

'I'll talk to you later, George,' I said hastily, already searching for the diary.

Why did the acronym BKC sound so familiar? And then I found it. 'Dr KQ. BKC.' Dr Kabir Qureshi.

Daanish had an entry about George's favourite plastic surgeon in his diary. Just like that, the ghost I was chasing assumed a very real, terrifying form.

★

In keeping with George's warning, I was fifteen minutes early. I was summoned into Dr Qureshi's office exactly as per schedule.

The clinic was everything I would expect from a luxury hotel. Pale colours, soft-spoken attractive reception staff, the smell of fresh flowers. From what I had managed to find out, Qureshi had left a promising job in a London hospital to start this clinic. Just as George said, it was generally impossible to get an appointment with him unless you had the right connections. What those connections were was also impossible to find out, because Qureshi was as discreet as they come.

He was in his late forties, and he had allowed himself a few wrinkles. Clean-shaven, with a sharp gaze and a nose so pleasant it may well have been the beneficiary of a surgeon's scalpel.

'George tells me I am to spill his deepest secrets to you,' he said with a smile.

'I am sure he has said no such thing.'

'Ah, it seems you know him well. But his true request was almost as surprising. He tells me you have some important questions to ask that are of vital importance for a number of top-secret reasons.' He smiled, though not with his eyes.

'We are working on a case that has links to the recent bomb blast at George's ashram in Goa.'

'And I am supposed to ignore that you look very much like one of the victims?'

'That wasn't me,' I said. I had rehearsed it many times by now, but the blatant lie felt so inadequate.

'You forget, it is my job to study faces.'

I gave him a tight little smile.

'No matter. You are not from the police,' he said.

'No.'

'So how can I help you?'

'I need information about one of your old patients.'

'I wish George had told me this is what you were after. I would have told him not to waste your time.'

'I don't need to know if you have worked with him. I don't need to know what procedures you have performed. I simply need to know whether he had ever come to meet you or not.'

'You have to understand. Not only am I ethically bound to protect my clients, in my line of work, it is almost the second most important thing, the first being able to hold a scalpel straight. I take privacy very, very seriously.'

'Dr Qureshi, I respect that, and I am also aware that under Indian law, there are provisions allowing for doctors to disclose information about their patients to protect persons at risk.'

'Is this person you speak of a risk to others?'

'If I am correct, he is responsible for the deaths of at least half a dozen people.'

'And if you are incorrect?'

'Then no harm done, because I am not going to use your statement in this form either way for any official purposes. I need only to know at this point. If we have cause, we will be visiting you through the proper police channels. If we don't, I leave and you don't hear about this ever again.'

He still looked unconvinced.

'It's quite simple, Dr Qureshi. I need you to only look at one picture, and tell me if you have met him in your office here.'

I presented the picture of Daanish Alam. Dr Qureshi glanced at it and then leaned back in his seat, elbows on the armrests, fingers forming a teepee. He looked at me for a long, tense moment before answering.

'Yes.'

I felt something in my chest constrict. 'Can you tell me when?'

Dr Qureshi tapped away at his computer. 'June 2010. The last time I saw him was January 2011. And now I will say no more. Good luck with your investigation.'

SIXTEEN

It was my first time in a private jet — unless you counted the air ambulance, which I most definitely did not.

'You can take a moment to enjoy it,' Shayak said with a smile.

'I didn't think it was that obvious.'

'You are not a cheap woman to impress, Ms Ray. My yacht had no effect on you. In fact, if anything, I think it stacked the deck against me.'

'And what makes you think I am any more pliable sitting in this plane?'

I think it took us both a moment to realize that we were flirting. We had studiously avoided letting the personal creep in while in Goa. But ever since the bomb blast, it felt like something had shifted.

'If I look pleased, it is because I really, really enjoy being right,' I said.

Shayak laughed. 'I'll let you gloat this time, but can you blame me for being sceptical?'

'Only because you should know by now that I am not given to wild flights of fancy.'

'You know, I think you've got me there. But at least give me credit for believing you once you showed me the evidence.'

'Yes, if you insist, I will give you credit for not being a complete ass.'

When I had gone to Shayak after my meeting with Qureshi, he went quieter than I had ever seen him. I had expected him to resist even in the face of what I had learned, but he did not. He seemed to reject as irrelevant any official confirmation. It was time we didn't have to waste, he said.

On his request, I had assembled all of the transcribed sheets of the diary that were connected to Goa and handed them over last night.

'Going through the diary, I felt he never had any intention of using the mass of data he had acquired for anything other than leverage. He spent years planning this,' he said.

He ran through the main findings. 'Daaku, of prime importance for Savarkar, probably the most important link established here. We have to assume Daanish had threatened Savarkar with Daaku's damning testimony to coerce cooperation in selling the drugs earlier this year. It is not clear how far that collaboration extended. Agree?'

'Yes.'

'Then there are the fraudulent companies that can be traced back to Fernandes, records of men he had taken with him on overseas trips as his assistants. George's Mumbai case. Dr KQ, BKC. These ones are obvious, now that we know how to connect the dots. But there are other names and case files, and who knows how he used them? Reams of information about corrupt officials in the Goan and central governments, only some of whom have been charge-sheeted in the mining scam.'

Now I could see why Shayak was such a force: overnight, he had been able to cast aside his personal bias and throw himself behind a theory that had been so abhorrent to him.

He continued. 'There are quite a lot of people in some

way connected to George, and George himself, and I think it is safe to assume that in some iteration of his plan, George was someone Daanish was hoping to manipulate for some use. Since we are now trusting George's information, I think we can accept he did not actually follow through with this plan. Possibly because George is himself so slippery that getting any kind of leverage to stick is tough. So he abandoned that angle, except tangentially, as you have discovered, to piggyback his way to the right people, such as the plastic surgeon.'

'And Rishi,' I pointed out.

'Yes, the all-important Rishi. A decision that turned out to be his biggest blunder.'

'After he found Rishi there, you think he moved on?'

'It's possible. George has always maintained a stranger had mentioned the Titanium job to him. Daanish must have stuck around long enough to ensure it worked before leaving. Remember, all of this happened before his physical transformation was complete. He would have had to be especially brazen to hang about for long at George's ashram. There are enough people from Mumbai and Goa there, and as a policeman not only did he meet a lot of people, but this was all happening after his alleged death, when they were flashing his photo on every media outlet. How he escaped identification is still a mystery to me.'

'Do you think if we take Daanish's photo around and ask, we might learn something?'

'It isn't a certainty. I have already sent a photograph to George and he doesn't remember seeing him around. But what we will certainly do is show our hand, which we can't afford at any cost. If he has any remaining connection with that place at all, he will get to know about it.'

'Why hang about in Goa at all? Why not move the product and get out of there? Things have been so hot of late that he has gone into all-out panic mode.'

'I can't figure it out either. Something that we aren't accounting for is in play.'

'What about the continuing pressure on the ministry of defence and police to freeze out Titanium?'

'I can't be sure, but from what I have seen of this diary, there are enough people that he could have tapped to do his bidding even in the highest offices. Businessmen, IPS officials, at least one cabinet minister.'

*

When we landed, I saw I had a missed call from Terrence. I called him back as soon as we were off the tarmac.

'You have opened quite a can of worms, Ray.'

'What do you mean?'

'I am sure it didn't make the papers in Mumbai, but the Goan media is abuzz with it.'

'What?'

'Fernandes is out on bail.'

'That's not a surprise, is it?'

'Word is he is singing like a contestant on *Indian Idol*.'

'About?'

'The nexus. Between mining and real estate and politics in Goa.'

'That's quite a risk.'

'Doesn't have much to lose any more, does he?'

'I'll call you in a bit, Terrence. How are you feeling now, by the way?'

'Trying not to think about it.'

Shayak had, as promised, set up an appointment with one of the foremost prosthetic specialists in the US and Terrence would be heading there as soon as he had healed sufficiently for fittings to begin.

Shayak got on the phone to try and set up a meeting with Fernandes, while I pulled out my tab and searched for all the news reports I could find on his release. There was predictably not much information we could use.

I switched off my data. We had all-new equipment, all-new numbers and data cards. I had had so many phone numbers in the past two weeks that I had stopped trying to memorize them. But we were still trying to spend as little time as possible online. So I found the airport bookshop and bought a couple of newspapers instead.

Shayak had arranged for a self-drive car to be dropped off for us at the airport. He got behind the wheel of the midnight-blue sedan and I opened the first newspaper. That Fernandes was out on bail was front-page news, but I found little of note in terms of information. The same was true of the bomb blast. The second paper was even less useful.

The apartment, it turned out, was just a few hundred metres from the beach, but I found myself robbed of the desire to even take a look at the view. The last time I had sand between my toes was not a happy occasion.

I went straight inside and dumped my bags in the corner. George had said there was a bed and a pullout. I couldn't help wonder, despite the circumstances, if George was trying to play matchmaker. Surely he had at his disposal a two- or even a one-bedroom apartment for me and Shayak to stay in, instead of this cramped studio?

I turned on the TV and tuned into the news. The solitary

Goan channel was showing a cookery show, and none of the national ones seemed to have picked up the Fernandes story yet.

★

If I were Fernandes, I would be so afraid I wouldn't talk to anyone. But luckily for us, his problems had been severely compounded by the selling of spurious cancer drugs in China. Perhaps that was why he wanted to meet us again. Having had a taste of jail, he was now eager to minimize his risk of being charged for other crimes, perhaps?

He had called us to room 409 of a deserted hotel that had, as far as I remembered, once been his. There were two very beefy guards outside the door who patted us down before allowing us entry.

'I have to say I am surprised you agreed to see us at all,' Shayak told Fernandes.

Fernandes gave me a withering look, which I should have expected given my role in his arrest. 'Then you must realize how urgent this is.'

'What can we do for you?'

'When I was in jail, I received a message from another inmate. A well-wisher, I was told, could help me if I kept my mouth shut.'

'About what?'

'It was left to me to figure that out. But given the method followed in silencing Savarkar, I could only imagine it was a reminder that I was very much within reach, and much more vulnerable in jail than I was out of it.'

'Does the name Daanish Alam mean anything to you?' I asked.

'Of course it does. He is one of the policemen who died in the blast that occurred over our drugs.'

'Which you still insist had nothing to do with you?'

'Why would I go to all that trouble and risk stealing something I could just make again?'

I pulled out Daanish's picture. 'Take a good look at this. Have you ever met this man?'

'No, but as I said, I have seen his picture in the papers.'

'Do you know if Savarkar had any contact with him?'

'Savarkar kept his methods very much to himself. I knew he was greasing palms in the police up and down the routes we used to move merchandise. But he never mentioned who was involved, and what his methods were.'

'You said at our last meeting that Savarkar denied having anything to do with the second shipment too. Did he say anything to indicate that he may have been approached by someone to become involved?'

'No, but he was a little vague about the details. I got the distinct impression it wasn't the first time he was hearing of it.'

'You had also mentioned that the transporter who called you had a sample of the drugs being moved. Do you know where he may have got it?'

'I assumed it was from his contact in the other trucking company hired to move the goods.'

'Could we meet this associate of yours?'

Fernandes grabbed a napkin, waving his hand around for a pen. I passed him one, and he scribbled a name and number.

'Tell him I asked you to call.'

'Why do you think he met us?' I asked Shayak on the way back to the car.

'Because he is genuinely scared? If we put this guy away, it means the target is off his back,' said Shayak.

We climbed in, and he called the transporter, Orvil Pereira, who agreed to meet immediately. Fernandes must have called ahead. When Shayak asked him to suggest a convenient, discreet location, he directed us to a church in Panjim.

*

'You have to understand how frightened we all were,' Pereira said. We were seated on a bench inside an empty, tube-lit modern building, with rain beating down on the new stained glass. 'Our first shipments had been seized, our drivers were still in jail, and we were very clear that we wanted out of the business. It was difficult, because of our relationship with Joaquim sir's family, but there came a point where I had to say no.'

'What relationship?'

'My family's business started with one truck, way back in '72. We were doing work for him, and he – and his father, who was still involved then – gave us the funding for two more as a soft loan, part of their plans to help encourage businesses run by Goan natives. From then, we grew one truck at a time, alongside the Fernandes Group. We have attended all of their family functions – weddings, funerals, parties – and they have come for all of ours. To say no to Joaquim sir for anything was very, very difficult. But it was only extreme measures that kept us out of jail, and we couldn't risk losing everything we had worked so hard to build.'

'So you suspended all business with them?'

'No, just the illegal stuff.'

'Can you tell us what you remember of the events of the night you discovered the second shipment?'

'I got a call from one of my former managers who had joined as GM of the company that finally moved the shipment. He was shaken. He had agreed to take the job on instructions from his boss, and when the time came for loading, he saw the product and he freaked out. His boss didn't know what was in the shipment, he said, and thought it was fake medicine. But having seen the stuff before, my former employee figured out what was really going on. He couldn't understand why some new guy was bringing the stuff, and got suspicious. When he spoke to his boss again, he apparently said Satish Savarkar would ensure the shipment would pass unchecked.'

And there was our connection. Savarkar's denial of involvement to Fernandes was a lie.

'What exactly did your former employee say?'

'He said there was this strange man he'd never seen before present at the time of loading. He didn't know whether he should go through with it, but didn't think he had much of a choice, with Savarkar involved.'

'How did you respond?'

'I called Joaquim sir. He asked me to find out as much as I could.'

'What did you do?'

'I went over to the warehouse and waited outside till the client came out.'

I felt my heart race. 'Did you see his face?'

'No. It was too dark. He had a big hat and sunglasses on.'

'Could you give us any sort of description?'

'About 5 feet 10 inches, maybe? Built, really built. But that's about it.'

'Anything else?'

'Well, I followed him for a while.'

My heart set off again. 'Where did he go?'

'Home, I think.'

'Why do you think?'

'It was a house. But while I waited, I got a call from Fernandes thanking me for the information, but not to worry about it any more because he had taken care of it. He said I should forget everything I had seen. So I went home.'

'Where was this house?'

He gave us an address. It wasn't far from the ashram, as far as I could tell, though distances in Goa were deceptive.

'What about your friend from the trucking company? He must have met the man, seen him?'

'He must have.'

'Do you think you can ask him to talk to us?'

'No way. Don't waste your time. He was skittish enough with me.'

'Wouldn't he prefer talking to us than the police?'

'Look, I can give you his number. But don't expect it to come to anything. With everything that's been going on, he is extra spooked. He even said something about shutting shop.'

'Doesn't he want to get paid?'

'That's just it. He was paid 50 per cent up front, and he decided it was enough money for him to keep his mouth zipped.'

'How did he stay out of jail while his drivers were imprisoned?'

'Paid off the drivers' families, so they all said he wasn't involved. Just like we had done before him.'

★

Driving through the wet, dark roads, Shayak and I stayed with our own thoughts for a long time. The windows were down, and as the wet air hit our faces, we were cocooned in a false sense of calm.

'To have had that much cash to pay the transport company, I would bet good money that Daanish had already sold some amount of the cargo,' said Shayak at last.

'Do we have an estimate on the approximate volume of drugs in the last shipment?' I asked.

'The first heist was supposed to be about 250 kg. The second one was closer to 175.'

'So the bulk of it was still intact. And we don't know if it was all from the old consignment or some of it had been swapped out,' I said.

'Assuming for the moment that he sold some for cash, and perhaps even held some back, I would say he could have been operating only with what he stole in that first heist.'

'He'd have had to pay for his plastic surgery.'

'He may have also been stashing money in a secret account, somewhere, ahead of his disappearance. Maybe in Mauritius,' said Shayak.

'He'd have had a fake ID for sure,' I said. Karan Johar could have been one of several. 'If you were Daanish,' I asked, 'how would you have sold the drugs?'

'I would have sold in Mumbai, given that speed must have been a concern. With the number of contacts he had made in the underworld during his seventeen years on the force, he was uniquely placed to reach out to the right people.'

I nodded. 'But based on how he operates, he wouldn't have met them either, given that it would be where he was most likely to be recognized.'

'If only we could get some lead as to where he is now. There is no chance the trucker will speak to us. How likely is Dr Qureshi to give us a photo of his masterpiece voluntarily? Archana is still working the warrants, but it seems like it will take more time than we have,' said Shayak.

'I can't see him cooperating unless we apply some official pressure.'

'What about a physical description?' he asked.

'At this point, he is stonewalling. And he's not been coming to the clinic either. We are being told he is on emergency leave.'

'So, what if we were to try to create an image ourselves?' he suggested.

'Based on what?'

'What makes the most sense. We could work from Daanish's old photographs.'

'It might not be anywhere near accurate,' I said.

'We could have a couple of different options based on the possible directions he could have taken. Plastic surgery isn't magic, after all.'

I had seen only old photos or headshots of him in uniform. Not necessarily the best way to get a sense of the man. 'Describe him to me,' I said.

'Average height – about 5 feet 9 inches. Not overweight, but had started to get a bit of a tummy. Hair straight, black.'

'Any grey?'

'No.'

'Dye job?'

'Probably.'

'Thinning?' I was taking notes now.

Shayak squinted his eyes. 'Yes. Quite a lot in the front.'

'Most striking features?'

'Definitely his eyes. They were light, expressive.'

'Nose was quite large too,' I said.

'I know that is how it seems in the pictures, but when you saw him, you really only saw the eyes. And he had this quiet sort of presence. You paid attention to him immediately.'

I rifled through the bag and pulled out a file, inside which was a photo. There he was. Just as Shayak described. 'Fair but not too fair, clean-shaven,' I murmured. 'He looks so weary.'

'He had a hard job, and he did it well. Or so I thought.'

Shayak was right: his nose was large for his face, with a pronounced hook, but it was his eyes — a light brown — that were the most arresting.

'A nose job must be the most obvious way to change your face. You could whittle this down quite a bit, and make quite a difference. I'd also change the hair, and definitely grow facial hair. And if he wore coloured contacts, it would probably make such a stark difference that it would be quite hard to recognize him at all.'

*

Archana had managed to locate a plastic surgeon who had worked on some radical transformations in the past, and back in the flat, we met via video conference. Shayak and I huddled in our room, over his laptop, while the other two were seated in the surgeon's plush Mumbai office.

'The picture you see,' said Shayak, 'is of a man who has since had extensive plastic surgery, and we need to get a sense of what he might look like now.'

'Archana told me that, but as I said to her as well, I am not sure how much accuracy I can provide.'

'We might be able to give you a direction. The objective of the transformation would be disguise. Not necessarily to look better. Does that make a difference?'

'Yes and no. Without any clue as to what procedures he has had, I am left to guess.'

'So why don't you create a few possible options of what he might have had done, and we can try to work out the rest?'

'How many options?'

'As many as seem likely.'

'There are so many things he could have done. His eyes have a little puffiness – getting rid of that could drastically alter his eye shape. His nose could have quite a lot of work done to it. Then chin implants might give him an even more masculine look.'

'As we said, it is up to you to use your professional skills to give us a few models of how he might look.'

'It'll take time.'

'How much?'

'I need two days.'

'If we doubled your pay and you cleared your schedule, and we also arranged an artist to work with you, how quickly could you deliver?'

'Twelve hours.'

It seemed we had a deal.

*

The next morning, I stepped out and went to a couple of stores to buy a newspaper; none seemed to have one. Goa was the kind of place where it was easier to buy a beer than a newspaper. Finally, I walked into the lobby of a small hotel, flicked a copy and met Shayak in the car outside.

'Anything?' he asked, pulling out on to the road. We were on our way to the address Pereira had provided, where Daanish had allegedly gone after loading the drugs on the trucks.

I scanned the headlines, and there at the bottom of the front page was the news. 'Fernandes is gone.'

'What do you mean, "gone"?'

'It says here that the police went to his house for a routine follow-up and no one answered the door. The servants had no idea where their employer was or when he would be back.'

'Why am I not surprised?'

'Do you think he has left for good?' I asked.

'There isn't anything holding him here, is there?'

'If he was going to leave anyway, why did he call us?'

'I am not sure. Let me see what Ajay can drum up through his contacts here.'

We reached the house, which was at the end of a quiet lane on the outskirts of Margao. It was a wooden structure, unusual in these parts, with big open windows and fluttering curtains. On the porch lay a dog, fast asleep on its back, clearly at home and not shy of displaying the goods.

Someone must be home.

So we waited. And as we waited, the strangest thing happened. In the heat of the dusty afternoon on that deserted road, Shayak started talking.

'I joined the army to spite my father. He had been pushing me into his business since I was a child. Heavy engineering. In many ways, I just didn't want anything to do with that.' The words poured out in a rush. And then he paused.

The last thing I wanted was for him to stop, so I prompted him. 'Why?'

'I don't know. It is good work, a good company, and it is
an industry of infinite possibility. Maybe it was this need for
perfection you accuse me of having. My father is an innovator.
Big shoes to fill. I was young, cocky and hungry to make my
own mark.'

'But you seem to have a natural affinity for business.'

'Depends on your measure of success. I built a successful
company, ground up, before I hit forty. But I also brought it
to the ground in less than six months.'

'I see you have appropriated the entire blame for
Titanium's troubles.'

'Who else is responsible?'

'How about the multiple criminals involved in a conspiracy
to bring you down? How about Daanish Alam? How about
corrupt officials who can be arm-twisted into backstabbing
their allies?'

'Reema, I appreciate the support, but I precipitated this.
I had been warned against investigating, and I pushed on
without thinking or taking necessary precautions. Rookie
mistakes that cost us dearly. I should have known better.'

'I don't buy that.'

'No, you wouldn't,' he said, with the whisper of a smile.

'What's that supposed to mean?'

'Only that you and I are more similar than I would like.
You do not respect caution. Following your nose without
consulting your head is not a virtue when there are lives on
the line. You have an excuse, at least. You are young, you are
supposed to be idealistic, you don't hold the livelihoods of
thousands in your hands. But I do, and that should inform
my choices. Especially when I have been there before.'

'How so?'

'A year before I left the special forces, we were in Burma on a recon mission. There was a pocket of insurgency, and the Indian government at the time wanted to talk with one of the rebel leaders. We were sent to bring him in. We set up a meet, but it turned out to be a trap. Vinod's father, who was then my driver, and I were taken hostage.'

'What did they want?'

'Not relevant,' he said. And I knew it must still be classified. 'The point is, we were held in that jungle camp for over three months. It gives you way too much time to think.'

'That is not what most people would have to say about that sort of situation.'

'I am not sure about that. Maybe it sounds more dangerous than it was. These were not bad people. They held us for leverage. They let us go unharmed. If I had really wanted to, I could have escaped, though finding our way out of dangerous and remote terrain blind would have been a challenge.'

'Is that what prompted you to leave the army?'

'No. Though I suppose that must be when I started to ask questions. When we returned, I was put on a month's forced leave, and then allowed to return to work. I guess it was meant to be an easy assignment. I was sent into Pakistan-occupied Kashmir with a small team. We had to bring out a close personal friend of the defence minister. We weren't told who we were meant to fetch. It was a journalist who had been told to evacuate a war zone weeks earlier. The extraction should have been simple enough, but we hit a mine and I lost two good men that day: one died instantly, and the other sustained serious injuries and retired well before his time.'

He paused, fiddling with a stray string protruding from the steering wheel cover. 'I have seen dozens of men go down. But the nature of the assignment made this loss different. It shook my confidence, and in that high-stress sort of position, I had to ask myself whether I would be able to take orders again, and when the answer was perhaps no, I had no choice but to leave. Any other decision could have put more men at risk.'

'So you could deal with being held hostage but not with corruption? I think that displays rare integrity.'

'Or simply the lack of ability to play in the sandbox of modern Indian life.'

'I prefer my explanation. You just accused me of being young and idealistic. It sounds to me like you were once as well.'

'Didn't I tell you we were alike?'

He looked at me, and there was a flash of something sweet that had been missing these past few months. I felt like reaching out, spreading my palm over his beautiful, tired, stubbled face.

'I don't talk about this much,' murmured Shayak.

'Ha! Don't I know it.'

'I mean it, Reema.'

I found I couldn't look at him, but I forced myself to. His mask was back in place, but mine was gone. I had become so used to his stonewalling that the honesty had caught me completely off guard.

And then he reached out, running the back of his fingers across my cheek. I had to smile.

'Poor Reema. I really have saved the worst of myself for you.'

But before I could ask him what he meant, there was movement at the house. The front door swung open, and a woman stepped out.

It was Arti.

And suddenly I had no need for a facial composite. I knew who Daanish Alam had died to become. I knew why he couldn't leave Goa. And I knew why he was in a rush to close up business.

Daanish Alam was Sid and Arti was the reason he could not leave. It was all I could do to not scream.

Seventeen

We were on Arti's trail, but she did not seem to be up to anything unusual. She got on her bike, went to the convenience store a couple of kilometres away, dropped her purchases off at home and then headed to the bar.

I could not be seen there, so Shayak went in while I went to a neighbouring shack. I had a view of Shayak, out of the corner of my eye, my floppy sunhat pulled down and my sunglasses not leaving their perch.

While I was waiting, I called Ajay. Daanish was the priority now, but we also needed to know where Joaquim Fernandes was.

'Really, so far, there have been no official reports. He was scheduled to appear in court and he missed that appointment, and he was not at home when officers went to check. But the authorities have deemed there is no indication that he has fled. I strongly disagree, of course, but there is nothing more I can do for the next twenty-four hours. All I know is he hasn't left the country, because he had been put on the no-fly list.'

After an hour, Shayak gave me a missed call, our signal to meet at the car. We were headed back to the apartment after Vinod had arrived at the Sundown Bar to keep an eye on Arti. She would have to be watched at all times in the hope of tracking down Daanish, aka Sid. Given our current constraints, this was quite a challenge.

'I can tail her,' I said. 'I cut my teeth following people and I'd like to think I am pretty good at it.'

'She knows you. Baby bump or not, she will recognize you, and then the game is up. The last thing you want her to do is to tell Daanish that you are alive and following her. It's a dead giveaway that we are on to him.'

'So then who?'

'Vinod can get started, and we can have two more people on the way within the hour. They need to stay on her. You are needed here. With me.'

'And what do we do?'

'We have to find Daanish. There is no guarantee that she will lead us to him in time.'

'In time for what?'

'I don't know. That is the biggest problem – but you can be sure he won't sit still for long. The blast had to be part of his exit plan.'

'George says he and Arti don't live together, that she is an independent spirit who spends much of her time alone,' I said. 'She is either at the bar or with friends, or in her house working on installation art, which is apparently her latest project. He also insists there is no way Arti is aware of her boyfriend's true identity or crimes.'

'You've met her, you've seen them together. Do you think he is right?'

'Meeting Arti isn't much help. She's perfected this elusive air almost as well as George. But what I do feel is that what she did, blowing the whistle in a manner wholly unconcerned with her own well-being, can only be the action of someone whose personal ethics, though unconventional, are operating at the highest levels. No chance someone like her would condone murder.'

'What about drugs?'

'That is harder to say.'

'If she is a user, or pro-decriminalization, she might take a less grim view of his drug-related crimes,' said Shayak.

'Still, I can't see her as an accomplice.'

We had asked George to casually enquire about Sid's whereabouts, and Arti had apparently been vague. To ask for his address was riskier, as it might tip him off.

It suddenly occurred to me that we had another option. 'What if we ask Olivia?' I said. 'Wasn't she scheduled to return to Goa a few days ago?' She had taken a bad blow, but she would be back on Arti's trail.

'We spoke in the aftermath of the blast, and she was friendly, if not forthcoming. It's worth a try.'

Shayak pulled over and made the call. 'She'll meet us today,' he said.

But first, though I was so certain of it that it seemed unnecessary, we stopped at home to check the images sent by the plastic surgeon. Having a composite of some likeness would help us in a search situation.

None of them was a perfect match, but I spoke to the artist, and with a little chopping and changing, the addition of the right kind of glasses, filling out the hair and lengthening it, a change in the shape of the beard line and the length of the beard itself, we arrived at an image of startling similarity.

'That's him,' I said to Shayak as the final image downloaded.

He looked at it. 'How close is it?' he asked.

'Eighty per cent, I would say. There is still something different about the eyes which I can't pin down. The nose might be a little narrower at the top here. But someone seeing this picture and Sid would definitely recognize it as the same person.'

Shayak took a good, long look. 'The whole vibe with the tattoos and hair and glasses is so different that someone who knew Daanish would not think in a million years that this could be him.'

'He is so lean now, and so muscular, that it changes his whole face, his whole gait. It takes ten years off his age.'

*

We met Olivia in her room on the grounds of a beautiful old Goan home in Morjim that had been converted into a guest house.

'What do you know about Siddharth, Arti's boyfriend?' asked Shayak.

'They have been together for about two years now. He is based in Goa, and claims to be a businessman of some description.'

'Why "claims"?'

'Because we haven't been able to find out anything about his business.'

'What about taxes, etc.?'

'Nothing. But there seems to be no dearth of people living double lives in Goa, and I had enough on my hands between Arti and George.'

'Olivia, when did you first come to Goa?'

'About six months ago.'

'How did you find out about Arti – Raya – being here?'

'I can't give you the details, but it was through our surveillance of her family who continue to live in the UK.'

'And you have been here since?'

'No, I first came for a brief visit, went back and then returned a couple of weeks later to start the investigation.'

'Have you ever got the sense that you were being watched?'

'I can't say I have. Till you two arrived at the ashram.'

'You knew who we were?'

'We had been listening to George's conversations for some time in the hope that he would lead us to Arti.'

'It was you who searched our room?' I asked.

She pursed her lips – the only answer I would get.

'What is the status now on your investigation?' Shayak asked.

'I really can't tell you that.'

'Olivia, you don't have to reveal any operational details. But this information could be critical to catching the bomber,' he said.

She looked from Shayak to me, and then took a long pause to consider her words carefully. 'I can say that I am now pretty close to making an arrest.'

'Do you have an address for Sid?'

'As a matter of fact, I do. Arti stays there sometimes.'

'We need that,' said Shayak.

Olivia wrote it on a piece of paper. 'It's a bit of trek from here. Call me if you need directions.'

*

We left and sat in the car for a while, processing what we had just heard.

'We need to go to his house,' said Shayak.

'Now?'

'Yes.'

'What if this whole thing is about Olivia?' I wondered aloud.

'Elaborate.'

'Daanish steals a crapload of drugs and disappears to Goa, where he means to live out his days. While living in George's shadow, he meets Arti, and finds himself blown away. Then, one day, a British operative comes looking for Arti. How does he protect her?'

'By disappearing once again.'

'Exactly. And suddenly the slow disposal of drugs is no longer an option. His need is for cash, and fast. So he goes into panic mode. He contacts Savarkar and presents him with a proposition to offload the drugs through his old channels. Savarkar says no, and Daanish threatens him with some of the ammunition he can urge Daaku to use against him. So Savarkar agrees to call the transporter and set things up. But what Daanish doesn't count on is the old loyalties. Fernandes finds out and wants vengeance, calling the Mumbai Police commissioner to ensure the consignment never reaches its destination. Now Daanish is short a whole lot of getaway money and is scrambling. So he tries to have it stolen back, but the Mumbai Police guard it better this time. When that fails, he initiates the whole Rishi plot, to steal the information only Titanium had which could connect the crimes and reveal his deceit. When Rishi botches the operation, Daanish goes into damage control mode by trying to kill Titanium's ties with the authorities.'

'That is quite a theory.'

'Does it make sense so far?'

'Yes. Continue.'

'Then he learns that Terrence and I are snooping around, and that we've paid a visit to Savarkar, who must be silenced before he talks as he's the only person who knows his identity. Also adding to the scramble is the fact that Olivia is now closing in, and they must leave soon, if they are to leave at all. In fact, I would go so far as to say that the bomb on the beach was not intended for Terrence and me – it was meant for Olivia. It was she who was supposed to be there at the DJ console, playing the music, next to which the bomb exploded. But she stepped away at the last moment, leaving young Victoria in her place.'

I had an image of Sid's – Daanish's – face, as he pulled Arti's arm. I couldn't be sure, but hadn't his eyes widened a fraction of a second before the blast? Didn't he seem very quick to respond? When I reacted, pulling Terrence down, hadn't I been feeding off his energy?

'So now what?' asked Shayak.

'That means the endgame is escape. For both of them.'

'And they could run anywhere in India without much problem – even as we speak they could be getting ready to flee,' said Shayak.

'We need to find Daanish now. Should we pay a visit to his house?'

'Yes. But, if you are right, Daanish won't leave without Arti. And we have her in our sights for now. Let's wait till morning – Palolem is a long way off and we need to prepare.'

I stared at the road as it rushed into us on our way back to the apartment. It took a while for me to notice Shayak repeatedly glancing at the rear-view mirror.

'What's the problem?' I asked.

'This guy has his high beam on. It's pissing me off,' he said.

I turned around in my seat. The vehicle seemed to be an SUV of some kind.

Shayak pulled over. 'Better to just let him pass,' he said. After the car went by, Shayak took to the road again.

But after a few moments, it was back, pulling out from a small lane behind us again.

'That's strange,' I said.

Shayak abruptly took the next turn.

'Do you know where you are going?' I asked.

'No.'

Sure enough, the car followed.

'What now?' I asked.

'We lose them.'

Shayak didn't increase the pace. He took a slow meandering route back to the main road. I said nothing, watching the car in the side mirror, which didn't drop its blinding glare for a minute.

Instead of heading for the highway, Shayak swung into a small lane that took us towards Calangute.

'Where are we going?'

'To get lost.'

There was much more traffic on this road. We crawled along at a more urban pace than I'd seen in Goa, and all the while, the SUV was never more than a couple of cars behind us.

'I need you to listen to me carefully, Reema. I am going to pull up into the first empty driveway I see. Behind this row of houses is an empty field, and then a smaller road that takes a route off the main road to Baga. We need to run as fast as we can to that road. We won't have much of a head start.'

'And then?' I asked, slinging my handbag across my body.

'We'll see.'

About 100 metres on, Shayak swung abruptly into the drive of a small house. There was no space for another car behind us, and I saw the SUV continue straight ahead.

'Get out!' screamed Shayak, and we jumped out of the car.

'This way,' he said, running towards the low boundary wall at the back.

We quickly scaled it and jumped over into an empty plot. We ran to the back road. It was much darker here.

It was too dark to see, but we had to assume that the man or men in the car would be close behind us. And soon enough I saw the bobbing beam of a flashlight.

'This is no good,' I yelled to Shayak.

'Keep moving!'

There was no place to hide, no opportunity to shake our pursuer off. I tried to keep up with Shayak's brutal pace. We followed a bend in the road, and there, in front of a tiny little restaurant, was a car parked by the side. We stopped.

'We need a drop to Baga,' I said to the driver between gasps for breath.

The man couldn't work up the energy to appear surprised, or even mildly curious about our state.

'I'm waiting for someone,' he said.

'I'll pay you ₹1,000 if you start the engine now,' said Shayak.

'Get in,' he said, swinging his leg off the dashboard and turning the key in the ignition.

Shayak hopped in behind the driver and I took the passenger seat.

'I'll give you another ₹1,000 if you get us there as fast as you can.'

As we raced away, I turned around and saw the beam of the flashlight, stationary now.

It wasn't more than a fifteen-minute drive, and we covered it in seven.

'How do you think they found us?' I asked when we were sure we were no longer being followed.

'Probably tailed us from Olivia's place. Daanish must have been having her watched. But we can't take any more chances now.'

'So we can't go back to the house?'

'Better not to. It is possible they followed us from there to Olivia's and I just didn't notice. It isn't worth the risk.'

'What do we do?'

'We need to regroup.'

That was all he offered for the time being, and I was, for once, too shaken to ask any more questions.

We reached the crowded stretch between Baga and Calangute beaches, overflowing with shops, restaurants, down- and mid-market hotels, taxis; scores and scores of tourists were out at this time of the evening.

'Get off here,' said Shayak, handing me his wallet. 'Buy some clothes, enough for a few days. For both of us. Then find a restaurant called Britto's, all the way at the end of the strip, and wait for me. I need to find somewhere safe for us to stay tonight.'

I got out of the car, and for the first 100 metres or so, I willed myself to slow down. The need now was to draw as little attention as possible to myself. I walked in and out of a few shops before I found one with a better selection of clothes. I bought myself a couple of cotton harem pants and tank tops, a summer dress, Shayak some shorts and T-shirts, and swimwear to stand in for underwear. And most importantly, hats.

I made another stop for toothbrushes and toothpaste, razor and foam. A small mirror. Neither Shayak nor I much needed a comb at this stage. I took my time walking down the road till I reached the restaurant, stopping at several more shops to browse and ensure I wasn't being followed.

I got to Britto's. It was crowded, and I found the darkest table in a corner, next to a loud family of eight. I took a seat and ordered a couple of whiskies.

No sign of Shayak yet. I was finishing my drink rather rapidly when the power went out. A hoot went up from the crowded beach, and the thumping of music suddenly stopped, leaving me feeling empty. All I could see was candlelight, like fireflies, all across the beach.

I don't know how Shayak found me in the darkness. But he did, collapsing into the chair across the table.

'Good idea,' he said, picking up the whisky that waited for him and downing it in one gulp.

He ordered a couple more drinks and a seafood platter. 'No more driving tonight, thankfully,' he said.

'What happens to the car?'

'I'll report it to the Goa Police. They can collect it.'

'Our laptops?'

'We'll retrieve them, if they are still there.'

The candlelight danced across his face. He looked more drained than ever. Behind him, the night sky illuminated the water, and without all the music emanating from every shack, you could hear the hypnotic crash of the waves.

Shayak got up and crossed over to the seat beside me, so he too could watch the sea. We didn't speak as clouds gathered and turned the lights out on us once again. Then, the power came back to a chorus of a thousand boos.

As the noise resumed, Shayak pointed to a constellation of lights shining down from a cliff standing guard over the beach.

'That is where we are going next,' he whispered. 'And we'd better be quick because it looks like it's going to come down.'

We left Britto's and hailed another taxi. The cliff, Shayak told me, was further away than it looked. The hotel turned out to be an old Goan villa that had been converted into an inn with a few cottages on the grounds.

'Sorry,' said Shayak, as he opened the door. 'It's peak season, and they only had one room available. I've asked for an extra bed.'

Once inside, Shayak called Vinod, telling him to organize two shifts and keep a watch out all night at Arti's place.

'All well?' I asked.

Shayak nodded. 'They are keeping an eye on her – she's back home now. Alone. No sign of Daanish.'

I plonked down on the bed, while Shayak slumped on the couch, looking utterly defeated.

'I fucked up, Reema,' he whispered.

'How can you say that?'

'Because it is true. In so many ways that to even list it all will be impossible.' He put his head in his hands. I didn't think he wanted to be with me at that moment.

'Take a minute alone. I need a shower,' I said, 'then we'll talk.'

I retreated to the bathroom, a whirlwind in my head. I stripped off my clothes – filthy from running through the muddy fields – and ran the shower. It wasn't hot enough, but I jumped under the jet and let it beat down on me. Thoroughly cleansed with the cheap bar of soap, I scrubbed down with the raspy towel and put on my new dress.

When I got out, Shayak was nowhere to be seen. I opened the door and walked out on to the wide balcony that looked silvery in the moonlight. My feet were bare, and I don't think he heard me.

I watched Shayak as he stood leaning over the railing, the waves throwing themselves against the rocks and giving a part of themselves up to the air.

I stood by his side, watching the water – violent, relentless, hypnotic. I could taste the sea on my tongue. For the longest time, we simply stood there. And then the wind seemed to drop ever so slightly, the waves backing off.

He had said no, but that was before our worlds had turned upside down. And hadn't I been saying no for months before that? I wouldn't want anyone to hold me to that, to my silly sense of priorities from before I had tasted death. Now, living in its shadow, my own rules had long ceased to matter. This was a man I had desired since the moment we had met; a desire I had felt compelled to hold at a safe distance for reasons I could no longer remember. And I had failed, anyhow: no distance was safe distance when it came to Shayak. The idea of him was so potent that I had to find out for myself if the truth came anywhere close.

Shayak turned his head, still not looking at me. I saw the tension in his jaw, and I reached out my hand to cover his on the railing, urging him to face me.

And he did at last. He seemed to share my need for wordlessness; but there was no space for silence between us. I will never forget his eyes, in that moment, even through the darkness. How tortured they were; how perfectly, how dangerously they mirrored my own. I saw his need, the naked vulnerability he had tried to hide these past few months and also the last vestiges of restraint.

I stepped forward, hands to my sides. I brushed my lips against his, cold from the sea breeze but warm from his breath. And then again. Warmer still. And again, my arms now around his neck, pulling him closer as he finally let out a ragged sigh, grabbing my face in his hands.

We clung to each other, impatient and yet not willing to lose a single moment to our haste. The music of the waves slowed us down while infecting us with its urgency.

To try and walk away from that moment was as futile as attempting to still the sea.

★

There is a zone, suspended between sleep and wakefulness, when all you remember is a feeling.

That morning, a slow, sunny joy filled me. I stretched and breathed deep, and then I knew.

A trace of aftershave, a distinct scent I hadn't known was his but which had been reeling me in all these days. A smell I would now never be able to forget, my brain having memorized it in the course of one night.

I opened my eyes. Shayak.

In my bed.

He was still asleep, as well he should be after the night we'd just had, and the weeks before it.

For a moment, I simply let myself enjoy how handsome he was. This was not an insignificant thing, given how hard I had pushed myself to blind myself to him.

What had I been thinking? How had I resisted for so long? I wanted him again, already.

I reached under the blanket and ran a hand up the outside of his thigh, ending at his hip.

And there its journey ended, trapped in a warm grip.

'Oh no, you don't,' said Shayak, eyes still closed. 'First we talk.'

'Bossy as ever.'

His eyes flew open. Amused, then serious. 'Out there, I am your boss. In here, no.'

'I get that part, but do you even have an unbossy bone in your body?'

'You did a pretty thorough search last night. Did you find one?'

'I can't say that I did. Maybe I should look again,' I suggested, moving my hand again.

The conversation had been averted for the moment, but would have to happen sooner or later.

Later, I thought as I snuck a little closer, was infinitely better.

EIGHTEEN

In my head, the million times this very situation had played out, the morning after with Shayak was always awkward. After the heat of the moment, I had told myself, it would have felt like a mistake.

What I got was the opposite. Even in that dingy little room, when we finally got out of bed, with nowhere to go and no one to be for the briefest glimmer of time, we were at ease. The talk Shayak had threatened me with seemed unnecessary. It was as though we both knew that as wondrous and remarkable as last night had been, it felt so much like all was finally as it should be – which made it, somehow, completely unremarkable. If that might sound unromantic, nothing could be further from the truth for me. Was there anything pedestrian about coming home?

How quickly that feeling passed, when my brain returned to our current predicament.

Shayak had been in touch with Vinod through the course of the night, and there had been no movement at Arti's house.

We went down to the reception and woke the person on duty. Six-thirty in the morning was a ridiculous hour to be up in Goa. We asked for tea and toast and eggs, and sat outside at a picnic table on that rocky cliff, waiting.

'What next?' I asked.

'It's time to reel him in. We can't risk any further delay. We must assume that Daanish will soon be on the move. If he thought he had bought some time after the explosion felled Olivia, he now knows that both she and we are back in play.'

'Do you have something in mind?'

'We use the investigation into the explosion to get in. They were witnesses, after all.'

'They won't talk to us.'

'He won't. But she might.'

I nodded. 'True. Do we attempt to tell her what is going on?'

'I think we need to play that part by the ear. And you will have to be left out of it, for now. You are still dead, remember.'

'Do you think Daanish knows Terrence and I are alive?'

'It is possible. Without any idea of who was following us last night, and what he saw, it's hard to say.'

★

We packed up our meagre possessions and set off in a car brought over by one of Titanium's men, a busload of whom had been brought into Goa from Mumbai. Sanjay was our driver, and he brought with him a fresh pair of cellphones.

About 3 km from Arti's house, we stopped and were met by Ramesh and Ajay. I was also pleasantly surprised to see Archana.

'This time I have official sanction to be here,' said Ajay. 'With what you learned, we were able to make Dr Qureshi talk, after which even the police commissioner couldn't protest any further.'

Shayak turned to me. 'This is where we part ways. We will be questioning Arti about the blast, and you can't be anywhere near here. Archana will take you somewhere safe, close at hand.'

★

I quietly seethed all the way to a local hotel.

'I know you had a near miss last night,' said Archana as we entered yet another strange room.

'Yes.'

'I was told you and Shayak had both lost your belongings, so before I came, I stopped by your flat and picked up a few things.'

'Archana, you are a lifesaver.' How I hoped she had packed some underwear – the tropical bikini I was wearing was not the most comfortable thing to be running about in. I rummaged through the bag: bingo.

I quickly changed into jeans and a crimson top. They were both a little loose – I had lost quite a bit of weight in the past six weeks – but it was a huge improvement on the tourist shop harem pants and tank tops.

I then grabbed the newspaper on the table as Archana ordered some coffee and snacks.

'How have you been?' I asked, as I scanned the headlines.

'Busy. Between the situation in Kyrgyzstan and here, there have been a lot of holes to plug.'

With the staff whittled down, the few experienced people were having to buckle down.

'What about you?' she asked.

'Nothing you don't already know.' Archana had brought me home-cooked meals for days while I was holed up in Mumbai after the explosion. She had heard it all by now.

I went back to the paper. It had little of note on the explosion. But, tucked into the business section, there was an article about how, though Fernandes was still missing, the maiden voyage of his cruise ship to Malaysia was nevertheless on that evening. The ship was to sail after an on-board party for Goa's glitterati. Though the paper speculated that several high-profile guests would not show up for fear of taint by association, the party – with Goa's best offshore gambling – would still proceed on schedule.

'A strange place, Goa,' I muttered.

'You are seeing sides of it most of us miss.'

'And I may have had just about enough of it.'

★

'She said she saw nothing suspicious on the day of the blast,' said Shayak, having arrived at the hotel post interview.

'So now what?' I asked.

'I've sent a team ahead to Daanish's address. There has been no sign of movement.'

'Is he there?'

'The curtains are all drawn. No noise. But we can't be sure yet.'

Shayak then disappeared into the bathroom, with some of his real clothes from Archana's scavenge. When he emerged – in all-black, his clothes also hanging off his frame – he continued.

'You seem to have made an impression on Arti. She was quite shaken while speaking of your death.'

'How heartening,' I said. 'That really takes the sting out of being left on the roadside for the second time during this investigation.'

Shayak looked confused, but Ajay laughed.

'What about Daanish aka Sid? Does she remember anything about his movements?'

'She says she can't account for his whereabouts on that or any other day. That they were seeing each other, so they went to the party together, but that was it.'

'When I saw them together a few days before, they looked very much into each other.'

'You think something has gone off there?' asked Shayak.

'Doesn't it sound that way to you? If Daanish is planning on skipping town, and she is supposed to go with him, don't you think she should be in the loop by now?'

Shayak nodded. 'Especially with Olivia so close to an arrest.'

'Can we search Daanish's house?' I asked.

'My fear is that he will have set up some surveillance or safety tools and we will give ourselves away,' said Shayak.

'What if we precipitated matters?' said Ajay.

'What do you have in mind?' Shayak asked.

'What if Olivia arrests her? Maybe that will draw him out,' he suggested.

'Or send him into hiding,' countered Shayak.

'What if we come clean with her? Maybe she will cooperate,' I said.

'I don't see her trusting us.'

'Not us, perhaps. But what about George?'

★

'So if what you are saying is true, I outed a government conspiracy and travelled halfway across the world to go into hiding, only to fall in love with a serial killer?' Arti said, bewildered.

George, sitting by her side, squeezed her hand.

'Did you ever get a sense that something was off?' I asked.

'Yeah, sure. Sid kept disappearing on these business trips, and was incredibly private, even by my standards. But I thought maybe he was cheating on me, maybe he even had a wife tucked away somewhere – or you know, something normal like that!'

'Have you ever asked him about it?'

'No. Our relationship – at least for me – didn't feel like that. I have never needed a partner by my side, and given my current situation, I preferred less questions to more.'

'But you've been fighting of late?' asked Shayak.

'He wanted me to go away with him.'

'And you didn't want to?'

'Well, we both knew our time was limited. Olivia was here, and George had her at his ashram, in some convoluted friends-close-enemies-closer deal.'

So she had always known. That was the conversation I had overheard – about how long 'she' would be here. It was Olivia they were talking about, not me.

'I just didn't see myself on the run with anyone.'

'He knew your past?'

'Yes.'

'You loved him?'

'What does that even mean when everything he has told me has been a lie?' She brushed a tear away.

'You will help us?' asked Shayak.

'What do you need me to do?'

'Get him to meet you.'

'Where?'

'Here? Somewhere private, contained, where we can bring him in safely.'

Arti disappeared into the bathroom. Emerging from it, she picked up the phone and dialled. 'Hello? Sid, where have you been?' Her face was blank as she listened. 'Look, it doesn't matter. Can you come over?'

Another silence.

'Okay, that works too,' she said, hanging up. 'His place, in an hour.'

I looked at my cellphone watch. 'That means 3 p.m.'

'He's there at the moment?' Shayak asked.

'Apparently.'

'It's too dangerous. We can't have any kind of surveillance inside,' said Shayak. 'We don't have any trackers or cameras, nothing to help us.'

'He won't hurt me, will he, after going to such elaborate lengths to be with me?' asked Arti.

'I can't allow you to take the risk.'

'I'm sorry, but it isn't only your decision. I am going.'

'Give me your phone,' I said.

She handed it over. It was fairly basic. I raised an eyebrow in her direction.

'I am off grid, remember?'

'At least it's a smartphone.' I searched and found the app I was looking for.

'There, it's installed. As long as your phone is on, we will know your location.'

'Good thinking,' said Shayak.

'Not exactly a James Bond-level gizmo, but it will do in a pinch.'

★

We left, Arti ahead of us, Ajay, Shayak and I in our car. George returned to the ashram, his task accomplished. We trailed her, 100 feet behind, till she gave a little flick of the hand to indicate the house was up ahead. Armed personnel had been sent ahead. Without the full strength of Titanium's heft behind us, it wasn't perfect, but it was the best that could be done under the circumstances.

We stopped well short of the house, but still had a clear view of it. There was a black SUV parked to the side. In the absence of a wire, we had improvised, sending her in with an active call to my phone. She was on speaker.

As she approached, Daanish opened the door.

'Arti,' he said.

'Still angry, are you?'

He stepped out.

'Who is this?' asked Arti, her voice rising in panic.

'Something's wrong!' I said.

'You don't recognize him? He's been all over the news of late,' we heard Daanish say.

'Joaquim Fernandes?'

'He's got Fernandes!' said Shayak.

'Why don't you ask your friends to join us,' said Daanish.

He looked over the wall, waved out, staring straight at our car.

'It's a set-up! Everyone wait here,' said Shayak.

He got out of the car and slowly moved towards the house, arms in the air.

I watched, with my heart in my throat, as Shayak approached them. 'Daanish,' he said.

'Shayak. Should have known it would be you, after all this time.'

'Should have killed me when you had the chance, Daanish.'

'Don't tempt me.'

'Let them go, Daanish.

'Don't worry, I have a peaceful solution in mind for our little face-off here. You call off your men, let us leave quietly, and no one gets hurt.'

'That might be a problem.'

'No, I don't think it will be. If you say no, I will press a button, and there is enough C-4 in my house to make a sizeable dent in this pretty little village.'

'You are lying.'

'Have you ever known me to bluff? But since you doubt, feel free to test me and find out for yourself.'

'Why are you doing this, Daanish? What happened to you?'

'I wish I had time to chat. You will let me go, and if I see anyone following me, the consequences are on your head. And I know just how much you hate being blamed for bloodshed.'

For a moment, Shayak stood there, head bowed, deciding what to do. Then he gave the order for all teams to stand down.

Daanish walked to the waiting SUV, with Arti by his side and a gun to Fernandes's head. As they got closer, I saw Arti's terrified face.

They drove away, and Shayak rushed into the house. His voice crackled in over the walky. 'Ajay, Ramesh, we need a bomb squad in here right away. And we need an evacuation along a 250-metre radius.'

We got out of the car, and I ran towards the house.

'Reema!' yelled Ajay.

I ignored him. I followed Shayak in, and was met by the most chilling sight I had ever beheld.

There, in Daanish's living room, was the biggest bomb I had ever seen.

'Get out, Reema.'

'Not till you do.'

'Then don't move a muscle.'

Shayak circled the mound – there was no other word for it – and located the detonator.

'There is no timer.'

'What does that mean?'

'It means it is all in his hands. And I hope it means that if we comply with his demands, he will not blow it up. It means he is buying time.'

'Where does that leave us?'

'We give him the head start he wants. Then we hunt that bastard down. He is desperate enough not to acknowledge that he is cornered.'

'Why not blow us up while he can?'

Shayak shook his head. 'Which part of his actions make sense any more? I think at the heart of it, Daanish is still Daanish. He hasn't been able to pull the trigger, so to speak, himself. Specially with Arti watching. Bombs, proxies, threats, intimidation – he has done everything possible to avoid feeling like he is a murderer.'

'Sick, deluded bastard, perhaps. But also a very clever, skilled criminal.'

We emerged. A police van was on its way, Ramesh said. Shayak called in his men and told them to split up into pairs with the police at hand to evacuate the area as fast as possible.

'There aren't that many houses nearby,' Ramesh said. 'It shouldn't take long.'

'How long will the bomb squad take to get here?'

'The Goan squad is about twenty minutes away, but I

have also requested support from the army – I don't think they will be here for another thirty minutes.'

'Now, about Daanish. What do we have in place?'

'Airports have already been alerted, but we need roadblocks. Along all major routes out of the state,' said Ramesh. 'We won't let them get away.' The car number and make had been sent out, as well as pictures of Arti, Fernandes and Daanish, which Ajay had managed to take during the confrontation with Shayak.

'We need to find out where they are going, and fast. Reema, the tracker app?'

'They are heading north on the highway,' I said, checking my phone for the latest location.

'You think they are going to the airport?' asked Ajay.

'Or any number of other places,' said Ramesh.

'Have you heard anything of note?'

'No.' My phone was on mute, still connected to Arti's, and so far it had been one long, frightening silence on the other end.

As we got into our car, there was suddenly some noise from the phone. It sounded like they were pulling over.

'What are we doing?' asked Arti. 'Is that gun really necessary?'

'Time to check whether our friends sent you over with any accessories,' said Daanish. I heard a ruffling noise.

'Where are we going?' she asked.

'Why are you so worried? I promised to keep you safe, remember?'

'This isn't exactly what you had suggested!'

'It'll be peaceful enough, soon enough.'

'They will be looking for us everywhere, Sid! And why don't you let this poor man go!'

'We need him,' he said. 'What's that under your thigh?'

And then the line was disconnected.

Shayak looked at me. 'Let's go.'

'Yes.'

We took the main road, Ajay following in his vehicle along with one of Ramesh's deputies. Ramesh had stayed behind to supervise the evacuation and coordinate with the bomb squad.

I kept checking my phone. But the tracker app was no longer moving.

'We have their last location,' said Shayak. 'It is more information than we could have hoped for.'

I looked at the map. The airport seemed like such a long shot. Though it was the direction they were headed in, there were only so many routes in Goa. Not even Joaquim Fernandes's private plane would make it through the security we had up there, and Daanish was smart enough to know it.

And then it hit me. '*Yahweh*!' I exclaimed.

'Huh?' said Shayak.

I grabbed my phone and did a search. 'That's it! They aren't going to the airport. They are going to Mormugao port. *Yahweh* is the name of Joaquim Fernandes's cruise liner, and it is leaving for Malaysia today on its maiden voyage!'

*

We reached Mormugao with only thirty minutes left before it was scheduled to set sail. We had called in the cavalry – the Goa Police, Titanium's men, Olivia's operatives were all at hand.

The port manager came out to meet us.

'We must organize a search immediately,' Olivia said.

'What evidence do you have that these people are even on board?' he asked.

Shayak showed the man the photograph of the C-4 in Daanish's room. 'We just found this in one of the suspect's homes. Do you want to take a chance that we are wrong?'

The port manager looked long and hard at the photograph. 'Let me call the captain.'

But when the captain arrived, he was far more dismissive of the situation.

'How can you ask us to delay our maiden voyage by what could be hours on the basis of speculation?' he said.

The argument escalated, with the port manager finally conceding that he could not order compliance without an official directive.

I pulled Shayak aside. 'Maybe the police will have more luck?'

So he called on Ramesh's deputy, Shankar, to intervene.

'Show me a warrant,' the captain kept insisting. 'Two of these people are not even wanted at the moment. And Joaquim Fernandes is the owner of this ship, so even if he is on it, I don't think you could stop him.'

'He is out on bail – he's not allowed to leave the country.'

'Even so, to stop this ship from sailing, you need to work fast and provide me with something more solid to go on.'

'Captain,' said the port manager, 'at least let them look around before departure. What if they are correct? What if there are explosives on board?'

The captain looked at his watch. 'You have twenty minutes. I can, at the most, delay departure by another thirty minutes, as we are still awaiting the arrival of our chief guest. But without an official permit, I cannot allow you to search the guest rooms.'

'How the hell is this supposed to work then?' asked Shankar.

'We'll take you to all the common areas, all the ship service areas, but you will not be disturbing our guests.'

'That's ludicrous! They could be hiding amongst them!'

'Bring me something official, and the ship is yours. Till then — and I am sorry —this is the best I can do.'

He walked away.

'He's been bought,' said Shankar.

'For sure. We need pressure,' said Shayak to Olivia.

'I'll get on it,' she said.

'As for our search, where do we even begin?' I said. 'We don't even know they are actually on board.'

'No, we don't. Which is why I have a hard time believing Olivia will manage anything in time. You sure about this?'

'As sure as I can be. Daanish needs to escape and a ship, with lax security, is the perfect vehicle. There are so many ways he can get away once they've set sail. Where would you hide if you were on a ship?'

'If Fernandes is with him, then it is well within his power to secure the cooperation of the crew, so I would say the captain's cabin.'

'So let's start there,' I said.

We started walking. 'Vinod,' I said, 'can you mingle with the crew, find out if anyone saw Fernandes in the past hour? Or if anyone has seen two men and one woman, possibly acting suspiciously, in and around the ship?'

After a brief resistance from the captain, we were in his three-room suite. There was no sign of anyone.

'It is the perfect hiding place,' I said. 'But maybe it's a little too perfect.'

'Too obvious?' asked Shayak.

'Daanish must have factored in the possibility that we would have worked it out.'

'There are plenty of other places to hide on board – too many.'

We left the cabin, and Shayak mustered the forces, ordering them to fan out and search whatever space they could. The captain sent his men scrambling after them, urging discretion.

'None of these men have ever seen the inside of a cruise ship. They need guidance,' said Shayak.

'You stay here,' I said. 'I'll get the others and search the docks.'

'Reema, no.'

'I won't be alone, Shayak. And you can always track my location.' I ran down the gangway before he could stop me.

George had arrived by now. He and his driver. Olivia and hers. Stragglers from the police – there were about a dozen people in total.

'We need to fan out, search the piers.'

'There are a million shipping containers, barges, boats. Where do we start?' asked George.

'Close to the water. They will want to move. They have to make it to the ship, either just before it sets sail, or before long. Look around for smaller unattended boats, any boats belonging to Fernandes's fleet.'

Descending down a flight of metal stairs, we were at water level, and looking up and around, the true scale of the dock struck me. Three barges, idling without a payload, a row of rusty containers, full or empty.

'We have to split up,' said George.

'We stay in twos,' I said.

We broke off, each pair going in an assigned direction. I found myself with George by my side.

'What would be your play, George?'

'Main goal would be to avoid detection. By now, I would have abandoned my cruise ship getaway plan.'

'Factor in his lack of options, his fear, his hostages.'

'Then I would lie low, prepared to wait it out. With Fernandes there, they have plenty of options for a water escape later.'

I walked up to the edge of the water and looked at the expanse before me. They had roughly an hour's lead at this point.

'Come, George, I have an idea.'

There were three speedboats on the pier. 'Look at the name on that one,' I said.

'Jahwe.'

'Another spelling for Yahweh. Deeply connected with the name Joaquim.'

'You are thinking it belongs to Fernandes?'

'It would make the perfect getaway vehicle: fast enough to slip out onto the water, and meet the cruise ship even on the open sea.' *Yahweh*'s first evening involved a party just off the coast, a night of music and gambling. It gave Daanish plenty of time to sneak on board, and with a cooperative crew, they could still sail in comfort to anywhere along the route, and escape before the next port, given the right boat and resources.

'Shall we?' said George. The speedboat was in front of us; all we needed to do was search it.

I followed him, despite the growing feeling of dread I had been working hard to ignore.

'You okay?' George asked.

'I'm fine.' There was no one on top. 'We need to search the cabin,' I said.

George opened the hatch.

'Stay up here,' I said. 'Keep watch.'

I descended into the small living quarters. The space was empty too. As I emerged, George pointed to a bag at the foot of the stairs.

'What's in that?' he asked.

I bent over to take a closer look.

But then I heard a voice that was not George's. 'Stay where you are, or your friend is dead.'

I froze.

'Without turning around, Reema,' said Daanish, 'take out your gun.'

I pulled it from my pocket.

'Now put it down by your feet,' he said.

I did as I was told, and also tucked my phone under the bag.

As I stood up, I fought the rising tide of panic. It had only been months since I had been held at gunpoint on sea. This went beyond an echo: it was a re-enactment.

'George?' Daanish asked.

'Guns aren't my style. You should know that by now.'

'Now turn around, Reema, slowly, and climb up the stairs.'

Once I was next to George, Daanish closed the hatch. 'Come on, off the boat. Now,' he said, waving the gun.

He led us to a container one row back from the dock. I tried to take it in, to look for any identifying features. But it was as though my mind was not processing what my eyes were seeing.

'Your phones,' he said, at the entrance to the container. George handed over his.

'I don't have mine,' I said.

'Lies. The tracking app was a very clever trick. Hand it over.'

'I lost it, I swear.'

Daanish got within an inch of my face, staring me down. Then he bent down and frisked me, before frisking George for good measure. Then he swung open the heavy metal door of the container.

At the far end were Arti, awake but listless, and Fernandes, who seemed to be in some sort of stupor. Neither was bound.

Had I felt a little more steady on my feet, I may have had the presence of mind to use Daanish's momentary distraction in the effort of opening the door to take him down. But I was still shaking. I stumbled on my way in, and George reached out to steady me.

'Uh-uh – no more of that,' warned Daanish.

Inside, I needed to get as close as I could to Arti. I slumped to the side and tried to calm myself. It was a panic attack, I told myself, one that I needed to get on top of if we were to get out of that container alive.

I closed my eyes. I had been working towards this moment for so long. I could not let my fear get the better of me.

I looked around. There were no bags. Were they on board? We knew Daanish had left with them. This was clearly an improvised part of the plan, and for once, Daanish seemed ill-equipped.

It made me even more convinced that their plan was still to get away on the cruise liner. That they had been given a tip – possibly while we were negotiating with the captain – and had escaped from the ship.

Daanish looked from me to Arti.

'You let this two-bit investigator get inside your head, did you? You believe everything she says?' he said to her.

'If she is wrong, tell me why are you doing this to me?'

I could see Daanish's growing anger. 'Always you, isn't it?'

Arti looked away. There was dirt smudged across her face, but she seemed unharmed.

He pulled out his phone and retreated to the corner, but there was only so far he could go. 'What is taking so much time!' he yelled to whoever was on the other end.

'You need to pretend,' I whispered to Arti. 'Act like you are having second thoughts.'

'And then?' she asked.

'I don't know, but it's our only chance. Cooperate with him. Wait for my signal.'

Daanish raged into the phone. 'I need you to clear the space for ten minutes. That's all!'

Now I knew his play – he had a man on the outside. The captain? He was waiting for the coast to be clear enough for the departure of the smaller vessel.

When the window opened, it would be tight.

'You say I am wrong, Sid?' said Arti, as he hung up. 'Then talk to me.'

'Why? You've made it clear you want nothing to do with this.'

'And yet you are still willing to risk everything to help me get away from Olivia? Why?'

'Because it is too late to stop now.'

'Stop what?'

'I have tied our fates together, Arti. Even if I wanted to dump you now, I would be stuck.'

'Why? It's not true, Sid, you still love me!'

'Why talk of love when you can talk about an idea?'

'Explain to me, please,' she pleaded.

'You are bigger than all of this pettiness. Bigger than justice and love. I thought I had given up on that, but I guess I haven't.'

'You were bigger than all of this, once, too.'

'No. I never was. I am a small guy. Following orders, that was my story. And when it comes down to it, our major flaw as a species is the need for a story.'

'You can write another one,' said Arti.

'I already did once.'

'With me!'

He appeared not to be listening. 'It's what made me so hard to catch,' he continued. 'A big crime needs a big criminal. But to succeed, you need to have no ego. To be faceless. I did that.'

He was pacing now, talking to me as much as to Arti.

'Daanish Alam didn't know that. But Sid does. Over the years, I have figured it out.'

'What do you mean?' said Arti.

'You wouldn't understand!'

'So help me understand! I want to understand!'

'You think I killed myself in order to steal some drugs? It was always the other way around. I felt I had no choice but to kill myself and so I stole. I took care to spill some blood. And then I set off the bomb and disappeared. To live anew.'

'What went wrong?'

'There was one person who knew the value of facelessness: Shayak Gupta,' he said, now looking at me. 'When he followed the scent and started to get close, I knew I had to shake him off.'

'How did you do it?' I asked.

'It was the simple matter of pulling a string. The biggest string in my network. Minister Satish Savarkar. He had you called off when your investigation started gaining steam. And in the process, we started a very profitable partnership. Everyone else I worked with was as small a person as you might expect to meet, operating on a small scale.'

'A cottage industry of crime?' I said.

A laugh, cold as a dip in the sea on a winter morning. 'You could call it that. Even the most perfect operations develop flaws, snags. Like the human cell, reproducing beautifully till, one day, one rogue goes malignant. From that point to death can take a startlingly short time. By keeping all the players apart, by controlling scale, by never creating any power hubs, I got a lot done. For a time.'

'Why did you need to disappear, Sid?' asked Arti.

'At some point you just ask yourself, why? Why bother with honesty at all? My daily life was a constant assault of the corruption of others. Why should they loot and pillage while I remained satisfied with a government salary, toiling to do a job without end, without redemption? Why should I remain bound to a life when others were free?

'There is a point of no return for everyone. I reached mine in the police. I watched them profit, rape, murder, pillage. What does that do to any soul? For years I tried to ignore it, but finally I was pushed so far that I had to get out, or die. I had nothing holding me back. Money was only ever a means to an end. I had no need for great amounts of wealth. But I did want enough to get by. I needed the drugs, enough to spend the rest of my days in comfort. I would sell them, in small increments, so as to not draw attention to myself. It was the perfect plan.'

'But six months ago,' I said, 'something changed. When Olivia showed up. You lost control of it. Because of Arti.'

'Murder had never been the plan. The people who were killed in the blast were collateral damage that couldn't be avoided, unfortunately. The rest was never meant to happen. I thought I knew enough of the system to be able to game it. Kill Titanium and kill the evidence to link the lost drugs to me. But as I said, there were malignancies within the system I had created.'

'Oh, Sid,' said Arti, burying her face in her hands.

'I had no problems leaving my wife, but I couldn't fade into oblivion after I met you. I could no longer even conceive of abandoning this life. So it became imperative to cover up the lies. Not just my lies, but yours as well. I've seen love mess people up, make them do crazy shit they should be smart enough not to do. I have always thought they were fools with no self-control. And then it happened to me. My marriage was dead and I thought I was done with romantic love. I was going to get the stash and disappear, but then there was you. I knew what I was doing when I stole the drugs. When I killed myself. What I didn't know was how difficult it would be to leave *you*.'

'You knew who she was?' I asked.

'Almost from the moment I saw her. It's not like she was hiding in those days. The piercings, the tattoos, *her*. No disguise.' A pause.

'I thought I would sell everything and run away with you. How many times did I try to convince you it was time to go? But offloading such enormous quantities of product in a hurry proved difficult. I couldn't take the stash with me, and I would definitely need the cash.'

'You didn't worry about how she would feel about it if she ever found out the truth?' I asked.

'The plan was to make sure that never, ever happened.'

'Why not just kill Shayak?' I asked.

'What purpose would that have served? He wouldn't have died with his knowledge, that was for sure. The records would have survived and an investigation at that point would have surely been more damaging.'

'Assassination has never been your preference. You prefer the safety of bright lights and loud noise. And excuses.'

'I never intended to kill anyone.'

'And yet you succeeded in killing so many.'

Daanish started pacing, tuning me out. He picked up his phone.

Where was Shayak now? By my guess, we had been inside for at least forty-five minutes. That was long enough for him to have at least tried to check in with me. How long would it take for him to grow concerned and track my phone? I wasn't sure how accurate the signal on the tracking app was, but it should be strong enough to get him to the vicinity.

Daanish was speaking to his man on the outside. It seemed there was news.

'Five minutes,' he said, hanging up. 'And then we move.'

As if on cue, I heard it: running feet. There were voices too and sounds of neighbouring containers opening.

Daanish grew still, listening. He held a finger to his lips, gun in the other hand.

They drew closer. Daanish ran towards me, grabbing me up by the arm, pressing the gun up against my temple.

'Out. Now,' he said to George.

He pushed open the doors and, with George as our shield,

we walked out and stood with our backs to the container, Daanish's arm like steel around my throat.

A shout went out among the search party.

'Any closer and I shoot!' he yelled, bringing the men to a grinding halt. He closed the door of the container behind us, locking Fernandes and Arti in. 'Bring me Shayak.'

In a minute, he was before us. I couldn't look at him. I knew it would send me over the precipice again.

'Daanish,' said Shayak, 'it's over.'

'Not if you value Reema's life. You will let me get on that boat and sail away.'

'You've used that card once today and failed.'

'You would rather I had blown you all up?'

'How far do you think you can go in that thing?'

'Fine, then. But if you are worried about the blood of another Titanium employee on your delicate hands, you'll do me one better.'

I forced myself to look at Shayak and mouthed one word: Arti.

There was a nod of his head, almost imperceptible. 'Take me instead,' he said.

'No can do. Get me transport out of here, with Reema and Arti. And no one gets hurt.'

'What about Fernandes?'

'He has outrun his utility. You will find him, unharmed, back there.'

'Where will you go?'

'None of your business. All I need is for you to ensure safe passage through the airport and use of an aircraft.'

'You know I am in no position to authorize that.'

'You have the duration of our drive to the airport to find someone who does.'

'My private plane is on standby at Dabolim. Give me time to make this work, then go wherever you need to go. I will ensure you pass through. But my condition is that before you reach the aircraft, you leave Reema behind.'

'Then what's there to stop you from shooting us out of the sky?'

'Arti and my pilot.'

'Arti is a wanted woman, just like me.'

'Take it or leave it, Daanish. Reema is a deal breaker.'

'Okay,' he said. 'Get me a car. A good one.'

Shayak called one of his men to bring an SUV. 'It's a Titanium car, Daanish. It's armoured. You'll be safe.'

Daanish shrugged. I knew in that moment what Shayak was really saying. And it wasn't to Daanish, it was to me.

Daanish inched forward. 'Let Arti out of there. Not you,' he said to Shayak who stepped up. 'George.'

George opened the doors to the container and Arti rushed out. Fernandes trailed behind her, just managing to make it out before collapsing in a heap. George stood by Arti's side.

'Clear the area,' commanded Daanish.

Shayak asked George and the men to leave, and they filtered away as the car arrived.

'You too,' he said. Shayak stepped away from the car.

Daanish led Arti to the driver's seat. 'If you were serious about what you said back there and you don't want Reema to get a bullet through the side of her head, you will drive,' he said.

Arti nodded. 'I was serious,' she said, leaning forward and planting a kiss on his mouth before jumping into the driver's seat.

'Open the back door,' Daanish told me. As I did so, I

knew I only had seconds. This was one of Titanium's VIP security vehicles, and it had a very special feature: a gun strapped to the bottom of the driver's seat.

There was a moment, a fraction of a breath, in which Daanish had to let me go so I could clamber into the high seat ahead of him. I reached under the seat. I had the gun in my hand.

Arti started the car. I looked at her in the rear-view mirror and nodded.

She put the car into reverse and gunned it. 'Wait!' yelled Daanish as he lost his footing behind me.

Twisting around, I fired.

As the tyres stopped spinning and the dust settled, I looked down and saw Daanish Alam lying on the ground in an expanding pool of red.

NINETEEN

It was all a rush of images, as though I wasn't there. Shayak running towards me, holding me. Arti sitting still in the driver's seat, till George coaxed her down. Police flooding the scene, an ambulance carrying Daanish away. Fernandes retching and retching in the corner. And Olivia, waiting in the wings.

We were all taken to hospital and Titanium's crew helped the police process our clothing for evidence. Fernandes was admitted, suffering from dehydration, in the presence of police who would keep guard round the clock. Despite his ordeal, he was still on his way to prison.

Daanish Alam did not make it to the hospital alive. He succumbed to abdominal injuries inflicted by the bullet from my gun.

And what about Arti? For the moment, at least, she was free to go. Shayak picked up the two of us in a car. I wasn't sure where we were going; I didn't think to ask.

Finally, Arti spoke. 'He told me he expected a payout for equity he held in a start-up. That it was being bought out and we could, if we wanted, go somewhere quiet, somewhere beautiful.'

'It's okay,' said Shayak.

'Is it?'

'He was a fine man, once.'

'I suppose my only consolation is that I said no. We fought. I agreed to at least think about it, and that is when you found me. How could I not see it?'

What could we say that wouldn't sound like a platitude? Silence hung over the car again. Shayak kept looking at me, waiting for me to speak, but I just couldn't find my voice. I couldn't bring myself to say I was okay just yet.

We exited the highway, and pulled onto a small village road. There, ahead of us, was George, standing on the shoulder, leaning against a black van.

Shayak pulled over. 'Wait here,' he said, getting out.

For a moment, it was just Arti and me in the back seat. 'Thank you,' she said.

'For what?'

'Getting us out alive. In all my time on the run, I have felt safe, somehow. But today, I would have died had you not been there. Of that I am sure. So thank you.'

Then Shayak was signalling to us to get out, and we joined them by the van.

George took Arti by the hands, and gave her a sweet, sad frown, his blue eyes filling with tears. He embraced her.

'Are you ready to run?' he asked.

'What do you mean?'

'Olivia is filing her paperwork. It's now or never.'

'But where will I go?'

'We'll figure that out.'

'What do you mean, "we"?'

'I thought you'd like some company. At least for a time.'

'I thought you were helping Olivia.'

'So does she.'

Arti broke into a grin, and I saw a light in George's eyes that I hadn't seen before.

He turned to me and wrapped me in his arms.

'George, you sly dog, you.'

'Shhh.'

'Are you done with gurudom?'

'Did I say that? I am a free agent after all.'

'Yeah, right. You know Olivia will come after you.'

'That's fine. I was getting bored anyway.'

'Good luck.'

'You too. You deserve a happy ending, Reema. As I said, you are one of the special ones.'

'Like Arti over there?'

He smiled, and leaned over to kiss my cheek.

'Let's just say I owe you one.'

'Take care, George.'

'Don't worry about me. I always land on my feet.'

'So it would seem.'

'As do you.'

'Yeah,' I said with a wink, 'except I would fall on my ankle at just the wrong angle, leaving me with a limp and pain in my back that lasts a decade, prompting me to question every decision leading up to that moment and every decision since.'

George, who had been listening with mock horror, burst into raucous laughter. 'No way that's you. I think you quite perfectly described that man over there, though,' he said, bobbing his head towards Shayak. 'But I think you can fix that.'

I smiled.

'Come visit, will you?' he said.

'Leave me an address.'

'I can guarantee that, when the time comes, you won't have any trouble finding me.'

George and Shayak shook hands. He and Arti got into the van and they drove away.

'Do you know where they are going?' I asked, watching the car as it disappeared around a bend.

'No, and I'd rather not know.'

'You will be questioned over her disappearance?'

'I don't see why I should be.' Shayak shrugged. 'Olivia has yet to make her position known. As far as I know, as of now, Arti and George are free to do exactly as they please.'

*

We returned to Shayak's home, still the war zone we had left it. There were soft boards and white boards filled with investigative material, machines and wires.

Shayak said nothing as I retreated to one of the bedrooms, where I miraculously found my clothes from the abandoned safe house.

I stripped down and stood under the shower for a good half hour. I methodically dried, moisturized and dressed before spending a long while sitting on the bed, mind numb. Finally, I went out into the living room.

And it was all gone. Shayak had swept away every last trace of the investigation. 'How did you manage that?' I asked.

'Just don't go into the spare room for now.' He smiled, walking up to me and cupping my face. 'Reema,' he began.

I shook my head, trying to stop the tears. 'Don't talk,' I said, as he put his arms around me.

'Can I at least ask if you are okay?' he asked after a long while.

'I will be.'

'Glass of wine?'

'A bottle would be better.'

He laughed and pulled away. I followed him into the kitchen and opened the fridge. I was happy to see it had been stocked with takeout. 'Now I know you are feeling better,' he said.

I ate hungrily. Afterwards, we took our glasses out to the terrace, and sat down.

'We'll leave first thing tomorrow,' he said. 'If that's okay.'

'That's fine,' I said.

'You will need some time off.'

'No, I won't.'

'It's not optional.'

'What will I do?'

'You will have to finish some paperwork, and I regret to say, some compulsory counselling, and then go on leave.'

'No.'

'What do you mean, "no"?'

'I am non-compliant with company policy. I refuse.'

'Sorry, no exceptions. Maybe you should go home?'

'Calcutta? Why would I do that?'

'I thought you'd like to be with family for a bit.'

'What I'd really like is to hit you over the head.'

'Me? What did I do?'

'Stop bossing me around.'

'I hate to say this again, but I am your boss! That is, if you still want to work for Titanium.'

'Where else would I work?'

'I don't know. I just thought you may have had enough.'

'No. I haven't.' I was feeling annoyed. Unreasonably so, except given the circumstances, being unreasonable was the only reasonable thing.

I put my glass down and stood up, turning to face him. 'Are you just going to sit there?' I asked.

'What?'

'For a very clever man, you can be very obtuse sometimes.'

'I am?' Now he stood up too. 'Tell me why I am obtuse.'

'Do you really want me to go home?' I asked.

'No.'

'Must we talk about this now?'

'No. But we must talk about it soon.'

'Soon is fine. Now, not so much.'

'Fair enough.'

'So moving on, the last time I threw myself at you, you turned me down.'

'What do you mean?'

'You said no.'

'Because –'

'The because doesn't matter. Throwing yourself repeatedly at the same man can be quite a challenge for the maintenance of a healthy self-respect.'

'Things have changed since then, haven't they?'

'Have they? Not necessarily.'

He reached out and pulled me towards him, kissing me till I was out of breath. 'After last night, how can you think this is anything apart from absolutely of the utmost necessity?'

'Was that only last night? It feels like a lifetime ago.'

Shayak quickly kissed me again.

When we finally headed downstairs, I paused on the bottom step.

'What's the matter?' asked Shayak.

'I know I've said it before to no effect, but now I really mean it.'

'What?'

'I am never, ever setting foot on a boat again.'

'Consider the yacht sold.'